PRAISE FOR THE NOVELS OF
#1 *NEW YORK TIMES* BESTSELLING AUTHOR

NICHOLAS SPARKS

THE CHOICE

"A heartrending love story . . . will have you entranced. And if *The Notebook* left you teary-eyed, his latest will have the same effect."   —*Myrtle Beach Sun News*

"Provides subtle lessons in love and hope . . . reinforces the theory that all choices, no matter how seemingly unimportant . . . often have far-reaching, rippling effects. Sparks has become a favorite storyteller because of his ability to take ordinary people, put them in extraordinary situations, and create unexpected outcomes."   —BookReporter.com

"Will leave the reader feeling warm of heart."
                                                            —CurledUp.com

"Will unleash a torrent of tears . . . But, the emotion will be emotionally cleansing, for it involves a choice each of us is likely to face one day. This is the stuff of serious romance novels."
                                              —ContemporaryLit.About.com

"As always, Nicholas Sparks touches readers' hearts and minds with THE CHOICE."   —BookLoons.com

more . . .

"Sheds light on the quirks couples discover in each other, and the frustration that can ensue . . . *At First Sight* delves deeper still—into the more serious realities of life and love."

—*New Bern Sun-Journal* (NC)

"A tender, poignant tale . . . Never expect the expected when you pick up a Nicholas Sparks novel . . . Prepare to laugh, cry, and fall in love all over again!"   —RoundTableReviews.com

TRUE BELIEVER

"Time for a date with Sparks . . . The slow dance to the couple's first kiss is a two-chapter guilty pleasure."   —*People*

"For romance fans, *True Believer* is a gem."   —EDGEBoston.com

"Another winner . . . a page-turner . . . has all the things we have come to expect from him: sweet romance and a strong sense of place."   —*Charlotte Observer*

"A story about taking chances and following your heart. In the end, it will make you, too, believe in the miracle of love."

—BusinessKnowhow.com

"Sparks does not disappoint his readers. He tells a fine story that entertains us."   —*Oklahoman*

more . . .

THE WEDDING

"Sweet but packs a punch . . . There is a twist that pulls everything together and makes you glad you read this."
—*Charlotte Observer*

"A slice of life readers will take to their hearts."   —*Tulsa World*

"Sparks tells his sweet story . . . [with] a gasp-inducing twist at the very end. Satisfied female readers will close the covers with a sigh."   —*Publishers Weekly*

THE GUARDIAN

"An involving love story . . . an edge-of-your-seat, unpredictable thriller."   —*Booklist*

"Nicholas Sparks is a top-notch writer. He has created a truly spine-tingling thriller exploring love and obsession with a kind of suspense never before experienced in his novels."   —*RedBank.com*

"Fans of Sparks won't be disappointed."
—*Southern Pines Pilot* (NC)

NIGHTS IN RODANTHE

"Bittersweet . . . romance blooms . . . You'll cry in spite of yourself."   —*People*

"Passionate and memorable . . . smooth, sensitive writing . . . This is a novel that can hold its own."   —Associated Press

"Extremely hard to put down . . . a love story, and a good love story at that."
—*Boston Herald*

A BEND IN THE ROAD

"Sweet, accessible, uplifting."
—*Publishers Weekly*

"A powerful tale of true love."
—*Booklist*

"Don't miss it; this is a book that's light on the surface but with subtle depths."
—BookLoons.com

THE RESCUE

"A romantic page-turner . . . Sparks's fans won't be disappointed."
—*Glamour*

"All of Sparks's trademark elements—love, loss, and small-town life—are present in this terrific read."
—*Booklist*

A WALK TO REMEMBER

"An extraordinary book . . . touching, at times riveting . . . a book you won't soon forget."
—*New York Post*

"A sweet tale of young but everlasting love."
—*Chicago Sun-Times*

"Bittersweet . . . a tragic yet spiritual love story."
—*Variety*

more . . .

MESSAGE IN A BOTTLE

"The novel's unabashed emotion—and an unexpected turn—will put tears in your eyes."
                                                              —People

"Glows with moments of tenderness . . . delve[s] deeply into the mysteries of eternal love."
                                                —Cleveland Plain Dealer

"Deeply moving, beautifully written, and extremely romantic."
                                                              —Booklist

THE NOTEBOOK

"Nicholas Sparks . . . will not let you go. His novel shines."
                                                —Dallas Morning News

"Proves that good things come in small packages . . . a classic tale of love."
                                              —Christian Science Monitor

"The lyrical beauty of this touching love story . . . will captivate the heart of every reader and establish Nicholas Sparks as a gifted novelist."
                                          —Denver Rocky Mountain News

The Choice

NICHOLAS SPARKS

The Choice

GRAND CENTRAL
PUBLISHING

NEW YORK   BOSTON

For the Lewis family:
Bob, Debbie, Cody, and Cole.
My family.

Grand Central Publishing
Hachette Book Group USA
237 Park Avenue
New York, NY 10017

Visit our Web site at www.HachetteBookGroupUSA.com.

Printed in the United States of America

Originally published in hardcover by Grand Central Publishing.

First Trade Edition: August 2008
10 9 8 7 6 5 4 3 2 1

Grand Central Publishing is a division of Hachette Book Group USA, Inc.
The Grand Central Publishing name and logo is a trademark of Hachette Book Group USA, Inc.

The Library of Congress has cataloged the hardcover edition as follows:

Sparks, Nicholas.
    The choice / Nicholas Sparks.—1st ed.
       p.   cm.
    ISBN-13 978-0-446-57992-6 (regular ed.)
    ISBN-10 0-446-57992-0 (regular ed.)
    ISBN-13 978-0-446-19509-6 (large print ed.)
    ISBN-10 0-446-19509-X (large print ed.)
    I. Title.

    PS3569.P363C47   2007
    813'.54—dc22
                                              2007029036

ISBN 978-0-446-69833-7 (pbk.)

Acknowledgments

Okay, I'll be honest. It's sometimes hard for me to write acknowledgments for the simple reason that my life as an author has been blessed with a kind of professional stability that strikes me as somewhat rare in this day and age. When I think back to my earlier novels and reread the acknowledgments in, say, *Message in a Bottle* or *The Rescue*, I see names of people with whom I still work today. Not only have I had the same literary agent and editor since I began writing, but I've worked with the same publicists, film agent, entertainment attorney, cover designer, and salespeople, and one producer has been responsible for three of the four film adaptations. While it's wonderful, it also makes me feel like something of a broken record when it comes to thanking these people. Nonetheless, each and every one of them deserves my gratitude.

Of course, I have to begin—as always—with thanking Cat, my wife. We've been married eighteen years and have shared quite a life together: five children, eight dogs (at various times), six different residences in three different states, three very sad funerals of various members of my family, twelve novels and another nonfiction work. It's been a whirlwind since the beginning, and I can't imagine experiencing any of it with any-one else.

My children—Miles, Ryan, Landon, Lexie, and Savannah—are growing up, slowly but surely, and while I love them dearly, I'm proud of each and every one of them.

Theresa Park, my agent at Park Literary Group, is not only one of my closest friends, but a fantastic one at that. Intelligent, charming, and kind, she's one of the great blessings of my life, and I'd like to thank her for everything she's done.

Jamie Raab, my editor at Grand Central Publishing, also deserves my gratitude for all she does. She puts the pencil to the manuscript in hopes of making it the best it can be, and I'm fortunate to have had access to her intuitive wisdom when it comes to novels. More than that, I'm lucky to call her a friend.

Denise DiNovi, the fabulous producer of *A Walk to Remember*, *Message in a Bottle*, and *Nights in Rodanthe*, is my best friend in Hollywood, and I look forward to those times on the film set, simply so we have a chance to visit.

David Young, the new CEO of Grand Central Publishing (well, not exactly new anymore, I suppose), has not only become a friend, but one who deserves my heartfelt thanks, if only because I have the nasty tendency to deliver my manuscripts at the very last possible moment. Sorry about that.

Both Jennifer Romanello and Edna Farley are publicists and friends, and I've adored working with them since *The Notebook* was published in 1996. Thanks for all that you do!

Harvey-Jane Kowal and Sona Vogel, who do the copy-editing, always deserve my thanks for catching the "little errors" that inevitably crop up in my novels.

Howie Sanders and Keya Khayatian at UTA deserve my thanks for the good fortune I've had in film adaptations. I appreciate all that both of you do.

Scott Schwimer always watches out for me, and I've come to think of him as a friend. Thanks, Scott!

Many thanks to Marty Bowen, the producer responsible for *Dear John*. I can't wait to see how it all turns out.

Thanks again to Flag for another wonderful cover.

And finally, many thanks to Shannon O'Keefe, Abby Koons, Sharon Krassney, David Park, Lynn Harris, and Mark Johnson.

Prologue

Stories are as unique as the people who tell them, and the best stories are those in which the ending is a surprise. At least, that's what Travis Parker recalled his dad telling him when he was a child. Travis remembered the way his dad would sit on the bed beside him, his mouth curling into a smile as Travis begged for a story.

"What kind of story do you want?" his dad would ask.

"The best one ever," Travis would answer.

Usually, his dad would sit quietly for a few moments, and then his eyes would light up. He'd put his arm around Travis and in a pitch-perfect voice would launch into a story that often kept Travis awake long after his dad had turned out the lights. There was always adventure and danger and excitement and journeys that took place in and around the small coastal town of Beaufort, North Carolina, the place Travis Parker grew up in and still called home. Strangely, most of them included bears. Grizzly bears, brown bears, Kodiak bears . . . his dad wasn't a stickler for reality when it came to a bear's natural habitat. He focused on hair-raising chase scenes through the sandy lowlands, giving Travis nightmares about crazed polar bears on Shackleford Banks until he was well into middle school. Yet no matter how frightened the stories had made him, he would inevitably ask, "What happened next?"

To Travis, those days seemed like the innocent vestiges of another era. He was forty-three now, and as he parked his car in the parking lot of Carteret General Hospital, where his wife had worked for the past ten years, he thought again about the words he'd always said to his father.

After stepping out of the car, he reached for the flowers he'd brought. The last time he and his wife had spoken, they'd had an argument, and more than anything he wanted to take back his words and make amends. He was under no illusions that the flowers would make things better between them, but he wasn't sure what else to do. It went without saying that he felt guilty about what had happened, but married friends had assured him that guilt was the cornerstone of any good marriage. It meant that a conscience was at work, values were held in high esteem, and reasons to feel guilty were best avoided whenever possible. His friends sometimes admitted their failures in this particular area, and Travis figured that the same could be said about any couple he'd ever met. He supposed his friends had said it to make him feel better, to reassure him that no one was perfect, that he shouldn't be so hard on himself. "Everyone makes mistakes," they'd said, and though he'd nodded as if he believed them, he knew they would never understand what he was going through. They couldn't. After all, their wives were still sleeping beside them every night; none of them had ever been separated for three months, none of them wondered whether their marriage would ever return to what it once had been.

As he crossed the parking lot, he thought about both of his daughters, his job, his wife. At the moment, none of them gave him much comfort. He felt as though he were failing in practically every area of his life. Lately, happiness seemed as distant and unattainable to him as space travel. He hadn't always felt this way. There had been a long period of time during which he remembered being very happy. But things change. People change. Change was one of the inevitable laws of nature, exacting its toll on people's lives. Mistakes are made, regrets form, and all that was left were repercussions that made something as simple as rising from the bed seem almost laborious.

Shaking his head, he approached the door of the hospital, picturing himself as the child he had been, listening to his father's stories. His own life had been the best story ever, he mused, the kind of story that should have ended on a happy note. As he reached for the door, he felt the familiar rush of memory and regret.

Only later, after he let the memories overtake him once again, would he allow himself to wonder what would happen next.

PART ONE

One

May 1996

"Tell me again why I agreed to help you with this." Matt, red-faced and grunting, continued to push the spa toward the recently cut square at the far edge of the deck. His feet slipped, and he could feel sweat pouring from his forehead into the corners of his eyes, making them sting. It was hot, way too hot for early May. Too damn hot for this, that's for sure. Even Travis's dog, Moby, was hiding in the shade and panting, his tongue hanging out.

Travis Parker, who was pushing the massive box alongside him, managed to shrug. "Because you thought it would be fun," he said. He lowered his shoulder and shoved; the spa—which must have weighed four hundred pounds—moved another couple of inches. At this rate, the spa should be in place, oh . . . sometime next week.

"This is ridiculous," Matt said, heaving his weight into the box, thinking that what they really needed was a team of mules. His back was killing him. For a moment, he visualized his ears blowing off the sides of his head from the strain, shooting in both directions like the bottle rockets he and Travis used to launch as kids.

"You've already said that."

"And it isn't fun," Matt grunted.

"You said that, too."

"And it isn't going to be easy to install."

"Sure it is," Travis said. He stood and pointed to the lettering on the box. "See? It says right here, 'Easy to Install.'" From his spot beneath the shady tree, Moby—a purebred boxer—barked as if in agreement, and Travis smiled, looking way too pleased with himself.

Matt scowled, trying to catch his breath. He hated that look. Well, not always. Most of the time he enjoyed his friend's boundless enthusiasm. But not today. Definitely not today.

Matt reached for the bandanna in his rear pocket. It was soaked with sweat, which had of course done wonders for the seat of his pants. He wiped his face and wrung the bandanna with a quick twist. Sweat dribbled from it like a leaky faucet onto the top of his shoe. He stared at it almost hypnotically, before feeling it soak through the light mesh fabric, giving his toes a nice, slimy feel. Oh, that was just dandy, wasn't it?

"As I recall, you said Joe and Laird would be here to help us with your 'little project' and that Megan and Allison would cook some burgers and we'd have beer, and that—oh yeah, installing this thing should only take a couple of hours at the most."

"They're coming," Travis said.

"You said that four hours ago."

"They must be running a little late."

"Maybe you never called them at all."

"Of course I called them. And they're bringing the kids, too. I promise."

"When?"

"Soon."

"*Uh-huh*," Matt answered. He stuffed the bandanna back in his pocket. "And by the way—assuming they don't arrive soon, just how on earth do you think the two of us will be able to lower this thing into place?"

Travis dismissed the problem with a wave as he turned toward the box again. "We'll figure it out. Just think how well we've done so far. We're almost halfway there."

Matt scowled again. It was Saturday—Saturday! His day of recreation and relaxation, his chance to escape from the grindstone, the break he *earned* after five days at the bank, the kind of day he *needed*. He was a loan officer, for God's sake! He was supposed to push paper, not hot tubs! He could have been watching the Braves play the Dodgers! He could have been golfing! He could have gone to the beach! He could have slept in with Liz before heading to her parents' house like they did almost every Saturday, instead of waking at the crack of dawn and performing manual labor for eight straight hours beneath a scalding southern sun. . . .

He paused. Who was he kidding? Had he not been here, he would have definitely spent the day with Liz's parents, which was, in all honesty, the main reason he'd agreed to Travis's request in the first place. But that wasn't the point. The point was, he didn't need this. He really didn't.

"I don't need this," he said. "I really don't."

Travis didn't seem to hear him. His hands were already on the box, and he was getting into position. "You ready?"

Matt lowered his shoulder, feeling bitter. His legs were shaking. Shaking! He already knew he'd be in serious, double-dose-of-Advil pain in the morning. Unlike Travis, he didn't make it into the gym four days a week or play racquetball or go running or go scuba diving in Aruba or surfing in Bali or skiing in Vail or anything else the guy did. "This isn't fun, you know?"

Travis winked. "You said that already, remember?"

"Wow!" Joe commented, lifting an eyebrow as he walked the perimeter of the hot tub. By then, the sun was beginning its descent, streams of gold reflecting off the bay. In the distance, a heron broke from the trees and gracefully skimmed the surface, dispersing the light. Joe and Megan, along with Laird and Allison, had arrived a few minutes before with kids in tow, and Travis was showing them around. "This looks great! You two did all of this today?"

Travis nodded, holding his beer. "It wasn't so bad," he said. "I think Matt even enjoyed it."

Joe glanced at Matt, who lay flattened in a lawn chair off to the side of the deck, a cold rag over his head. Even his belly—Matt had always been on the pudgy side—seemed to sag.

"I can see that."

"Was it heavy?"

"Like an Egyptian sarcophagus!" Matt croaked. "One of those gold ones that only cranes can move!"

Joe laughed. "Can the kids get in?"

"Not yet. I just filled it, and the water will take a little while to heat up. The sun will help, though."

"The sun will heat it within minutes!" Matt moaned. "Within seconds!"

Joe grinned. Laird and the three of them had gone to school together since kindergarten.

"Tough day, Matt?"

Matt removed the rag and scowled at Joe. "You have no idea. And thanks for showing up on time."

"Travis said to be here at five. If I had known you needed help, I would have come earlier."

Matt slowly shifted his gaze to Travis. He really hated his friend sometimes.

"How's Tina doing?" Travis said, changing the subject. "Is Megan getting any sleep?"

Megan was chatting with Allison at the table on the far end of the deck, and Joe glanced briefly in her direction. "Some. Tina's cough is gone and she's been able to sleep through the night again, but sometimes I just think that Megan isn't wired to sleep. At least, not since she became a mom. She gets up even if Tina hasn't made a peep. It's like the quiet wakes her up."

"She's a good mom," Travis said. "She always has been."

Joe turned to Matt. "Where's Liz?" he asked.

"She should be here any minute," Matt answered, his voice floating up as if from the dead. "She spent the day with her parents."

"Lovely," Joe commented.

"Be nice. They're good people."

"I seem to recall you saying that if you had to sit through one more of your father-in-law's stories about his prostate cancer or listen to your mother-in-law fret about Henry getting fired again—even though it wasn't his fault—you were going to stick your head in the oven."

Matt struggled to sit up. "I never said that!"

"Yes, you did." Joe winked as Matt's wife, Liz, rounded the corner of the house with Ben toddling just in front of her. "But don't worry. I won't say a word."

Matt's eyes darted nervously from Liz to Joe and back again, checking to see if she'd heard.

"Hey, y'all!" Liz called out with a friendly wave, leading little Ben by the hand. She made a beeline for Megan and Allison. Ben broke away and toddled toward the other kids in the yard.

Joe saw Matt sigh in relief. He grinned and lowered his voice. "So . . . Matt's in-laws. Is that how you conned him into coming here?"

"I might have mentioned it," Travis smirked.

Joe laughed.

"What are you guys saying?" Matt called out suspiciously.

"Nothing," they said in unison.

Later, with the sun down and the food eaten, Moby curled up at Travis's feet. As he listened to the sound of the kids splashing away in the spa, Travis felt a wave of satisfaction wash over him. This was his favorite kind of evening, whiled away to the sound of shared laughter and familiar banter. One minute Allison was talking to Joe; the next minute she was chatting with Liz and then Laird or Matt; and so on for everyone seated around the outdoor table. No pretenses, no attempts to impress, no one trying to show anyone up. His life, he sometimes thought, resembled a beer commercial, and for the most part, he was content simply to ride the current of good feeling.

Every now and then, one of the wives would get up to check on the kids. Laird, Joe, and Matt, on the other hand, reserved their child-rearing duties at times like these to periodically raising their voices in hopes of calming down the kids or preventing them from teasing or accidentally hurting one another. Sure, one of the kids would throw a tantrum now and then, but most problems were solved with a quick kiss on a scraped knee or a hug that was as tender to watch from a distance as it must have been for the kid to receive.

Travis looked around the table, pleased that his childhood friends not only had become good husbands and fathers, but were still a part of his life. It didn't always turn out that way. At thirty-two, he knew that life was sometimes a gamble, and he'd survived more than his share of accidents and falls, some of which should have inflicted far more serious bodily injury than they had. But it wasn't just that. Life was unpredictable. Others he'd known growing up had already died in car accidents, been married and divorced, found themselves addicted to drugs or booze, or simply moved away from this tiny town, their faces already blurring in his memory. What were the odds that the four of them—who'd known one another since kindergarten—would find themselves in their early thirties still spending weekends together? Pretty small, he thought. But somehow, after hanging together through all the adolescent acne and girl troubles and pressure from their parents, then heading off to four different colleges with differing career goals, they had each, one by one, moved back here to Beaufort. They were more like family than friends, right down to coded expressions and shared experiences that no outsiders could ever fully understand.

And miraculously, the wives got along, too. They'd come from different backgrounds and different parts of the state, but marriage, motherhood, and the endless gossip of small-town America were more than enough to keep them chatting regularly on the phone and bonding like long-lost sisters. Laird had been the first to marry—he and Allison had tied the knot the summer after they graduated from Wake Forest; Joe and Megan walked the aisle a year later, after falling in love during their senior year at North Carolina. Matt, who'd gone to Duke, met Liz here in Beaufort, and they were married a year after that. Travis had been the best man in all three weddings.

Some things had changed in the past few years, of course, largely because of the new additions to the families. Laird wasn't always available to go mountain biking, Joe couldn't join Travis on the spur of the moment to go skiing in Colorado as he used to, and Matt had all but given up trying to keep up with him on most things. But that was okay. They were all still available enough, and among the three of them—and with enough planning—he was still able to make the most of his weekends.

Lost in thought, Travis hadn't realized that the conversation had lapsed.

"Did I miss something?"

"I asked if you'd talked to Monica lately," Megan said, her tone letting Travis know he was in trouble. All six of them, he thought, took a bit too much interest in his love life. The trouble with married people was that they seemed to believe that everyone they knew should get married. Every woman Travis dated was thus subjected to subtle, though unyielding, evaluation, especially by Megan. She was usually the ringleader at moments like these, always trying to figure out what made Travis tick when it came to women. And Travis, of course, loved nothing more than to push her buttons in return.

"Not recently," he said.

"Why not? She's nice."

She's also more than a little neurotic, Travis thought. But that was beside the point.

"She broke up with me, remember?"

"So? It doesn't mean she doesn't want you to call."

"I thought that's exactly what it meant."

Megan, along with Allison and Liz, stared at him as if he were just plain dense. The guys, as usual, seemed to be enjoying this. It was a regular feature of their evenings.

"But you were fighting, right?"

"So?"

"Did you ever think she might have simply broken up with you because she was angry?"

"I was angry, too."

"Why?"

"She wanted me to see a therapist."

"And let me guess—you said you didn't need to see one."

"The day I need to see a therapist is the day you see me hike up my skirt and crochet some mittens."

Joe and Laird laughed, but Megan's eyebrows shot up. Megan, they all knew, watched Oprah nearly every day.

"You don't think men need therapy?"

"I know I don't."

"But generally speaking?"

"Since I'm not a general, I really couldn't say."

Megan leaned back in her chair. "I think Monica might be on to something. If you ask me, I think you have commitment issues."

"Then I'll make sure not to ask you."

Megan leaned forward. "What's the longest you've ever dated someone? Two months? Four months?"

Travis pondered the question. "I dated Olivia for almost a year."

"I don't think she's talking about high school," Laird cracked. Occasionally, his friends enjoyed throwing him under the bus, so to speak.

"Thanks, Laird," Travis said.

"What are friends for?"

"You're changing the subject," Megan reminded him.

Travis drummed his fingers on his leg. "I guess I'd have to say . . . I can't remember."

"In other words, not long enough to remember?"

"What can I say? I've yet to meet any woman who could measure up to any of you."

Despite the growing darkness, he could tell she was pleased by his words. He'd learned long ago that flattery was his best defense at moments like these, especially since it was usually sincere. Megan, Liz, and Allison were terrific. All heart and loyalty and generous common sense.

"Well, just so you know, I like her," she said.

"Yeah, but you like everyone I date."

"No, I don't. I didn't like Leslie."

None of the wives had liked Leslie. Matt, Laird, and Joe, on the other hand, hadn't minded her company at all, especially when she wore her bikini. She was definitely a beauty, and while she wasn't the type he'd ever marry, they'd had a lot of fun while it lasted.

"I'm just saying that I think you should give her a call," she persisted.

"I'll think about it," he said, knowing he wouldn't. He rose from the table, angling for an escape. "Anyone need another beer?"

Joe and Laird lifted their bottles in unison; the others shook their heads. Travis started for the cooler before hesitating near the sliding glass door of his house. He darted inside and changed the CD, listening to the strains of new music filtering out over the yard as he brought the beers back to the table. By then, Megan, Allison, and Liz were already chatting about Gwen, the woman who did their hair. Gwen always had good stories, many of which concerned the illicit predilections of the town's citizens.

Travis nursed his beer silently, looking out over the water.

"What are you thinking about?" Laird asked.

"It's not important."

"What is it?"

Travis turned toward him. "Did you ever notice how some colors are used for people's names but others aren't?"

"What are you talking about?"

"White and Black. Like Mr. White, the guy who owns the tire store. And Mr. Black, our third-grade teacher. Or even Mr. Green from the game Clue. But you never hear of someone named Mr. Orange or Mr. Yellow. It's like some colors make good names, but other colors just sound stupid. You know what I mean?"

"I can't say I've ever thought about it."

"Me neither. Not until just a minute ago, I mean. But it's kind of strange, isn't it?"

"Sure," Laird finally agreed.

Both men were quiet for a moment. "I told you it wasn't important."

"Yes, you did."

"Was I right?"

"Yep."

When little Josie had her second temper tantrum in a fifteen-minute span—it was a little before nine—Allison scooped her into her arms and gave Laird *the look*, the one that said it was time to go so they could get the kids in bed. Laird didn't bother arguing, and when he stood up from the table, Megan glanced at Joe, Liz nodded at Matt, and Travis knew the evening was at an end. Parents might believe themselves to be the bosses, but in the end it was the kids who made the rules.

He supposed he could have tried to talk one of his friends into staying, and might even have gotten one to agree, but he had long since grown accustomed to the fact that his friends lived their lives by a different schedule from his. Besides, he had a sneaking suspicion that Stephanie, his younger sister, might swing by later. She was coming in from Chapel Hill, where she was working toward a master's degree in biochemistry. Though she would stay at their parents' place, she was usually wired after the drive and in the mood to talk, and their parents would already be in bed. Megan, Joe, and Liz rose and started to clean up the table, but Travis waved them off.

"I'll get it in a while. No big deal."

A few minutes later, two SUVs and a minivan were being loaded with children. Travis stood on the front porch and waved as they pulled out of the driveway.

When they were gone, Travis wandered back to the stereo, sorted through the CDs again, and chose *Tattoo You* by the Rolling Stones, then cranked up the volume. He pulled at another beer on his way back to his chair, threw his feet up on the table, and leaned back. Moby sat beside him.

"Just you and me for a while," he said. "What time do you think Stephanie will be rolling in?"

Moby turned away. Unless Travis said the words *walk* or *ball* or *go for a ride* or *come get a bone*, Moby wasn't much interested in anything he had to say.

"Do you think I should call her to see if she's on her way yet?"

Moby continued to stare.

"Yeah, that's what I thought. She'll get here when she gets here."

He sat drinking his beer and stared out over the water. Behind him, Moby whined. "You want to go get your ball?" he finally said.

Moby stood so quickly, he almost knocked over the chair.

It was the music, she thought, that proved to be the clincher in what had already been one of the most miserable weeks of her life. Loud music. Okay, nine o'clock on a Saturday night wasn't so bad, especially since he obviously had company, and ten o'clock wasn't all that unreasonable, either. But eleven o'clock? When he was alone and playing fetch with his dog?

From her back deck, she could see him just sitting there in the same shorts he'd worn all day, feet on the table, tossing the ball and staring at the river. What on earth could he be thinking?

Maybe she shouldn't be so hard on him; she should simply ignore him. It was his house, right? King of the castle and all that. He could do what he wanted. But that wasn't the problem. The problem was that he had neighbors, including her, and she had a castle, too, and neighbors were supposed to be considerate. And truth be told, he'd crossed the line. Not just because of the music. In all honesty, she liked the music he was listening to and usually didn't really care how loud or how long he played it. The problem was with his dog, Nobby, or whatever he called him. More specifically, what his dog had done to her dog.

Molly, she was certain, was pregnant.

Molly, her beautiful, sweet, purebred collie of prize-winning lineage—the first thing she'd bought herself after finishing her physician assistant rotations at the Eastern Virginia School of Medicine and the kind of dog she'd always wanted—had noticeably gained weight during the last couple of weeks. Even more alarming, she noticed that Molly's nipples seemed to be growing. She could feel them now whenever Molly rolled over to have her tummy scratched. And she was moving more slowly, too. Add it up, and Molly was definitely on her way to birthing a litter of puppies that no one on earth was ever going to want. A boxer and a collie? Unconsciously she squinched up her face as she tried to imagine how the puppies would look before finally forcing the thought away.

It had to be that man's dog. When Molly was in heat, that dog had practically staked out her house like a private detective, and he was the only dog she'd seen wandering around the neighborhood in weeks. But would her neighbor even consider fencing his yard? Or keeping the dog inside? Or setting up a dog run? No. His motto seemed to be "My dog shall be free!" It didn't surprise her. He seemed to live his own life by the same irresponsible motto. On her way to work, she saw him running, and when she got back, he was out biking or kayaking or in-line skating or shooting baskets in his front drive with a group of neighborhood kids. A month ago, he'd put his boat in the water, and now he was wakeboarding as well. As if the man weren't active enough already. God forbid the man should work a minute of overtime, and she knew that he didn't work at all on Fridays. And what kind of job let you head off every day wearing jeans and T-shirts? She had no idea, but she suspected—with a grim sort of satisfaction—that it more than likely required an apron and name tag.

Okay, maybe she wasn't being entirely fair. He was probably a nice guy. His friends—who appeared normal enough and had kids to boot—seemed to enjoy his company and were over there all the time. She realized she'd even seen a couple of them at the office before, when their kids had come in with the sniffles or an ear infection. But what about Molly? Molly was sitting near the back door, her tail thumping, and Gabby felt anxious at the thought of the future. Molly would be okay, but what about the puppies? What was going to happen to them? What if no one wanted them? She couldn't imagine taking them to the pound or the SPCA or whatever it was they called it here, to be put to sleep. She couldn't do that. She wouldn't do that. She wasn't going to have them murdered.

But what, then, was she going to do with the puppies?

It was all his fault, and he was just sitting there on his deck with his feet propped up, acting as if he didn't have a care in the world.

This wasn't what she'd dreamed about when she'd first seen the house earlier this year. Even though it wasn't in Morehead City, where her boyfriend, Kevin, lived, it was just minutes across the bridge. It was small and almost half a century old and a definite fixer-upper by Beaufort standards, but the view along the creek was spectacular, the yard was big enough for Molly to run, and best of all, she could afford it. Just barely, what with all the loans she'd taken out for PA school, but loan officers were pretty understanding when it came to making loans to people like her. Professional, educated people.

Not like Mr. My Dog Shall Be Free and I Don't Work Fridays.

She drew a deep breath, reminding herself again that the man might be a nice guy. He always waved to her whenever he saw her pulling in from work, and she vaguely remembered that he'd dropped off a basket of cheese and wine to welcome her to the neighborhood when she'd moved in a couple of months back. She hadn't been home, but he'd left it on the porch, and she'd promised herself that she'd send a thank-you note, one that she never quite got around to writing.

Her face squinched unconsciously again. So much for moral superiority. Okay, she wasn't perfect, either, but this wasn't about a forgotten thank-you note. This was about Molly and that man's wandering dog and unwanted puppies, and now was as good a time as any for them to discuss the situation. He was obviously awake.

She stepped off the back deck and started toward the tall row of hedges that separated his house from hers. Part of her wished Kevin were with her, but that wasn't going to happen. Not after their spat this morning, which started after she'd casually mentioned that her cousin was getting married. Kevin, buried in the sports section of the newspaper, hadn't said a word in response, preferring to act as if he hadn't heard her. Anything about marriage made the man get as quiet as a stone, especially lately. She supposed she shouldn't have been surprised—they'd been dating almost four years (a year less than her cousin, she was tempted to point out), and if she'd learned one thing about him, it was that if Kevin found a topic uncomfortable, then more than likely he wouldn't say anything at all.

But Kevin wasn't the problem. Nor was the fact that lately she felt as though her life weren't quite what she'd imagined it would be. And it wasn't the terrible week at the office, either, one in which she'd been puked on three—*three!*—times on Friday alone, which was an all-time office record, at least according to the nurses, who didn't bother to hide their smirks and repeated the story with glee. Nor was she angry about Adrian Melton, the married doctor at her office who liked to touch her whenever they spoke, his hand lingering just a bit too long for comfort. And she surely wasn't angry at the fact that through it all, she hadn't once stood up for herself.

Nosiree, this had to do with Mr. Party being a responsible neighbor, one who was going to own up to the fact that he had as much of a duty to find a solution to their problem as she did. And while she was letting him know that, maybe she'd mention that it was a little late for him to be blaring his music (even if she did like it), just to let him know she was serious.

As Gabby marched through the grass, the dew moistened the tips of her toes through her sandals and the moonlight reflected on the lawn like silver trails. Trying to figure out exactly where to begin, she barely noticed. Courtesy dictated that she head first to the front door and knock, but with the music roaring, she doubted he'd even be able to hear it. Besides, she wanted to get this over with while she was still worked up and willing to confront him head-on.

Up ahead, she spotted an opening in the hedges and headed toward it. It was probably the same one that Nobby snuck through to take advantage of poor, sweet Molly. Her heart squeezed again, and this time she tried to hold on to the feeling. This was important. Very important.

Focused as she was on her mission, she didn't notice the tennis ball come flying toward her just as she emerged from the opening. She did, however, distantly register the sound of the dog galloping toward her—but only distantly—a second before she was bowled over and hit the ground.

As she lay on her back, Gabby noted dully that there were way too many stars in a too bright, out-of-focus sky. For a moment, she wondered why she couldn't draw breath, then quickly became more concerned with the pain that was coursing through her. All she could do was lie on the grass and blink with every throb.

From somewhere far away, she heard a jumble of sounds, and the world slowly started coming back into focus. She tried to concentrate and realized that it wasn't a jumble; she was hearing voices. Or, rather, a single voice. It seemed to be asking if she was okay.

At the same time, she gradually became conscious of a succession of warm, smelly, and rhythmic breezes on her cheek. She blinked once more, turned her head slightly, and was confronted with an enormous, furry, square head towering over her. Nobby, she concluded fuzzily.

"Ahhhh . . . ," she whimpered, trying to sit up. As she moved, the dog licked her face.

"Moby! Down!" the voice said, sounding closer. "Are you okay? Maybe you shouldn't try to get up yet!"

"I'm okay," she said, finally raising herself into a seated position. She took a couple of deep breaths, still feeling dizzy. Wow, she thought, that really hurt. In the darkness, she sensed someone squatting beside her, though she could barely make out his features.

"I'm really sorry," the voice said.

"What happened?"

"Moby accidentally knocked you down. He was going after a ball."

"Who's Moby?"

"My dog."

"Then who's Nobby?"

"What?"

She brought a hand to her temple. "Never mind."

"Are you sure you're okay?"

"Yeah," she said, still dizzy but feeling the pain subside to a low throb. As she began to rise, she felt her neighbor place his hand on her arm, helping her up. She was reminded of the toddlers she saw at the office who struggled to stay balanced and remain upright. When she finally had her feet under her, she felt him release her arm.

"Some welcome, huh?" he asked.

His voice still sounded far away, but she knew it wasn't, and when she faced him, she found herself focusing up at someone at least six inches taller than her own five feet seven. She wasn't used to that, and as she tilted her head upward, she noticed his angled cheekbones and clean skin. His brown hair was wavy, curling naturally at the ends, and his teeth gleamed white. Up close, he was good-looking—okay, really good-looking—but she suspected that he knew it as well. Lost in thought, she opened her mouth to say something, then closed it again, realizing she'd forgotten the question.

"I mean, here you are, coming over to visit, and you get slammed by my dog," he went on. "Like I said, I'm really sorry. Usually he pays a bit more attention. Say hey, Moby."

The dog was sitting on his haunches, acting pleased as punch, and with that, she suddenly remembered the purpose of her visit. Beside her, Moby raised a paw in greeting. It was cute—and he *was* cute for a boxer—but she wasn't about to fall for it. This was the mutt who'd not only tackled her, but ruined Molly as well. He probably should have been named Mugger. Or better yet, Pervert.

"You sure you're okay?"

The way he asked made her realize that this wasn't the sort of confrontation she'd wanted, and she tried to summon the feeling she'd had on her way over.

"I'm fine," she said, her tone sharp.

For an awkward moment, they eyed each other without speaking. Finally he motioned over his shoulder with his thumb. "Would you like to sit on the deck? I'm just listening to some music."

"Why do you think I want to sit on the deck?" she snapped, feeling more in control.

He hesitated. "Because you were coming over?"

Oh yeah, she thought. That.

"I mean, I suppose we could stand here by the hedges if you'd rather," he continued.

She held up her hands to stop him, impatient to get this over with. "I came over here because I wanted to talk to you . . ."

She broke off when he slapped at his arm. "Me, too," he said before she could get started again. "I've been meaning to drop by to officially welcome you to the neighborhood. Did you get my basket?"

She heard a buzzing near her ear and waved at it. "Yes. Thank you for that," she said, slightly distracted. "But what I wanted to talk about . . ."

She trailed off when she realized he wasn't paying attention. Instead, he was fanning the air between them. "You sure you don't want to head to the deck?" he pressed. "The mosquitoes are vicious around the bushes here."

"What I was trying to say was—"

"There's one on your earlobe," he said, pointing.

Her right hand shot up instinctively.

"The other one."

She swatted at it and saw a smear of blood on her fingers as she pulled her hand back. Gross, she thought.

"There's another right by your cheek."

She waved again at the growing swarm. "What's going on?"

"Like I said, it's the bushes. They breed in the water, and it's always moist in the shade. . . ."

"Fine," she relented. "We can talk on the deck."

A moment later they were in the clear, moving quickly. "I hate mosquitoes, which is why I've got some citronella candles going on the table. That's usually enough to keep them away. They get much worse later in the summer." He left just enough space between them so they wouldn't accidentally bump. "I don't think we've formally met, by the way. I'm Travis Parker."

She felt a flicker of uncertainty. She wasn't here to be his buddy, after all, but expectation and manners prevailed, and she answered before she could stop herself. "I'm Gabby Holland."

"Nice to meet you."

"Yeah," she said. She made a point to cross her arms as she said it, then subconsciously brought a hand to her ribs where a dull ache remained. From there, it traveled to her ear, which was already beginning to itch.

Staring at her profile, Travis could tell that she was angry. Her mouth had a tight, pinched look he'd seen on any number of girlfriends. Somehow he knew the anger was directed at him, though he had no idea why. Aside from being tackled by the dog, that is. But that wasn't quite it, he decided. He remembered the expressions that his kid sister, Stephanie, was famous for, ones that signaled a slow buildup of resentment over time, and that's how Gabby seemed to be acting now. As if she'd worked herself up to this. But there the similarities with his sister ended. While Stephanie had grown up to become a certifiable beauty, Gabby was attractive in a similar but not quite perfect kind of way. Her blue eyes were a little too wide set, her nose was just a bit too big, and red hair was always hard to pull off, but somehow these imperfections lent an air of vulnerability to her natural good looks, which most men would find arresting.

In the silence, Gabby tried to collect her thoughts. "I was coming over because—"

"Hold on," he said. "Before you begin, why don't you sit down? I'll be right there." He started for the cooler, then rotated in midstride. "Would you like a beer?"

"No, thank you," she said, wishing she could get this over with. Refusing to sit down, she turned with the hope of confronting him as he strode past. But, too quickly, he dropped into his chair, leaned back, and put his feet on the table.

Flustered, Gabby continued to stand. This was not working out as she'd planned.

He popped open his beer and took a short pull. "Aren't you going to sit?" he asked over his shoulder.

"I'd rather remain standing, thank you."

Travis squinted and shaded his eyes with his hands. "But I can barely see you," he said. "The porch lights are shining behind you."

"I came over here to tell you something—"

"Can you move just a few feet to the side?" he asked.

She made an impatient noise and moved a few steps.

"Better?"

"Not yet."

By then, she was almost against the table. She threw up her hands in exasperation.

"Maybe you should just sit," he suggested.

"Fine!" she said. She pulled out a chair and took a seat. He was throwing this whole thing completely out of whack. "I came over because I wanted to talk to you . . . ," she began, wondering if she should start with Molly's situation or what it generally meant to be a good neighbor.

He raised his eyebrows. "You've already said that."

"I know!" she said. "I've been trying to tell you, but you haven't let me finish!"

He saw her glare at him just the way his sister used to but still had no idea what she was so wound up about. After a second, she began to speak, a bit hesitantly at first, as if wary that he was going to interrupt her again. He didn't, and she seemed to find her rhythm, the words coming more and more quickly. She talked about how she'd found the house and how excited she'd been, and how owning a home had been her dream for a long time, before the topic wandered to Molly and how Molly's nipples were getting bigger. At first, Travis had no idea who Molly was—which lent that part of the monologue a surreal quality—but as she continued, he gradually realized that Molly was Gabby's collie, which he'd noticed her walking occasionally. After that, she began talking about ugly puppies and murder and, strangely, something about neither "Dr. Hands-on-me" nor vomit having anything to do with the way she was feeling, but in all honesty, it made little sense until she started gesturing at Moby. That allowed him to put two and two together until it dawned on him that she believed Moby was responsible for Molly getting pregnant.

He wanted to tell her that it wasn't Moby, but she was on such a roll, he thought it best to let her finish before protesting. By that point, her story had veered back on itself. Bits and pieces of her life continued to come tumbling out, little snippets that sounded unrehearsed and unconnected, along with bursts of anger randomly directed his way. It felt as though she went on for a good twenty minutes or so, but Travis knew it couldn't have been that long. Even so, being on the receiving end of a stranger's angry accusations about his failures as a neighbor wasn't exactly easy, nor did he appreciate the way she was talking about Moby. Moby, in his opinion, was just about the most perfect dog in the world.

Sometimes she paused, and in those moments, Travis tried unsuccessfully to respond. But that didn't work, either, because she immediately overrode him. Instead, he listened and—at least in those moments when she wasn't insulting him or his dog— sensed a trace of desperation, even some confusion, as to what was happening in her life. The dog, whether she realized it or not, was only a small part of what was bothering her. He felt a surge of compassion for her and found himself nodding, just to let her know he was paying attention. Every now and then, she asked a question, but before he could respond, she would answer for him. "Aren't neighbors supposed to consider their actions?" Yes, obviously, he started to say, but she beat him to it. "Of course they are!" she cried, and Travis found himself nodding again.

When her tirade finally wound down, she ended up staring at the ground, spent. Although her mouth was set in that same straight line, Travis thought he saw tears, and he wondered whether he should offer to bring her a tissue. They were inside the house—too far away, he realized—but then he remembered the napkins near the grill. He rose quickly, grabbed a few, and brought them to her. He offered her one, and after debating, she took it.

She wiped the corner of her eyes. Now that she'd calmed down, he noted she was even prettier than he'd first realized.

She drew a shaky breath. "The question is, what are you going to do?" she finally asked.

He hesitated, trying to draw a bead on what she meant. "About what?"

"The puppies!"

He could hear the anger beginning to percolate again, and he raised his hands in an attempt to calm her. "Let's start at the beginning. Are you sure she's pregnant?"

"Of course I'm sure! Didn't you hear a word I said?"

"Have you had her checked by a vet?"

"I'm a physician assistant. I spent two and a half years in PA school and another year in rotations. I know when someone's pregnant."

"With people, I'm sure you do. But with dogs, it's different."

"How would you know?"

"I've had a lot of experience with dogs. Actually, I—"

Yeah, I'll bet, she thought, cutting him off with a wave. "She's moving slower, her nipples are swollen, and she's been acting strangely. What else could it be?" Honestly, every man she'd ever met believed that having a dog as a kid made him an expert on all things canine.

"What if she has an infection? That would cause swelling. And if the infection is bad enough, she might be in some pain, too, which could explain the way she's acting."

Gabby opened her mouth to speak, then closed it when she realized that she hadn't thought of that. An infection *could* cause swelling in the nipples—mastitis or something like that—and for a moment, she felt a surge of relief wash through her. As she considered it further, however, reality came crashing back. It wasn't one or two nipples, it was all of them. She twisted the napkin, wishing he would just *listen*.

"She's pregnant, and she's going to have puppies. And you're going to have to help me find homes for them, since I'm not bringing them to the pound."

"I'm sure it wasn't Moby."

"I knew you were going to say that."

"But you should know—"

She shook her head furiously. This was so typical. Pregnancy was always a woman's problem. She stood up from her chair. "You're going to have to take some responsibility here. And I hope you realize it's not going to be easy to find homes for them."

"But—"

"What on earth was that about?" Stephanie asked.

Gabby had disappeared into the hedge; a few seconds later, he'd seen her enter her home through the sliding glass door. He was still sitting at the table, feeling slightly shell-shocked, when he spotted his sister approaching.

"How long have you been here?"

"Long enough," she said. She saw the cooler near the door and pulled out a beer. "For a second there, I thought she was going to punch you. Then I thought she was going to cry. And then she looked like she wanted to punch you again."

"That's about right," he admitted. He rubbed his forehead, still processing the scene.

"Still charming the girlfriends, I see."

"She's not my girlfriend. She's my neighbor."

"Even better." Stephanie took a seat. "How long have you been dating?"

"We're not. Actually, that's the first time I've ever met her."

"Impressive," Stephanie observed. "I didn't think you had it in you."

"What?"

"You know—making someone hate you so quickly. That's a rare gift. Usually you have to know a person better first."

"Very funny."

"I thought so. And Moby . . ." She turned toward the dog and lifted a scolding finger. "You should know better."

Moby wiggled his tail before getting to his feet. He walked toward her, nuzzling Stephanie in her lap. She pushed the top of the head, which only made Moby push back harder.

"Easy there, you old hound dog."

"It's not Moby's fault."

"So you said. Not that she wanted to hear it, of course. What's with her?"

"She was just upset."

"I could tell. It took me a little while before I could figure out what she was talking about. But I must say that it was entertaining."

"Be nice."

"I am nice." Stephanie leaned back, evaluating her brother. "She was kind of cute, don't you think?"

"I didn't notice."

"Yeah, sure you didn't. I'd be willing to bet it was the first thing you noticed. I saw the way you were ogling her."

"My, my. You're in quite a mood this evening."

"I should be. The exam I just finished was a killer."

"What does that mean? You think you missed a question?"

"No. But I had to really think hard about some of them."

"Must be nice being you."

"Oh, it is. I've got three more exams next week, too."

"Poor baby. Life as a perpetual student is so much harder than actually earning a living."

"Look who's talking. You were in school longer than me. Which reminds me . . . how do you think Mom and Dad would feel if I told them I wanted to stay in for another couple of years to get my PhD?"

At Gabby's house, the kitchen light flashed on. Distracted, he took a moment to answer.

"They'd probably be okay with it. You know Mom and Dad."

"I know. But lately I get the feeling that they want me to meet someone and settle down."

"Join the club. I've had that feeling for years."

"Yeah, but it's different for me. I'm a woman. My biological clock is ticking."

The kitchen light next door flashed off; a few seconds later, another flashed on in the bedroom. He wondered idly whether Gabby was turning in for the night.

"You've got to remember that Mom was married at twenty-one," Stephanie went on. "By twenty-three, she already had you." She waited for a response but got nothing. "But then again, look how well you turned out. Maybe I should use that as my argument."

Her words filtered in slowly, and he furrowed his brow when they finally registered.

"Is that an insult?"

"I tried," she said with a smirk. "Just checking to see if you're paying attention to me or whether you're thinking about your new friend over there."

"She's not a friend," he said. He knew he sounded defensive but he couldn't help it.

"Not now," his sister said. "But I get a funny feeling she will be."

Two

Gabby wasn't sure how she felt after leaving her neighbor's, and all she could do after closing her door was to lean against it while she tried to regain her equilibrium.

Maybe she shouldn't have gone over there, she thought. It certainly hadn't done any good. Not only hadn't he apologized, he'd gone so far as to deny that his dog was responsible. Still, as she finally moved away from the door, she found herself smiling. At least she'd done it. She'd stood up for herself and told him exactly how it was going to be. It had taken courage to do that, she told herself. She normally wasn't very good at speaking her mind. Not to Kevin about the fact that his plans for their future seemed to go only as far as the next weekend. Or to Dr. Melton about the way she felt when he touched her. Not even to her mom, who always seemed to have opinions on how Gabby could improve herself.

She stopped smiling when she caught sight of Molly sleeping in the corner. A quick peek was enough to remind her that the end result hadn't changed and that maybe, just maybe, she could have done a better job of convincing him that it was his duty to help her. As she replayed the evening, she felt a wave of embarrassment. She knew she'd been rambling, but after being knocked down, she had lost her focus, and then her frustration had rendered her completely unable to stop talking. Her mother would have had a field day with that one. She loved her mother, but her mother was one of those ladies who never lost control. It drove Gabby crazy; more than once during her teenage years, she'd wanted to take her mother by the arms and shake her, just to elicit a spontaneous response. Of course, it wouldn't have worked. Her mother would have simply allowed the shaking to continue until Gabby was finished, then smoothed her hair and made some infuriating comment like "Well, Gabrielle, now that you've gotten that out of your system, can we discuss this like ladies?"

Ladies. Gabby couldn't stand that word. When her mother said it, she was often plagued by a sweeping sense of failure, one that made her think she had a long way to go and no map to get there.

Of course, her mother couldn't help the way she was, any more than Gabby could. Her mother was a walking cliché of southern womanhood, having grown up wearing frilly dresses and being presented to the community's elite at the Savannah Christmas Cotillion, one of the most exclusive debutante balls in the country. She had also served as treasurer for the Tri Delts at the University of Georgia, another family tradition, and while in college, she had apparently been of the opinion that academics were far less important than working toward a "Mrs." degree, which she believed the only career choice for a proper southern lady. It went without saying that she wanted the "Mr." part of the equation to be worthy of the family name. Which essentially meant rich.

Enter her father. Her dad, a successful real estate developer and general contractor, was twelve years older than his wife when they'd married, and if not as rich as some, he was certainly well-off. Still, Gabby could remember studying the wedding photos of her parents as they stood outside the church and wondering how two such different people could have ever fallen in love. While her mom loved the pheasant at the country club, Dad preferred biscuits and gravy at the local diner; while Mom never walked as far as the mailbox without her makeup, Dad wore jeans, and his hair was always a bit disheveled. But love each other they did—of this, Gabby had no doubt. In the mornings, she would sometimes catch her parents in a tender embrace, and never once had she heard them argue. Nor did they have separate beds, like so many of Gabby's friends' parents, who often struck her as business partners more than lovers. Even now, when she visited, she would find her parents snuggled up on the couch together, and when her friends marveled, she would simply shake her head and admit that for whatever reason, they were perfectly suited to each other.

Much to her mother's endless disappointment, Gabby, unlike her three honey blond sisters, had always been more like her father. Even as a child, she preferred overalls to dresses, adored climbing in trees, and spent hours playing in the dirt. Every now and then, she would traipse behind her father at a job site, mimicking his movements as he checked the seals on newly installed windows or peeked into boxes that had recently arrived from Mitchell's hardware store. Her dad taught her to bait a hook and to fish, and she loved riding beside him in his old, rumbly truck with its broken radio, a truck he'd never bothered to trade in. After work, they would either play catch or shoot baskets while her mom watched from the kitchen window in a way that always struck Gabby as not only disapproving, but uncomprehending. More often than not, her sisters could be seen standing beside her, their mouths agape.

While Gabby liked to tell people about the free spirit she'd been as a child, in reality she'd ended up straddling both her parents' visions of the world, mainly because her mom was an expert when it came to the manipulative power of motherhood. As she grew older, Gabby acquiesced more to her mother's opinions about clothing and *the proper behavior for ladies,* simply to avoid feeling guilty. Of all the weapons in her mother's arsenal, guilt was far and away the most effective, and Mom always knew just how to use it. Because of a raised eyebrow here and a little comment there, Gabby ended up in cotillion classes and dance lessons; she dutifully learned to play the piano and, like her mother, was formally presented at the Savannah Christmas Cotillion. If her mother was proud that night—and she was, by the look on her face—Gabby by that time felt as if she were finally ready to make her own decisions, some of which she knew her mother wouldn't approve. Sure, she wanted to get married and have children someday just like Mom, but by then she'd realized that she also wanted a career like Dad. More specifically, she wanted to be a doctor.

Oh, Mom said all the right things when she found out. In the beginning, anyway. But then the subtle guilt offensive began. As Gabby aced exam after exam in college, her mom would sometimes frown and wonder aloud whether it was possible to both work full-time as a doctor and be a full-time wife and mother.

"But if work is more important to you than family," her mom would say, "then by all means, become a doctor."

Gabby tried to resist her mother's campaign, but in the end, old habits die hard and she eventually settled on PA school instead of medical school. The reasons made sense: She'd still see patients, but her hours would be relatively stable and she'd never be on call—definitely a more family-friendly option. Still, it sometimes bugged her that her mother put the idea in her mind in the first place.

But she couldn't deny that family was important to her. That's the thing about being the product of happily married parents. You grow up thinking the fairy tale is real, and more than that, you think you're entitled to live it. So far, though, it wasn't working out as planned. She and Kevin had dated long enough to fall in love, survive the ordinary ups and downs that break most couples apart, and even talk about the future. She had decided that he was the one she wanted to spend her life with, and she frowned, thinking about their most recent argument.

As if sensing Gabby's distress, Molly struggled to her feet and waddled over, nuzzling Gabby's hand. Gabby stroked her fur, allowing it to run through her fingers.

"I wonder if it's stress," Gabby said, wishing her life could be more like Molly's. Simple, without cares or responsibilities . . . well, except for the pregnancy part. "Do I seem stressed to you?"

Molly didn't answer, but she didn't have to. Gabby knew she was stressed. She could feel it in her shoulders whenever she paid the bills, or when Dr. Melton leered at her, or when Kevin played stupid about what she'd expected by agreeing to move closer to him. It didn't help that, aside from Kevin, she didn't really have any friends here. She'd barely gotten to know anyone outside the office, and truth be told, her neighbor was the first person she'd spoken with since she'd moved in. Thinking back, she supposed she could have been nicer about the whole thing. She felt a twinge of remorse about spouting off the way she had, especially since he did seem like a friendly guy. When he'd helped her up, he'd seemed almost like a friend. And once she'd started babbling, he hadn't interrupted her once, which was sort of refreshing, too.

It was remarkable now that she thought about it. Considering how crazy she must have sounded, he hadn't gotten upset or snapped at her, which was something Kevin would have done. Just thinking about the gentle way he'd helped her to her feet made the blood rush to her cheeks. And then there had been a moment after he'd handed her the napkin that she'd caught him staring at her in a way that suggested he'd found her attractive as well. It had been a long time since something like that had happened, and even though she didn't want to admit it, it made her feel good about herself. She missed that. Amazing what a little truthful confrontation could do for the soul.

She went into the bedroom and slipped into a pair of comfy sweats and a soft, worn shirt she'd owned since her freshman year in college. Molly trailed behind her, and when Gabby realized what she needed, she motioned toward the door.

"You ready to go outside?" she asked.

Molly's tail started to wag as she moved toward the door. Gabby inspected her closely. She still looked pregnant, but maybe her neighbor had a point. She should bring her to the vet, if only to be sure. Besides, she had no idea how to care for a pregnant dog. She wondered if Molly needed extra vitamins, which reminded her again that she was falling behind in her own resolution to lead a healthier life. Eating better, exercising, sleeping regularly, stretching: She'd planned to start as soon as she'd moved into the house. A new-house resolution of sorts, but it hadn't really taken hold. Tomorrow, she'd definitely go jogging, then have a salad for lunch and another one for dinner. And since she was ready to get on with some serious life changes, she might just ask Kevin point-blank about his plans for their future.

Then again, maybe that wasn't such a good idea. Standing up to the neighbor was one thing; was she ready to accept the consequences if she wasn't happy with Kevin's answer? What if he had no plans? Did she really want to quit her first job after a couple of months? Sell her house? Move away? Just how far was she willing to go?

She wasn't sure of anything, other than the fact that she didn't want to lose him. But trying to be healthier—now that, she could definitely do. One step at a time, right? Her decision made, she stepped onto the back deck and watched as Molly padded down the steps and headed toward the far end of the yard. The air was still warm, but a light breeze had picked up. The stars spread across the sky in random, intricate patterns that, aside from the Big Dipper, she'd never been able to discern, and she resolved that she'd buy a book on astronomy tomorrow, right after lunch. She'd spend a couple of days learning the basics, then invite Kevin to spend a romantic evening at the beach, where she'd point to the sky and ever so casually mention something astronomically impressive. She closed her eyes, imagining the scene, and stood straighter. Tomorrow, she'd start becoming a new person. A better person. And she'd figure out what to do about Molly, too. Even if she had to beg, she'd find homes for every one of those puppies.

But first, she'd bring her to the vet.

Three

It was shaping up to be one of those days when Gabby wondered why she'd decided to work in a pediatric office. She had the chance, after all, to work in a cardiology unit at the hospital, which had been her plan all the way through PA school. She had loved assisting in challenging surgeries, and it seemed like a perfect fit until her final rotation, when she happened to work with a pediatrician who filled her head with ideas about the nobility and joy of caring for infants. Dr. Bender, a gray-haired medical veteran who never stopped smiling and knew practically every child in Sumter, South Carolina, convinced her that while cardiology might pay better and seem more glamorous, there was nothing quite as rewarding as holding newborns and watching them develop over the critical first years of life. Usually she nodded dutifully, but on her last day, he'd forced the issue by placing an infant in her arms. As the baby cooed, Dr. Bender's voice floated toward her: "In cardiology, everything is an emergency and your patients always seem to get sicker, no matter what you do. After a while, that has to be draining. It can burn you out quick if you're not careful. But caring for a little fella like this . . ." He paused, motioning to the baby. "This is the highest calling in the world."

Despite a job offer in cardiology at a hospital in her hometown, she'd taken a job with Drs. Furman and Melton in Beaufort, North Carolina. Dr. Furman struck her as oblivious, Dr. Melton struck her as a flirt, but it was an opportunity to be nearer to Kevin. And on some level, she'd believed that Dr. Bender just might be right. He'd been right about the infants. For the most part, she loved working with them, even when she had to give them shots and their screams made her wince. Toddlers were okay, too. Most of them had darling personalities, and she loved to watch as they cuddled their blankets or teddy bears and stared at her with guileless expressions. It was the parents who drove her crazy. Dr. Bender had failed to mention one critical point: In cardiology, you dealt with a patient who came to the office because he or she wanted or needed to; in pediatrics, you dealt with a patient who was often under the care of neurotic, know-it-all parents. Eva Bronson was a case in point.

Eva, who was holding George on her lap in the exam room, seemed to be looking down her nose at Gabby. The fact that she wasn't technically a physician and was relatively young made many parents believe she was little more than an overpaid nurse.

"Are you sure Dr. Furman can't squeeze us in?" She emphasized the word *doctor*.

"He's at the hospital," Gabby replied. "He won't be in until later. Besides, I'm pretty sure he'd agree with me. Your son seems fine."

"But he's still coughing."

"Like I said before, toddlers can cough for up to six weeks after a cold. Their lungs take longer to heal, but it's perfectly normal at this age."

"So you're not going to give him an antibiotic?"

"No. He doesn't need one. His ears were clear, his sinuses were clear, and I didn't hear any evidence of bronchitis in his lungs. His temperature is normal, and he looks healthy."

George, who'd just turned two, was squirming in Eva's lap, trying to get free, a bundle of happy energy. Eva tightened her grip.

"Since Dr. Furman's not here, maybe Dr. Melton should see him.

I'm pretty sure he needs an antibiotic. Half the kids in his day care are on antibiotics right now. Something's going around."

Gabby pretended to write something in the chart. Eva Bronson always wanted an antibiotic for George. Eva Bronson was an antibiotic junkie, if there was such a thing.

"If he spikes a fever, you can bring him back and I'll examine him again."

"I don't want to bring him *back*. That's why I brought him in *today*. I think he should see a *doctor*."

Gabby did her best to keep her tone steady. "Okay, I'll see if Dr. Melton can squeeze in a couple of minutes for you."

As she left the room, Gabby paused in the hallway, knowing she needed to prepare herself. She didn't want to talk to Dr. Melton again; she'd been doing her best to avoid him all morning. As soon as Dr. Furman had left for the hospital to be present at an emergency C-section at Carteret General Hospital in Morehead City, Dr. Melton had sidled up next to her, close enough for her to notice that he'd recently gargled with mouthwash.

"I guess we'll be on our own this morning," he'd said.

"Maybe it won't be too busy," she'd said neutrally. She wasn't ready to confront him, not without Dr. Furman around.

"Mondays are always busy. Hopefully we won't have to work through lunch."

"Hopefully," she'd echoed.

Dr. Melton had reached for the file on the door of the exam room across the hall. He'd scanned it quickly, and just as Gabby was about to leave, she'd heard his voice again. "Speaking of lunch, have you ever had a fish taco?"

Gabby blinked. "Huh?"

"I know this great place in Morehead near the beach. Maybe we could swing by. We could bring some back for the staff, too."

Though he had maintained a pretense of professionalism—he would have sounded the same way had he been speaking to Dr. Furman—Gabby had felt herself recoil.

"I can't," she'd said. "I'm supposed to bring Molly to the vet. I made an appointment this morning."

"And they can get you in and out of there in time?"

"They said they would."

He had hesitated. "Okay then," he'd said. "Maybe another time."

As Gabby reached for a file, she'd winced. "You okay?" Dr. Melton had asked.

"I'm just a little sore from working out," she'd said before disappearing into the room.

Actually, she was really sore. Ridiculously sore. Everything from her neck to her ankles throbbed, and it seemed to be getting worse. Had she simply jogged on Sunday, she figured she probably would have been okay. But that hadn't been enough. Not for the new, improved Gabby. After jogging—and proud of the fact that even though her pace had been slow, she hadn't had to stop once to walk—she'd headed to Gold's Gym in Morehead City to sign up for a membership. She'd signed the paperwork while the trainer explained the various classes with complicated names that were scheduled almost every hour. As she got up to leave, he'd mentioned that a new class called Body Pump was about to start in a few minutes.

"It's a fantastic class," he'd said. "It works the whole body. You get strength and cardio in a single workout. You should try it."

So she had. And may God forgive him for how it made her feel.

Not immediately, of course. No, during the class, she'd been fine. Though deep down she knew she should pace herself, she found herself trying to keep up with the scantily clad, surgically enhanced, mascara-wearing woman next to her. She'd lifted and pushed weights, jogged in place to the beat, then lifted some more and jogged in place, over and over. By the time she left, with muscles quivering, she'd felt as if she'd taken the next step in her evolution. She'd ordered herself a protein shake on the way out the door, just to complete the transformation.

On the way home, she'd swung by the bookstore to buy a book on astronomy, and later, as she was about to fall asleep, she'd realized she felt better about the future than she had in a long time, except for the fact that her muscles seemed to be stiffening by the minute.

Unfortunately, the new, improved Gabby had found it exceptionally painful to rise from bed the following morning. Everything hurt. No, scratch that. It was beyond hurt. Way beyond. It was excruciating. Every muscle in her body felt as if it had been run through a juice blender. Her back, her chest, her stomach, her legs, her butt, her arms, her neck . . . even her fingers ached. It took three attempts to sit up in bed, and after staggering to the bathroom, she'd found that brushing her teeth without screaming took a herculean amount of self-control. In the medicine cabinet, she'd found herself reaching for pretty much everything—Tylenol, Bayer aspirin, Aleve—and in the end, she'd decided to take them all. She'd washed down the pills with a glass of water and watched herself wince while swallowing.

Okay, she admitted, maybe she'd overdone it.

But it was too late now, and even worse, the painkillers hadn't worked. Or maybe they had. She was, after all, able to function in the office, as long as she moved slowly. But the pain was still there, and Dr. Furman was gone, and the last thing she wanted was to deal with Dr. Melton.

Without another option, she asked one of the nurses which room he was in and, after knocking on the door, poked her head in. Dr. Melton looked up from his patient, his expression becoming animated as soon as he saw her.

"Sorry to interrupt," she said. "Can I talk to you for a second?"

"Sure," he said. He rose from his stool, set aside the file on his way out, and closed the door behind him. "Did you change your mind about lunch?"

She shook her head and told him about Eva Bronson and George; he promised he'd talk to them as quickly as he could. As she left, she could feel his eyes lingering on her as she limped down the hall.

It was half-past noon when Gabby finished with her last patient of the morning. Clutching her purse, she hobbled toward her car, knowing she didn't have much time. Her next appointment was in forty-five minutes, but assuming she wasn't held up at the vet, she would be okay. It was one of the nice things about living in a small town of fewer than four thousand people. Everything was only minutes away. While Morehead City—five times the size of Beaufort—was just across the bridge that spanned the Intracoastal Waterway and the place where most people did their weekend shopping, the short distance was enough to make this town feel distinct and isolated, like most of the towns *down east,* which was what the locals called this part of the state.

It was a pretty place, especially the historic district. On a day like today, with temperatures perfect for strolling, Beaufort resembled what she imagined Savannah to be in the first century of its existence.

Wide streets, shade trees, and a little more than a hundred restored homes occupied several blocks, eventually giving way to Front Street and a short boardwalk that overlooked the marina. Slips were occupied by leisure and working boats of every shape and size; a magnificent yacht worth millions might be docked next to a small crab boat on one side, with a lovingly maintained sailboat on the other. There were a couple of restaurants with gorgeous views: old, homegrown places with local character, complete with covered patios and picnic tables that made customers feel as if they were on vacation in a place where time stood still. On occasional weekend evenings, bands would perform at the restaurants, and last summer on the Fourth of July, when she was visiting Kevin, so many people came to hear the music and see the fireworks that the marina literally filled with boats. Without enough slips to accommodate them, the boats were simply tied up to one another, and their owners would walk from boat to boat until they reached the dock, accepting or offering beers to strangers as they went.

On the opposite side of the street, there were real estate offices mingled with art shops and tourist traps. In the evenings, Gabby liked to stroll through the art shops to examine the work. When she was young, she'd dreamed of painting or drawing for a living; it took a few years before she realized that her ambition far exceeded her talent. That didn't mean she couldn't appreciate quality work, and every now and then she found a photograph or painting that made her pause. Twice, she'd actually made purchases, and both paintings now hung in her house. She'd considered buying a few more to complement them, but her monthly budget prevented it, at least for the time being.

A few minutes later, Gabby pulled into her driveway and yelped as she got out of the car before gamely making her way to the front door. Molly met her on the porch, took her sweet time smelling the flower bed until she took care of business, then hopped into the passenger seat. Gabby yelped again as she got back in, then rolled down the window so Molly could hang her head out, something she loved to do.

The Down East Veterinary Clinic was only a couple of minutes away, and she pulled into the parking lot, listening to the crunch of gravel beneath her wheels. A rustic and weathered Victorian, the clinic building appeared less like an office than a home. She slipped a leash on Molly, then stole a glance at her watch. She prayed the vet would be quick.

The screen door opened with a loud squeak, and she felt Molly tug at the leash as she was confronted with odors typical of animal clinics. Gabby approached the front desk, but before she could speak, the receptionist stood up from behind her desk.

"Is this Molly?" she asked.

Gabby didn't bother to hide her surprise. Living in a small town still took some getting used to. "Yeah. I'm Gabby Holland."

"Nice to meet you. I'm Terri, by the way. What a beautiful dog."

"Thank you."

"We were wondering when you'd get here. You have to get back to work, right?" She grabbed a clipboard. "Let me go ahead and get you set up in a room. You can do the paperwork there. That way, the vet can see you right away. It shouldn't be long. He's almost done."

"Great," Gabby said. "I really appreciate it."

The receptionist led them to an adjoining room; just inside was a scale, and she helped Molly get on it. "It's no big deal. Besides, I bring my kids to your pediatric office all the time. How do you like it so far?"

"I'm enjoying it," she said. "It's busier than I thought it would be."

Terri recorded the weight, then proceeded down the hallway. "I just love Dr. Melton. He's been wonderful with my son."

"I'll tell him," Gabby said.

Terri motioned to a small room furnished with a metal table and plastic chair and handed the clipboard to Gabby. "Just fill that out, and I'll let the doctor know you're here."

Terri left them alone, and Gabby gingerly took a seat, wincing as she felt the muscles in her legs plead in agony. She took a couple of deep breaths, waiting until the pain passed, then filled out the paperwork while Molly wandered the room.

Less than a minute later, the door opened and the first thing Gabby noticed was the white smock; an instant later, the name embroidered in blue letters. Gabby was just about to speak, but sudden recognition made it impossible.

"Hi, Gabby," Travis said. "How are you?"

Gabby continued to stare, wondering what on earth he was doing here. She was about to say something when she realized that his eyes were blue, when she'd thought they were brown. Strange. Still—

"I take it this is Molly," he said, interrupting her thoughts. "Hey, girl . . ." He squatted and rubbed Molly's neck. "You like that? Oh, you're a sweet one, aren't you? How you feeling, girl?"

The sound of his voice brought her back, and memories of their argument the other night followed. "You're—you're the vet?" Gabby stammered.

Travis nodded as he continued to scratch Molly's neck. "Along with my dad. He started the clinic, I joined him after I finished school."

This couldn't be happening. Of all the people in this town, it had to be him. Why on earth couldn't she have an ordinary, uncomplicated day?

"Why didn't you say anything the other night?"

"I did. I told you to bring her to the vet, remember?"

Her eyes narrowed. The man seemed to enjoy infuriating her. "You know what I mean."

He looked up. "You mean about me being the vet? I tried to tell you, but you wouldn't let me."

"You should have said something anyway."

"I don't think you were in any mood to hear it. But that's water under the bridge. No hard feelings." He smiled. "Let me check this girl out, okay? I know you have to get back to work, so I'll make this quick."

She could feel her anger rising at his nonchalant "No hard feelings." Part of her wanted to leave right then. Unfortunately, he was already beginning to prod Molly's belly. Nor, she realized, could she rise quickly, even if she tried, since right now her legs seemed to be on strike. Chagrined, she crossed her arms and felt something akin to a knife blade plunging into her back and shoulders while Travis readied the stethoscope. She bit her lip, proud of the fact she hadn't yelped again.

Travis glanced at her. "You okay?"

"I'm fine," she said.

"You sure? You seem like you're in pain."

"I'm fine," she repeated.

Ignoring her tone, he returned his attention to the dog. He moved the stethoscope, listened again, then examined one of her nipples. Finally, he slipped on a rubber glove with a snap and did a quick internal.

"Well, she's definitely pregnant," he said, removing the glove and tossing it into the bin. "And from the looks of things, she's about seven weeks along."

"I told you." She glared at him. *And Moby is responsible,* she refrained from adding.

Travis stood and put the stethoscope back into his pocket. He reached for the clipboard and flipped the page.

"Just so you know, I'm pretty sure Moby's not responsible."

"Oh, no?"

"No. Most likely it's that Labrador I've seen around the neighborhood. I think he's old man Cason's, but I'm not positive about that. It might be his son's dog. I know he's back in town."

"What makes you so sure it's not Moby?"

He started making notes, and for a moment, she wasn't sure he'd heard her.

He shrugged. "Well, for one thing, he's been neutered."

There are moments when mental overload can render words impossible. All at once, Gabby saw a mortifying montage of herself babbling and crying and finally storming off in a huff. She *did* have a vague memory of him trying to tell her something, all of which served to make her feel queasy.

"Neutered?" she whispered.

"Uh-huh." He looked up from the clipboard. "Two years ago. My dad did it here in the office."

"Oh . . ."

"I tried to tell you that, too. But you left before I had a chance.

I felt sort of bad about it, so I stopped by on Sunday to tell you then, but you were out."

She said the only thing that came to mind. "I was at the gym."

"Yeah? Good for you."

It took some effort, but she uncrossed her arms. "I guess I owe you an apology."

"No hard feelings," he said again, but this time it made her feel even worse. "But listen, I know you're in a rush, so let me tell you a bit about Molly, okay?"

She nodded, feeling as if she'd been placed in the corner by her teacher, still thinking about her tirade on Saturday night. The fact that he was being gracious about it somehow made it even worse.

"The gestation period lasts nine weeks, so you've got another two weeks. Her hips are wide enough, so you don't have to worry about that, which was why I wanted you to bring her in. Collies sometimes have small hips. Now, normally, there's nothing you need to do, but keep in mind that most likely she'll want a cool, dark place to have her puppies, so you might want to put some old blankets down in the garage. You have a door from the kitchen, right?"

She nodded again, feeling as if she were shrinking.

"Just leave it open, and she'll probably start wandering in there. We call it nesting, and it's perfectly normal. Odds are she'll have the puppies when it's quiet. At night, or while you're at work, but remember this is completely natural, so there's nothing to worry about. The puppies will know how to wean right away, so you don't need to be concerned about that, either. And you'll most likely throw out the blankets, so don't use anything fancy, okay?"

She nodded for the third time, feeling ever smaller.

"Other than that, there's not much more you need to know. If there are any problems, you can bring her to the office. If it's after hours, you know where I live."

She cleared her throat. "Okay."

When she said nothing else, he smiled and began to move toward the door. "That's it. You can bring her back home if you'd like. But I'm glad you brought her in. I didn't think it was an infection, but I'm happy I made sure."

"Thanks," Gabby mumbled. "And again, I'm really sorry. . . ."

He held up his hands to stop her. "It's no problem. Really. You were upset, and Moby does wander the neighborhood. It was an honest mistake. I'll see you around, okay?" By the time he gave Molly a final pat, Gabby felt six inches tall.

Once Travis—Dr. Parker—left the exam room, she waited for a long moment to be certain he was gone. Then slowly, painfully, she rose from her chair. She peeked out the door and, after making sure the coast was clear, went to the receptionist's desk, where she quietly paid her bill.

By the time she got back to work, the only thing Gabby knew for certain was that as forgiving as he'd been, she'd never live down what she'd done, and since there wasn't a rock large enough for her to crawl under, it was in her best interest to find a way to avoid him for a while. Not forever, of course. Something reasonable. Like the next fifty years.

Four

~~~

Travis Parker stood by the window, watching as Gabby led Molly back to the car. He was smiling to himself, amused by her expressions. Though he barely knew her, he'd seen enough to conclude that she was one of those people whose expressions were a window to their every feeling. It was a rare quality these days. He often felt that too many people lived their lives acting and pretending, wearing masks and losing themselves in the process. Gabby, he felt certain, would never be that way.

Pocketing his keys, he headed for his truck, with the promise that he'd be back from lunch in half an hour. He retrieved his cooler—he packed his lunch every morning—and drove to his usual spot. A year ago he'd purchased a plot of land overlooking Shackleford Banks at the end of Front Street, with the thought that one day he'd build his dream home there. The only problem was that he wasn't quite sure what that entailed. For the most part, he led a simple life and dreamed of throwing up a rustic little shack like the kind he'd seen in the Florida Keys, something with lots of character that appeared a hundred years old on the outside but was surprisingly bright and roomy on the inside. He didn't need much space—a bedroom and maybe an office in addition to the living area—but as soon as he'd start the process, he'd reason that the lot was better suited for something more family-friendly. That rendered the image of his dream home fuzzier, since it no doubt included a future wife and kids, neither of which he was even close to imagining.

Sometimes, the way he and his sister had turned out struck him as strange, since she, too, was in no hurry to marry. Their parents had been married for almost thirty-five years, and Travis could no more picture either of them single than he could picture himself flapping his arms and zooming into the clouds. Sure, he'd heard the stories of how they'd met on a church group camping trip while they were in high school, how Mom had cut her finger while slicing a piece of pie for dessert, and how dad had clamped his hand over the wound like a surgical bandage to stem the bleeding. One touch and "Bing, bang, boom, just like that," Dad would say, "I knew she was the one for me."

So far, there'd never been a bing, bang, boom for Travis. Nothing even close, for that matter. Sure, there was his high school girlfriend, Olivia; everyone at the school seemed to think they were perfect for each other. She lived across the bridge in Morehead City these days, and every now and then he'd run into her at Wal-Mart or Target. They'd chat for a minute or so about nothing important and then amicably go their separate ways.

There had been countless girlfriends since Olivia, of course. He wasn't clueless when it came to women, after all. He found them attractive and interesting, but more than that, he was genuinely fond of them. He was proud of the fact that he'd never had what could even remotely be considered a painful breakup for either him or one of his exes. The breakups were almost always mutual, petering out like a soggy fuse on a firecracker as opposed to the big kaboom of fireworks overhead. He considered himself friends with all of his exes—Monica, his latest, included—and figured they'd say the same thing about him. He wasn't right for them, and they weren't right for him. He'd watched three former girlfriends get married off to great guys, and he'd been invited to all three weddings. He seldom thought about finding *permanence* or *his soul mate*, but in the rare times he did, he always ended up imagining finding someone who shared the same active, outdoor passions he did. Life was for living, wasn't it? Sure, everyone had responsibilities, and he didn't mind those. He enjoyed his work, earned a good living, owned a house, and paid his bills on time, but he didn't want a life where those things constituted all there was. He wanted to experience life. No, change that. He *needed* to experience life.

He'd been that way for as long as he could remember. Growing up, Travis had been organized and capable when it came to school, getting good grades with a minimum of fuss or anxiety, but, more often than not, just as happy with a B instead of an A. It drove his mother crazy—"Imagine how well you could do if you applied yourself," she repeated every time a report card came home. But school didn't excite him the way riding his bike at breakneck speed or surfing in the Outer Banks did. While other kids thought about sports in terms of baseball and soccer, he thought of floating on air on his motorbike as he soared off a dirt ramp or the rush of energy he felt when he successfully landed it. He was an X Games kind of kid, even before there was such a thing, and by thirty-two, he'd pretty much done it all.

In the distance, he could see wild horses congregating near the dunes of Shackleford Banks, and as he watched them, he reached for his sandwich. Turkey on wheat with mustard, an apple, and a bottle of water; he had the same thing every day, after the exact same breakfast of oatmeal, scrambled egg whites, and a banana. As much as he craved the occasional adrenaline rush, his diet couldn't be more boring. His friends marveled at the rigidity of his self-control, but what he didn't tell them was that it had more to do with his limited palate than discipline. When he was ten, he'd been forced to finish a plate of Thai noodles drenched in ginger, and he'd vomited most of the night. Ever since then, the faintest whiff of ginger would send him gagging to the bathroom, and his palate had never been the same. He became timid about food in general, preferring plain and predictable to anything with exotic flavor; then gradually, as he grew older, he cut out the junk. Now, after more than twenty years, he was too afraid to change.

As he enjoyed his sandwich—plain and predictable—he wondered at the direction of his thoughts. It wasn't like him. He usually wasn't prone to deep reflection. (Another cause of the inevitable soggy fuse, according to Maria, his girlfriend of six years ago.) Usually he just went about his life, doing what needed to be done and figuring out ways to enjoy the rest of his time. That was one of the great things about being single: A person could pretty much do what he wanted, whenever he wanted, and introspection was only an option.

It had to be Gabby, he thought, though for the life of him, he couldn't understand why. He barely knew her, and he doubted whether he'd even had a chance to meet the real Gabby Holland yet. Oh, he'd seen the angry one the other night and the mea culpa one just a little while ago, but he had no idea how she behaved under ordinary circumstances. He suspected that she had a good sense of humor, though on closer reflection, he couldn't pin down the reason he thought so. And she was no doubt intelligent, though he could have deduced that on the basis of her job. But other than that . . . he tried and failed to picture her on a date. Still, he was glad she'd come by, if only to give them a chance to start over as neighbors. One thing he'd learned was that bad neighbors could make a person miserable. Joe's neighbor was the kind of guy who burned leaves on the first gorgeous day of spring and mowed his lawn first thing Saturday mornings, and the two of them had nearly come to blows more than once after a long night with the baby. Common courtesy, it sometimes seemed to Travis, was going the way of the dinosaurs, and the last thing he wanted was for Gabby to feel any reason to avoid him. Maybe he'd invite her over the next time his friends came by. . . .

Yeah, he thought, I'll do that. The decision made, he gathered his cooler and started back toward his truck. On tap that afternoon were the regular assortment of dogs and cats, but at three, someone was supposed to be bringing in a gecko. He liked treating geckos or any exotic pet; the idea that he knew what he was talking about, which he did, always impressed the owners. He enjoyed their awed expressions: *I wonder if he knows the exact anatomy and physiology of every creature on earth.* And he pretended that he did. But fact was a bit more prosaic. No, he of course didn't know the ins and outs of every creature on earth—who could?—but infections were infections and pretty much treated the same way regardless of species; only the medication dose was different, and that he had to verify in a reference book he kept on his desk.

As he got in the car, he found himself thinking about Gabby and wondering whether she'd ever gone surfing or snowboarding. It seemed unlikely, but at the same time, he had the strange feeling that, unlike most of his exes, she would be up for either of those two things, given the opportunity. He wasn't sure why, and as he started the engine he tried to dismiss the notion, doing his best to convince himself it didn't matter. Except for the fact that, somehow, it did.

Five

Over the next two weeks, Gabby became an expert in making a covert entry and exit, at least when it came to her house.

She had no other choice. What on earth could she say to Travis? She'd made a fool of herself, and he'd compounded the matter by being so forgiving, which obviously meant that coming and going required a new set of rules, one in which avoidance was Rule #1. Her only saving grace—the only positive thing to come out of the whole experience—was that she'd apologized in his office.

It was getting harder to keep it up, though. At first, all she'd had to do was park her car in the garage, but now that Molly was getting close to her due date, Gabby had to start parking in the driveway so Molly could nest. Which meant that Gabby thenceforth had to come and go when she was certain Travis wasn't around.

She'd come down on the fifty-year limit, though; now, she figured a couple of months or maybe half a year would suffice. Whatever amount of time seemed long enough for him to forget, or at least diminish the memory of, the way she'd acted. She knew that time had a funny way of dimming the edges of reality until only something blurry remained, and when that happened, she'd go back to a more normal routine. She'd start small—a wave here or there as she got in the car, maybe a wave from her back deck if they happened to see each other—and they'd go on from there. In time, she figured they'd be fine—maybe they'd even share a laugh someday at the way they'd met—but until then, she preferred to live like a spy.

She'd had to learn Travis's schedule, of course. It wasn't hard—a quick peek at the clock when he was about to pull out in the morning while she watched from her kitchen. Returning home from work was even easier; he was usually out on the boat or the Jet Ski by the time she arrived, but on the downside, that made the evenings the worst problem of all. Because he was *out there*, she had to stay *in here*, no matter how glorious the sunset, and unless she went over to Kevin's, she'd find herself studying the astronomy book, the one she'd purchased in hopes of impressing Kevin while they did some stargazing. Which, unfortunately, hadn't happened yet.

She supposed she could have been more grown up about the whole thing, but she had the funny feeling that if she came face-to-face with Travis, she'd find herself *remembering* instead of *listening*, and the last thing she wanted was to make an even worse impression than she already had. Besides, she had other things on her mind.

Kevin, for one. Most evenings, he swung by for a little while, and he'd even stayed over last weekend, after his customary round of golf, of course. Kevin adored golf. They'd also gone out to three dinners and two movies and had spent part of Sunday afternoon at the beach, and a couple of days ago, while sitting on the couch, he'd slipped off her shoes while they were sipping wine.

"What are you doing?"

"I figured you'd like your feet rubbed. I'll bet they're sore after spending all day standing."

"I should rinse them off first."

"I don't care if they're clean. And besides, I like to look at your toes. You've got cute toes."

"You don't have a secret foot fetish, do you?"

"Not at all. Well, I'm crazy about your feet," he said, beginning to tickle them, and she tugged her foot away, laughing. A moment later, they were kissing passionately, and when he lay beside her afterward, he told her how much he loved her. By the way he was talking, she kind of got the impression that she should consider moving in with him.

Which was good. It was the closest he'd come to talking about their future, but . . .

But what? That's what it always came down to, wasn't it? Was living together a step toward the future or just a way to continue the present? Did she really need him to propose? She thought about it. Well . . . *yes*. But not until he was ready. Which led, of course, to questions that had begun to creep into her thoughts whenever they were together: When would he be ready? Would he ever be ready? And, of course, Why wasn't he ready to marry her?

Was it wrong to want to get married instead of simply live with him? Lord knows she wasn't even sure about that anymore. It's like some people grew up knowing they'd be married by a certain age, and it happened just the way they planned; others knew they wouldn't for a while and moved in with the ones they loved, and that worked fine, too. Sometimes, she felt she was the only one without a clear plan; for her, marriage had always been a vague idea, something that would just . . . happen. And it would. Right?

Thinking about this stuff gave her a headache. What she really wanted to do was sit outside on the deck with a glass of wine and forget everything for a while. But Travis Parker was on his back deck, flipping through a magazine, and that just wouldn't do. So she was stuck inside on a Thursday night again.

She wished Kevin weren't working late so they could do something together. He had a late meeting with a dentist who was opening an office and thus needed all sorts of insurance. That wasn't so bad—she knew he was dedicated to building the business—but he was heading off with his dad to Myrtle Beach for a convention first thing in the morning, and she wouldn't have a chance to see him until next Wednesday, which meant she'd have to spend even more time cooped up like a chicken. Kevin's dad had started one of the largest insurance brokerages in eastern North Carolina, and Kevin was taking on more responsibility with every passing year at their office in Morehead City while his dad edged closer to retirement. Sometimes she wondered what that must have been like—having a career path already charted from the time he could walk—but she supposed there were worse things, especially since the business was successful. Despite the whiff of nepotism, it wasn't as if Kevin didn't earn his way; his dad spent fewer than twenty hours a week in the office these days, which usually left Kevin working closer to sixty. With almost thirty employees, management problems were endless, but Kevin had a knack for dealing with people. At least, that's what a few of them had told her at the company Christmas party both times she'd gone.

Yes, she was proud of him, but it still left her stuck inside on nights like this, which seemed like a waste. Maybe she should just head over to Atlantic Beach, where she could drink a glass of wine and watch the sun go down. For a moment, she considered doing just that. Then she decided against it. It was okay to be alone at home, but the thought of drinking at the beach alone made her feel like a loser. People would think she didn't have a single friend in the world, which wasn't true. She had lots of friends. It just happened that none of them was within a hundred miles of here, and the realization didn't make her feel much better.

If she brought the dog, though . . . now, that was different. That was a perfectly ordinary thing to do, even healthy. It had taken a few days and most of the painkillers she'd had in her medicine cabinet, but the soreness of the first workout had finally passed. She hadn't returned to the Body Pump class again—people in there were obviously masochists—but she had started to keep a fairly regular routine at the gym. For the last few days, anyway. She'd gone on both Monday and Wednesday, and she was determined to make time to go tomorrow as well.

She got up from the couch and turned off the television. Molly wasn't around, and guessing she was in the garage, she headed that way. The door to the garage was propped open, and when she walked in and turned on the light, the first thing she noticed was the collection of wiggling, whining furballs surrounding her. Gabby called out to her; a moment later, however, she began to scream.

Travis had just gone into the kitchen to pull a chicken breast from the refrigerator when he heard the sudden, frantic pounding on his door.

"Dr. Parker? . . . Travis? . . . Are you in there?"

It took only an instant to recognize the voice as Gabby's. When he opened the door, her face was pale and terrified.

"You've got to come." Gabby gasped. "Molly's in trouble."

Travis reacted on instinct; as Gabby began racing back to her house, he retrieved a medical bag from behind the passenger seat in the truck, the one he used for the occasional livestock call that required him to treat animals on farms. His father had always stressed the importance of keeping it fully stocked with anything he might need, and Travis had taken the message to heart. By then, Gabby was almost at her door, and she left it open, disappearing into the house. Travis followed a moment later and spotted her in the kitchen, near the open door that led to the garage.

"She's panting and vomiting," she said as he hurried to her side. "And . . . something's hanging out of her." Travis took in the scene instantly, recognizing the prolapsed uterus and hoping he wasn't too late.

"Let me wash my hands," he said quickly. He scrubbed his hands briskly at the kitchen sink, going on as he scrubbed: "Is there any way you can get some more light in there? Like a lamp or something?"

"Aren't you going to bring her into the clinic?"

"Probably," he said, keeping his voice level. "But not this instant. I want to try something first. And I do need a light, okay? Can you do that for me?"

"Yeah, yeah . . . of course." She vanished from the kitchen, returning a moment later with a lamp. "Is she going to be okay?"

"I'll know in a couple of minutes how serious it is." Holding up his hands like a surgeon, he nodded toward the bag on the floor. "Could you bring that in for me, too? Just put the bag over there and find a place to plug in the lamp. As close to Molly as you can get, okay?"

"Okay," she said, trying not to panic.

Travis approached the dog carefully as Gabby plugged in the light, noting with some relief that Molly was conscious. He could hear her whimpering, which was normal in a situation like this. Next, he focused on the tubular mass that protruded from her vulva and looked over at the puppies, fairly certain that whelping had occurred within the last half hour, which was good, he thought. Less chance of necrosis . . .

"What now?" she asked.

"Just hold her and whisper to her. I need you to help keep her calm."

When Gabby was in place, Travis squatted next to the dog,

listening as Gabby murmured and whispered to her, their faces close together. Molly's tongue lapped out, another good sign. He gently checked the uterus, and Molly twitched slightly.

"What's wrong with her?"

"It's a uterine prolapse. It means that part of the uterus has turned inside out, and it's protruding." He felt the uterus, turning it gently to see if there were any ruptures or necrotic areas. "Were there any problems with the whelping?"

"I don't know," she said. "I didn't even know it was happening. She's going to be okay, right?"

Focused on the uterus, he didn't answer. "Reach into the bag," he said. "There should be some saline. And I'll need the jelly, too."

"What are you going to do?"

"I need to clean the uterus, and then I'm just going to manipulate it a bit. I want to try to manually reduce it, and if we're lucky, it'll contract back in on its own. If not, I'll have to bring her in for surgery. I'd rather avoid that if at all possible."

Gabby found the saline and the jelly and handed them over. Travis rinsed the uterus, then rinsed it two more times before reaching for the lubricating jelly, hoping it would work.

Gabby couldn't bear to watch, so she concentrated on Molly, her mouth close to Molly's ear as she whispered over and over what a good dog she was. Travis stayed quiet, his hand moving rhythmically over the uterus.

She didn't know how long they were in the garage—it could have been ten minutes or it could have been an hour—but finally, she saw Travis lean back, as if trying to relieve the tension in his shoulders. It was then she noticed that his hands were free.

"Is it over?" she ventured. "Is she all right?"

"Yes and no," he said. "Her uterus is back in place, and it seemed to contract without any problems, but she needs to go to the clinic. She's going to need to take it easy for a couple of days while she gets her strength back, and she'll need some antibiotics and fluids. I'll have to do an X-ray as well. But if there are no further complications, she should be good as new. What I'm going to do now is back my truck up to the garage. I've got some old blankets she can lie on."

"And it won't . . . fall back out?"

"It shouldn't. Like I said, it contracted normally."

"What about the puppies?"

"We'll bring them. They need to be with their mama."

"And that won't hurt her?"

"It shouldn't. But that's why she needs fluids. So the puppies can nurse."

Gabby felt her shoulders relax; she hadn't realized how tense they'd become. For the first time, she smiled. "I don't know how to thank you," she said.

"You just did."

After cleaning up, Travis carefully loaded Molly into the truck while Gabby started with the puppies. Once all six were settled, Travis repacked the bag and tossed it onto the front seat. He walked around the truck and opened the driver's-side door.

"I'll let you know how it goes," he said.

"I'm coming."

"It would be better if she got some rest, and if you're in the room, that might not happen. She needs to recover. Don't worry—I'll take good care of her. I'll be with her all night. You have my word on that."

She hesitated. "Are you sure?"

"She'll be fine. I promise."

She considered what he'd said, then offered a tremulous smile. "You know, in my line of work, we're taught never to promise anything. We're told to say that we'll do our best."

"Would you feel better if I didn't promise?"

"No. But I still think I should come with you."

"Don't you have to work tomorrow?"

"Yes. But so do you."

"True, but this is my job. It's what I do. And besides, I have a cot. If you came, you'd have to sleep on the floor."

"You mean you wouldn't give me the cot?"

He climbed into the truck. "I suppose I could if I had to," he said, grinning. "But I'm concerned about what your boyfriend would think if you and I spent the night together."

"How did you know I have a boyfriend?"

He reached for the door. "I didn't," he said, sounding faintly disappointed. Then he smiled, recovering. "Let me bring her in, okay? And call me tomorrow. I'll let you know how it went."

"Yeah," she relented. "Okay."

Travis closed the door, and she heard the engine rattle to a start. He leaned out the window. "Don't worry," he said again. "She's going to be fine."

He eased toward the road, then turned left. In the distance, he waved at her out the window. Gabby waved in return, though she knew he couldn't see it, watching the red lights fade as they rounded the corner.

After he left, Gabby wandered to the bedroom and stood in front of the bureau. She'd always known she'd never be the type to stop traffic, but for the first time in ages, she found herself staring into the mirror and wondering what someone besides Kevin thought when he saw her.

Despite her exhaustion and unruly hair, she didn't look as bad as she feared. The thought pleased her, though she wasn't sure why. Unaccountably, she recalled the disappointment on Travis's face when she'd told him about her boyfriend, and she flushed. It wasn't as if she felt any differently toward Kevin. . . .

She'd certainly been wrong about Travis Parker, wrong about everything from the beginning. He'd been so steady during the emergency. It still amazed her, though she shouldn't have been surprised. It was his job, after all, she reminded herself.

With that, she decided to call Kevin. He was immediately sympathetic, promising to be there within minutes.

"How're you holding up?" Kevin asked.

Gabby leaned into him. His arm felt good around her. "Anxious, I guess."

He pulled her closer, and she could smell him, fresh and clean, as if he'd showered right before coming over. His hair, unkempt and windblown, made him look like a college student.

"I'm glad your neighbor was there," he said. "Travis, right?"

"Yeah." She looked over. "Do you know him?"

"Not really," he said. "We do the insurance for the clinic, but that's one of the accounts my dad still handles."

"I thought this was a small town and you knew everyone."

"It is. But I grew up in Morehead City, and as a kid, I didn't hang out with anyone from Beaufort. Besides, I think he's a few years older than me. He was probably off to college by the time I started high school."

She nodded. In the silence, her thoughts circled back to Travis, his serious expression as he worked on Molly, the quiet assurance in his voice as he explained what was wrong. In the silence, she felt a vague current of guilt, and she leaned in to nuzzle Kevin's neck. Kevin stroked her shoulder, his touch comforting in its familiarity. "I'm glad you came over," she whispered. "I really needed you here tonight."

He kissed her hair. "Where else would I be?"

"I know, but you had that meeting, and you're leaving early tomorrow."

"No big deal. It's just a convention. It'll take me ten minutes to pack, tops. I just wish I could have gotten here sooner."

"You probably would have been grossed out."

"Probably. But I still feel bad."

"Don't. There's no reason to."

He stroked her hair. "Do you want me to postpone my trip? I'm sure my dad would understand if I stay around here tomorrow."

"No, that's okay. I've got to work anyway."

"You sure?"

"Yeah," she said. "But thanks for asking. That means a lot to me."

Six

After finding his son crashed on the cot and a dog in the recovery room, Max Parker listened as Travis explained what had happened. Max filled two cups with coffee and brought them both to the table.

"Not bad for your first time," Max said. With his white hair and bushy white eyebrows, he was the picture of a well-liked small-town veterinarian.

"Have you ever treated a dog for it?"

"Never," Max admitted. "Treated a horse once, though. You know how rare it is. Molly seems to be doing fine now. She sat up and wagged her tail when I came in this morning. How late were you up with her?"

Travis sipped the coffee with gratitude. "Most of the night. I wanted to make sure it didn't recur."

"It usually doesn't," he said. "It's a good thing you were there. Have you called the owner yet?"

"No. But I will." He wiped his face. "Man, I'm exhausted."

"Why don't you go get some sleep? I can handle things here, and I'll keep an eye on Molly."

"I don't want to put you out."

"You're not," Max said with a grin. "Don't you remember? You're not supposed to be here. It's Friday."

A few minutes later, after checking in on Molly, Travis pulled into his driveway and got out of the car. He stretched his arms overhead, then headed over to Gabby's place. As he crossed her driveway, he saw the newspaper poking out of the box and, after a brief hesitation, pulled it out. On her porch a moment later, he was just about to knock when he heard the sound of approaching footsteps and the door swung open. Gabby straightened, surprised to see him.

"Oh, hey . . . ," she said, letting go of the door. "I was just thinking that I should call you."

Though barefoot, she was dressed in slacks and an off-white blouse, her hair fastened loosely by an ivory clip. He noted again how attractive she was, but today it struck him that her appeal lay more in an unfeigned openness than conventional good looks. She just seemed so . . . *real*. "Since I was on my way home, I thought I'd let you know in person. Molly's doing fine."

"You're sure?"

He nodded. "I did an X-ray, and I didn't see any indication of internal bleeding. Once she got some fluids in, she seemed to get her strength back. She could probably come home later today, but I'd like to keep her one more night, just to be safe. Actually, my dad will watch her for a while. I was up most of the night, so I'm going to bed, but I'll check on her myself later."

"Can I see her?"

"Sure," he said. "You can see her anytime. Just remember that she might still be a little doped up, though, since I had to administer some sedatives so she'd be calm for the X-ray and to help with the pain." He paused. "The puppies are doing well, too, by the way. They're cute as bugs."

She smiled, liking the gentle twang of his accent, surprised that she hadn't noticed it before. "I just want to thank you again," she said. "I don't know how I can ever repay you."

He waved it off. "I was glad to help." He held out the newspaper. "Which reminds me, I grabbed this for you, too."

"Thanks," she said, taking it.

For an awkward beat, they faced each other silently.

"Would you like a cup of coffee?" she offered. "I just brewed a pot."

She felt a mixture of relief and disappointment when he shook his head.

"No thanks. I'd rather not be awake when I'm trying to sleep."

She laughed. "Funny."

"I try," he said, and for an instant she pictured him leaning against a bar and offering the same response to an attractive woman, which left her with the vague feeling that he was flirting with her.

"But listen," he went on, "I know you're probably getting ready for work and I'm bushed, so I'm going home to crash for a while." He turned to step off the porch.

Despite herself, Gabby crossed the threshold and called to him as he reached the yard. "Before you go, could you tell me what time you think you'll be at the clinic? To check on Molly, I mean?"

"I'm not sure. I guess it depends on how long I sleep."

"Oh . . . okay," she said, feeling foolish and wishing she hadn't asked.

"But how about this," he went on. "You tell me what time you take lunch, and I'll meet you at the clinic."

"I didn't mean—"

"What time?"

She swallowed. "A quarter to one?"

"I'll be there," he promised. He took a couple of steps backward. "And by the way, you look fantastic in that outfit," he added.

What on earth just happened?

That pretty much summed up Gabby's mental state for the rest of the morning. It didn't matter whether she was doing a well-baby check (twice), diagnosing ear infections (four times), giving a vaccination (once), or recommending an X-ray (once); she felt herself operating on autopilot, only half-present, while another part was still back on the porch, wondering if Travis had actually been flirting with her and whether maybe, just maybe, she'd sort of liked it.

She wished for the umpteenth time that she had a friend in town to talk to about all this. There was nothing like having a close girlfriend to confide in, and though there were nurses in the office, her status as a physician assistant seemed to set her apart. Frequently, she'd hear the nurses talking and laughing, but they tended to get quiet as soon as she approached. Which left her feeling as isolated as she had been when she'd first moved to town.

After finishing with her last patient (the child needed a referral to an ear, nose, and throat specialist for a possible tonsillectomy), Gabby stuffed her stethoscope into the pocket of her lab coat and retreated to her office. It wasn't much; she had the sneaking suspicion that before her arrival it had been used as a storeroom. There was no window, and the desk took up most of the room, but as long as she kept the clutter under control, it was still nice to have a place to call her own. There was a small, nearly empty filing cabinet in the corner, and she retrieved her purse from the bottom drawer. Checking her watch, she saw that she had a few minutes until she had to leave. She pulled up her chair and ran a hand through her undisciplined curls.

She was definitely making too big a deal about it, she decided. People flirted all the time. It was human nature. Besides, it probably didn't mean anything. After all they'd gone through the night before, he'd become something like a friend. . . .

Her friend. Her first friend in a new town at the start of her new life. She liked the sound of that. What was wrong with having a friend? Nothing at all. She smiled at the thought before it gave way to a frown.

Then again, maybe it wasn't such a good idea. Being friendly with a neighbor was one thing, making friends with a flirty guy was something completely different. Especially a good-looking flirty guy. Kevin wasn't normally the jealous type, but she wasn't dumb enough to think he'd be overjoyed at the thought of Gabby and Travis having coffee on the back deck a couple of times a week, either, which was exactly the sort of thing friendly neighbors did. As innocent as the visit to the vet might be—and it was going to be innocent, mind you—it had a vaguely *unfaithful* feeling about it.

She hesitated. I'm going crazy, she thought. I really am going crazy.

She'd done nothing wrong. He hadn't, either. And nothing was going to come of their little flirtation, even if they were neighbors. She and Kevin had been a couple since their senior year at the University of North Carolina—they'd met on a cold, miserable evening when her hat had blown off after she'd left Spanky's with her friends. Kevin had darted onto Franklin Street and threaded between cars to retrieve it, and if sparks hadn't flown at that moment, there might have been an ember, even if she wasn't fully aware of it.

At the time, the last thing she'd wanted was anything as complicated as a relationship, for it felt as though there were enough complications in her life already. Finals were looming, the rent was due, and she didn't know where she was going to PA school. Though it seemed preposterous now, at the time it seemed like the single most important decision she'd ever faced. She'd been accepted to the programs at both MUSC in Charleston and Eastern Virginia in Norfolk, and her mother was lobbying fiercely for Charleston: "Your decision is simple, Gabrielle. You'd only be a couple of hours from home, and Charleston is far more cosmopolitan, dear." Gabby was leaning toward Charleston as well, although deep down she knew that Charleston was tempting for all the wrong reasons: the nightlife, the excitement of living in a beautiful city, the culture, the lively social circuit. She reminded herself that she really wouldn't have time to enjoy any of those things. With the exception of a few key classes, PA students had the same curriculum as medical school students but had only two and a half years to complete the program, as opposed to four. She'd already heard horror stories of what to expect: that classes were taught and information passed on with all the delicacy of a fire hose opened to maximum velocity. When she'd visited both campuses, she'd actually preferred the program at Eastern Virginia; for whatever reason, it felt more comfortable, a place where she could focus on what she needed to do.

So which would it be?

She'd been fretting about the choice that winter evening when her hat blew off and Kevin had retrieved it. After thanking him, she promptly forgot all about him until he spotted her from across the quad a few weeks later. Though she'd forgotten him, he remembered her. His easygoing manner contrasted sharply with that of the many arrogant frat guys she'd met up to that point, most of whom tended to drink inordinate amounts and painted letters on their bare chests whenever the Tarheels played Duke. Conversation led to coffee, coffee led to dinner, and by the time she tossed her cap in the air at graduation, she figured she was in love. By then, she'd made her decision about which school to attend, and with Kevin planning to live in Morehead City, only a few hours to the south of where she'd be for the next few years, the choice seemed almost predestined.

Kevin commuted to Norfolk to see her; she drove down to Morehead City to see him. He got to know her family, and she got to know his. They fought and made up, broke up and reunited, and she'd even played a few rounds of golf with him, although she wasn't fond of the game; and through it all, he'd remained the laid-back, easygoing guy he always had been. His nature seemed to reflect his upbringing in a small town, where—let's be honest—things were mighty slow most of the time. Slowness seemed ingrained in his personality. Where she would worry, he would shrug; in her pessimistic moments, he remained unconcerned. That was why, she thought, they got along so well. They balanced each other. They were good for each other. There would be no contest if the choice came down to Kevin or Travis, not even close.

Having reached clarity on the issue, she decided it didn't matter whether Travis was flirting. He could flirt all he wanted; in the end, she knew exactly what she wanted in her life. She was sure of it.

Just as Travis had promised, Molly was better than Gabby had hoped. Her tail thumped with enthusiasm, and despite the presence of her puppies—most of which were sleeping and resembled furry little balls—she got up without a struggle when Gabby entered and trotted toward her before applying a few sloppy licks. Molly's nose was cold, and she wiggled and whined as she circled Gabby, not with her usual abandon, but enough to let Gabby know she was fine, and then sat beside Gabby.

"I'm so glad you're better," Gabby whispered, stroking her fur.

"I am, too," Travis's voice echoed behind her from the doorway. "She's a real trouper, and she's got a wonderful disposition."

Gabby turned around and saw him leaning against the door.

"I think I was wrong," he said, walking toward her, holding a Fuji apple. "She could probably go home tonight, if you want to pick her up after work. I'm not saying you have to. I'd be happy to keep her here if you'd be more comfortable with it. But Molly's doing even better than I predicted." He squatted and lightly snapped his fingers, turning his attention away from Gabby. "Aren't you a good girl," he said, using what can best be described as an "I love dogs and won't you come to me?" kind of voice. Surprising her, Molly left Gabby's side to go to him, where he took over the petting and whispering, leaving Gabby feeling like an outsider.

"And these little guys are doing great, too," he went on. "If you do bring them home, make sure you put together some sort of pen to keep them contained. Otherwise, it can get kind of messy. It doesn't have to be fancy—just prop a few boards against some boxes—and make sure to line it with newspaper."

She barely heard him as, despite herself, she noted again how good-looking he was. It annoyed her that she couldn't get past that every time she saw him. It was as if his appearance constantly set off alarm bells in her, and for the life of her, she didn't know why. He was tall and lean, but she'd seen lots of guys like that. He smiled a lot, but that wasn't unusual. His teeth were almost too white—he was a definite bleacher, she decided— but even if she knew the color wasn't natural, it still had an effect. He was fit, too, but guys like that could be found in every gym in America—guys who worked out religiously, guys who never ate anything but chicken breasts and oatmeal, guys who ran ten miles a day—and none of them had ever had the same effect on her.

So what was it about him?

It would have been so much easier had he been ugly. Everything from their initial confrontation to her present discomfort would have been different, simply because she wouldn't have felt so off-kilter. But that was done now, she resolved. She wouldn't be taken in anymore. Nosiree. Not this gal. She'd finish up here, wave to him in a neighborly way in the future, and get back to living her life without distraction.

"You okay?" he said, scrutinizing her. "You seem distracted."

"Just tired," she lied. She motioned to Molly. "I guess she's taken a liking to you."

"Oh yeah," he said. "We've been getting along great. I think it was the jerky treats I gave her this morning. Jerky treats are the way to a dog's heart. That's what I tell all the FedEx and UPS guys when they ask what to do about dogs that dislike them."

"I'll remember that," she said, quickly regaining composure.

When one of the puppies began to whine, Molly stood up and returned to the open cage, the presence of Travis and Gabby suddenly extraneous. Travis stood and polished the apple on his jeans. "So what do you think?" he asked.

"About what?"

"About Molly."

"What about Molly?"

He frowned. When he spoke, the words came out slowly. "Do you want to take her home tonight or not?"

"Oh, that," she said, flustered as a high school freshman meeting the varsity quarterback. She felt like kicking herself but instead cleared her throat. "I think I'll take her home. If you're sure it won't hurt her."

"She'll be fine," he assured her. "She's young and healthy. As scary as it was, it could have been a whole lot worse. Molly was a lucky dog."

Gabby crossed her arms. "Yes, she was."

For the first time, she noticed that his T-shirt advertised a Key West hangout, something about Dog's Saloon. He took a bite of his apple, then motioned toward her with it. "You know, I thought you'd be more excited about the fact she's okay."

"I am excited."

"You don't seem excited."

"What's that supposed to mean?"

"I don't know," he said. He took another bite of his apple. "Based on the way you showed up at my door, I guess I figured that you'd show a bit more emotion. Not only about Molly, but the fact that I happened to be there to help."

"And I've already told you I appreciate it," she said. "How many times do I have to thank you?"

"I don't know. How many do you think?"

"I wasn't the one who asked."

He lifted an eyebrow. "Actually, you were."

Oh yeah, she thought. "Well, fine," she said, throwing up her hands. "Thank you again. For all you did." She enunciated the words carefully, as if he were hard of hearing.

He laughed. "Are you like this with your patients?"

"Like what?"

"So serious."

"As a matter of fact, I'm not."

"How about with your friends?"

"No . . ." She shook her head in confusion. "What's this got to do with anything?"

He took another bite of his apple, letting the question hang. "I was just curious," he finally said.

"About what?"

"About whether it was your personality, or whether you're just serious around me. If it's the latter, I'm flattered."

She could feel the flame rising in her cheeks. "I don't know what you're talking about."

He smirked. "Okay."

She opened her mouth, wanting to say something witty and unexpected, something to put him in his place, but before anything sprang to mind, he tossed the remains of the apple in the garbage and turned to rinse his hands before going on.

"Listen. I'm glad you're here for another reason, too," he said over his shoulder. "I'm having a little get-together tomorrow with friends, and I was hoping you'd be able to swing by."

She blinked, unsure if she'd heard him right. "To your house?"

"That's the plan."

"Like a date?"

"No, like a get-together. With friends." He turned off the faucet and began to dry his hands. "I'm hooking up the parasail for the first time this year. It should be a blast."

"Are they mainly couples? The people going?"

"Except for my sister and me, all of them are married."

She shook her head. "I don't think so. I have a boyfriend."

"Great. Bring him along."

"We've been together almost four years."

"Like I said, he's more than welcome to come."

She wondered if she'd heard him right and stared at him, trying to tell if he was serious. "Really?"

"Of course. Why not?"

"Oh, well . . . he can't come anyway. He'll be out of town for a few days."

"Then if you've got nothing else to do, come on over."

"I'm not so sure that's a good idea."

"Why not?"

"I'm in love with him."

"And?"

"And what?"

"And . . . you can be in love with him at my place. Like I said, it's going to be fun. Temperature is supposed to get close to eighty. Have you ever been parasailing?"

"No. But that's not the point."

"You don't think he'd be happy if you came over."

"Exactly."

"So he's the kind of guy who wants to keep you pretty much locked up when he's away."

"No, not at all."

"Then he doesn't like you to have fun?"

"No!"

"He doesn't want you to meet new people?"

"Of course he does!"

"It's settled, then," he said. He headed toward the door before pausing. "People will start showing up around ten or eleven. All you need to bring is a bathing suit. We'll have beer and wine and soda, but if you're particular about what you drink, you might want to bring your own."

"I just don't think . . ."

He held up his hands. "I'll tell you what. You're welcome to come if you'd like. But no pressure, okay?" He shrugged. "I just figured it would give us a chance to get to know each other."

She knew she should have said no. But instead, she swallowed through the sudden dryness in her throat. "Maybe I will," she said.

Seven

~~~

Saturday morning started out well—as the sun came slanting through the blinds, Gabby found her fuzzy pink slippers and shuffled to the kitchen to pour herself a cup of coffee, looking forward to a leisurely morning. It was only afterward that things started to go wrong. Even before she'd taken her first sip, she remembered that she needed to check on Molly and was happy to find that she was nearly back to normal. The puppies seemed healthy, too, not that she had the slightest idea of what, if anything, she was supposed to watch for. Aside from latching themselves onto Molly like fuzzy barnacles, they tottered and toppled and whimpered and cried, all of which seemed like nature's way of making them adorable enough so their mother wouldn't eat them. Not that Gabby was falling for it. Granted, they weren't as ugly as they might have been, but that didn't make them nearly as beautiful as Molly, and she still worried that she might not find homes for them. And she had to find homes for them; that much was certain. The stench in the garage was enough to convince her of that.

It didn't just smell—the odor assailed her like the Force in a *Star Wars* movie. As she began to gag, she vaguely remembered that Travis had suggested she build a pen of some sort to keep the puppies contained. Who on God's green earth knew puppies could poop so much? There were piles *everywhere*. The smell seemed to have leached into the walls; even opening the garage door didn't help. She spent the next half hour holding her breath and trying to keep from getting sick as she cleaned up the garage.

By the time she was finished, she had pretty much convinced herself that they had been part of some sort of evil plan designed to ruin her weekend. Really. It was the only reasonable explanation for the fact that the puppies seemed to favor the long, jagged crack in the garage floor, and their accuracy had been uncanny enough to force her to use a toothbrush to clean it. It was disgusting.

And Travis . . . let's not leave him out of it, either. It was as much his fault as the puppies'. Granted, he had mentioned in passing that she should keep them contained, but he hadn't really made a point of it, had he? He hadn't explained what would happen if she didn't listen to him, did he?

But he'd known what would happen. She was sure of that. Sneaky.

And now that she considered it, she realized that it hadn't been the only thing he'd been sneaky about. The way he'd pressed her to answer the whole "Do I go out boating with my neighbor who happens to be a flirty hunk?" She decided she didn't want to go, if only because he'd been so manipulative about getting her to agree. All those ridiculous questions insinuating that Kevin kept her under lock and key. As though she were Kevin's property or something! As if she had no mind of her own! And here she was now, cleaning up a million mounds of poop. . . .

What a way to start the weekend. To top it off, her coffee was cold, her newspaper had been soaked by an errant sprinkler, and the water had gone frigid before her shower was finished.

Great. Just great.

Where was the fun? she grumbled to herself as she threw on her clothes. Here it was, the weekend, and Kevin was nowhere to be found. Even when he was around, their weekends weren't anything like the ones she'd had when she'd visited him during her school breaks. Back then, it seemed as if every visit were fun, filled with new experiences and people. Now he spent at least part of every weekend at the golf course.

She poured herself another cup of coffee. Granted, Kevin had always been the quiet type, and she knew he needed to unwind after a hard week at work. But she couldn't deny that since she'd moved here, their relationship had changed. Not that it was completely his fault, of course. She'd played a role, too. She had wanted to move in, settle in, so to speak. Which was exactly what had happened. So what was the problem?

The problem, she heard a little voice answer, *was that it seemed as though there should be . . . more.* She wasn't exactly sure what that entailed, other than that *spontaneity* seemed to be an integral part of it.

She shook her head, thinking she was making too much of it. Their relationship was just going through some growing pains. Moving out onto her back deck, she saw that outside, it was one of those impossibly beautiful mornings. Perfect temperature, light breeze, not a cloud in the sky. In the distance, she watched a heron break from the marsh grass, gliding above sun-drenched water. As she stared in that direction, she caught sight of Travis heading down to the dock, wearing nothing but low-slung plaid Bermudas that stretched almost to his knees. From her vantage point, she could see the muscle striations in his arms and back as he walked, and she took a step backward, toward the sliding glass door, hoping he wouldn't spot her. In the next instant, however, she heard him calling out to her.

"Hey, Gabby!" He waved, reminding her of a kid on the first day of summer vacation. "Can you believe how beautiful the day is already?"

He started to jog toward her, and she stepped into the sun just as he pushed through the hedges. She took a deep breath.

"Hey, Travis."

"It's my favorite time of year." He opened his arms wide to take in the sky and trees. "Not too hot, not too cold, and blue skies that stretch forever."

She smiled, refusing to eye his admittedly sexy hip muscles, which, she always thought, were far and away the sexiest muscles on men.

"How's Molly doing?" he chattered. "I assume she made it through the night okay."

Gabby cleared her throat. "She's fine. Thanks."

"And the puppies?"

"They seem okay, too. But they made quite a mess."

"They'll do that. That's why it's a good idea to keep them in a smaller area."

He flashed those bleached teeth in a familiar grin, way too familiar, even if he was the hunk-who-saved-her-dog.

She crossed her arms, reminding herself how sneaky he'd been the day before. "Yeah, well, I didn't quite get to it yesterday."

"Why not?"

Because you distracted me, she thought. "I guess I just forgot."

"Your garage must smell to high heaven."

She shrugged without responding, not wanting to give him the satisfaction.

He didn't seem to notice her carefully choreographed response. "Listen, it doesn't have to be complicated. But pooping is all puppies do for the first couple of days. It's like the milk runs right through them. But you've got the pen up now, right?"

She tried her best to keep a poker face but obviously failed.

"You don't?" he asked.

Gabby shifted from one foot to the other. "Not exactly," she admitted.

"Why not?"

Because you keep distracting me, she thought. "I'm not sure I need one."

Travis scratched at his neck. "Do you like cleaning up after them?"

"It's not so bad," she mumbled.

"You mean you're going to give them the run of your whole garage?"

"Why not?" she said, knowing that the first thing she was going to do after this was to build the tiniest pen she could.

He stared at her in obvious bafflement. "Just so you know, as your vet, I'm going to come right out and say that I don't think you've made the right decision."

"Thanks for your opinion," she snapped.

He continued to stare at her. "All right, then. Suit yourself. You're going to come to my house around ten, right?"

"I don't think so."

"Why not?"

"Because I don't think it's a good idea."

"Why not?"

"Because."

"I see," he said, sounding exactly like her mother.

"Good."

"Is something bothering you?"

"No."

"Have I done something to upset you?"

Yes, the little voice answered. *You and your damn hip muscles.* "No."

"Then what's the problem?" he asked.

"There's no problem."

"Then what's up with the way you're acting?"

"I'm not acting any way."

The teeth-baring smile was gone, as was all the friendliness he'd shown earlier. "Yeah, you are. I drop a basket off to welcome you to the neighborhood, I save your dog and stay awake all night to make sure she's okay, I invite you over to have some fun on my boat today—all this after you screamed at me for no reason, mind you—and now you're treating me like I have the plague. Since you moved next door, I've tried to be nice, but every time I see you, you seem angry at me. I just want to know why."

"Why?" she parroted.

"Yeah," he said, his voice steady. "Why."

"Because," she repeated, knowing she sounded like a sulky fifth-grader. She just couldn't think of anything else to say.

He studied her face closely. "Because why?"

"It's none of your business."

He let her answer settle into the silence.

"Whatever," he finally said. He turned on his heels, shaking his head as he walked toward the steps. He was already on the grass when Gabby took a step forward.

"Wait!" she called out.

Travis slowed, took another couple of steps, then came to a halt. He turned to face her. "Yeah?"

"I'm sorry," she offered.

"Yeah?" he said again. "What are you sorry for?"

She hesitated. "I don't know what you mean."

"I didn't expect that you would," he grunted. When she sensed him getting ready to turn again—a turn that Gabby knew would signal the end of cordial relations between them—she took a step forward, almost against her will.

"I'm sorry for all of it." To her ears, her own voice sounded strained and tinny. "For the way I've been treating you. For the way I've made you think I'm not grateful for the things you've done."

"And?"

She felt herself shrink, something that seemed to happen only in his presence.

"And," she said, her tone softening, "I've been wrong."

He paused, hand on hip. "About what?"

Gee, where should I start? the little voice answered. *Maybe*

I haven't been wrong. Maybe my intuition has been warning me about something I don't quite understand but shouldn't be underestimated. . . .

"About you," she said, ignoring the little voice. "And you're right. I haven't been treating you the way I should, but to be honest, I'd rather not go into the reasons why." She forced a smile, one that wasn't reciprocated. "Would it be possible for us to start over?"

He seemed to mull this over. "I don't know."

"Huh?"

"You heard me," he said. "The last thing I need in my life is a crazy neighbor. I don't mean to hurt your feelings, but I learned a long time ago to call 'em like I see 'em."

"That's not fair."

"No?" He didn't bother to hide his skepticism. "Actually, I think I'm being more than fair. But I'll tell you what—if you're willing to start over, I'm willing to start over. But only if you're certain you want that."

"I am."

"Okay, then," he said. He retraced his steps to the deck. "Hi," he offered, holding out his hand. "My name is Travis Parker, and I want to welcome you to the neighborhood."

She stared at his hand. After a moment, she took it and said, "I'm Gabby Holland. It's a pleasure to meet you."

"What do you do?

"I'm a physician assistant," she said, feeling slightly ridiculous. "How about you?"

"I'm a veterinarian," he said. "Where are you from?"

"Savannah, Georgia," she answered. "And you?"

"From here," he said. "Born and raised."

"Do you like it here?"

"What's not to like? Beautiful weather, zero traffic." He paused. "And for the most part, nice neighbors, too."

"I've heard that," she said. "In fact, I know the vet here in town might even make an emergency house call now and then. Can't find that in the city."

"No, I don't suppose you would." He motioned over his shoulder. "Hey, by the way, my friends and I are heading out on the boat today. Would you like to join us?"

She squinted up at him. "I would, but I have to build a pen for the puppies my dog, Molly, had two nights ago. I don't want you to have to wait for me."

"Need some help? I've got some extra planks of wood and some crates in the garage. It won't take long."

She hesitated, then looked up with a smile. "In that case, I'd love to go."

Travis was as good as his word. He arrived—still half-naked, to her dismay—carrying four long boards beneath his arms. After dropping those off, he jogged back to his garage. He returned with the crates, along with a hammer and a handful of nails.

Though he pretended not to notice the smell, she noticed that he put the pen together far faster than she would have imagined possible.

"You should probably line this area with newspapers. Do you have enough?"

When she nodded, he motioned toward his house again. "I've still got a few things to take care of, so I'll see you in a little while, okay?"

Gabby nodded again, feeling a roiling sensation in her stomach, something akin to nervousness. Which was why, after she'd watched him enter his house and had lined the pen, she found herself standing in the bedroom, evaluating the merits of swimwear. More specifically, whether she should wear her bikini or her one-piece.

There were pros and cons to each. Normally, she would have worn her bikini. She was, after all, twenty-six and single, and even if she wasn't a supermodel, she was honest enough to admit she liked the way she looked in a bikini. Kevin certainly did—if she even suggested that she wear a one-piece, Kevin would pout until she changed her mind. On the other hand, Kevin wasn't around, she would be hanging out with a neighbor (guy!), and considering the size of her bikini, she might as well be wearing a bra and panties, none of which would make her feel very comfortable and all of which added up to the one-piece.

Still, her one-piece was sort of old and a little faded from chlorine and sun. Her mother had purchased it for her a few years ago, for afternoons spent at the country club (God forbid she expose herself like a harlot!). It wasn't a particularly flattering cut, as far as one-pieces went. Instead of a high cut on her thighs, the suit was cut low on the sides, which made her legs look short and stumpy.

She didn't want her legs to look short and stumpy. On the other hand, did it really matter? Of course not, she thought, while simultaneously thinking, Of course it did.

The one-piece, she decided. At the very least, she wouldn't give any of them the wrong impression about her. And there were going to be kids on the boat, too. It was better to err on the conservative side than to be a bit too . . . exposed. She reached for the one-piece, and all at once she could hear her mother telling her that she'd made the right decision.

Tossing it back on the bed, she reached for the bikini.

Eight

You invited the new neighbor over, huh?" Stephanie asked. "What's her name again?"

"Gabby," Travis answered, pulling the boat closer to the dock. "She should be here any minute." The rope tightened and then slackened as the boat was maneuvered into place. They'd just lowered it into the water and were tying it up to the dock to load the coolers.

"She's single, right?"

"Technically. But she has a boyfriend."

"So?" Stephanie grinned. "When have you ever let that stop you?"

"Don't read anything into this. He's out of town and she had nothing to do, so being the good neighbor, I invited her along."

"Uh-huh." Stephanie nodded. "Sounds just like you to do something honorable like that."

"I am honorable," he protested.

"That's what I just said."

Travis finished tying the boat. "But you didn't sound like you meant it."

"I didn't? That's strange."

"Yeah, yeah. Keep it up."

Travis grabbed the cooler and hopped in the boat.

"Umm . . . you think she's attractive, don't you?"

Travis put the cooler in place. "I guess."

"You guess?"

"What do you want me to say?"

"Nothing."

Travis looked at his sister. "Why do I get the feeling that this is going to be a long day?"

"I have no idea."

"Do me a favor, okay? Go easy on her."

"What do you mean?"

"You know what I mean. Just . . . let her get used to everyone before you start in on her."

Stephanie cackled. "You do realize who you're talking to, right?"

"I'm just saying that she might not understand your humor."

"I promise to be on my best behavior."

"So . . . you ready to go skinny-dipping?" Stephanie asked.

Gabby blinked, unsure she'd heard her right. "Excuse me?"

A minute earlier, Stephanie had walked over wearing a long T-shirt and holding a couple of beers. Handing one to Gabby, she'd introduced herself as Travis's sister and led her to some chairs along the back deck while Travis finished up.

"Oh, not right now." Stephanie waved. "It usually takes a couple of beers before everyone is loose enough to drop their drawers."

"Skinny-dipping?"

"You did know that Travis is a nudist, right?" She nodded toward the slip-and-slide Travis had set up earlier. "After that, we generally go slip-and-sliding."

Though her head felt as though it were spinning, Gabby nodded almost imperceptibly as she felt things click into place: the fact that Travis usually seemed only half-dressed, his utter lack of discomfort at conversing with his chest bared, an explanation for why he worked out so much.

Her thoughts were interrupted by the sound of Stephanie's laughter.

"I was kidding!" she hooted. "Do you honestly think I'd go skinny-dipping with my brother around? Ewww! That's gross!"

Gabby felt a red-hot flush work its way up from her neck to her face. "I knew you were kidding."

Stephanie eyed Gabby over her beer. "You did think I was serious! Oh, that's a hoot! But I'm sorry. My brother warned me to take it easy on you. For whatever reason, he thinks my humor takes some getting used to."

Gee, I wonder why. "Really?" Gabby said instead.

"Yeah, but if you ask me, we're two peas in a pod. Where do you think I learned it?" Stephanie leaned back in her seat as she adjusted her sunglasses. "Travis tells me you're a physician assistant?"

"Yeah. I work at the children's clinic."

"How is it?"

"I enjoy it," she said, thinking it best not to mention her pervert boss or the occasionally overbearing parent. "How about you?"

"I'm a student," she said. She took a sip of beer. "I'm thinking of making it my career."

For the first time, Gabby laughed and felt herself begin to relax. "Do you know who else is coming?"

"Oh, probably the same old crew. Travis has these three friends he's known forever, and I'm sure they'll be here along with their wives and kids. Travis doesn't bring the parasail boat out too much anymore, which is why he keeps it docked at the marina. Usually he uses the ski boat, because wakeboarding or skiing is a lot easier. Just get in the boat, lower the lift, and go. You can wakeboard or ski or skurf almost anywhere. But parasailing is great. Why do you think I'm here? I should be studying, and I actually ditched some lab work I was supposed to do this weekend. Have you ever been parasailing?"

"No."

"You'll love it. And Travis knows what he's doing. That's how he earned extra spending money while he was in college. Or, at least, that's what he claims. Actually, I'm fairly certain that everything he earned was used to buy the boat; they're manufactured by CWS exclusively for parasailing, and they're very expensive. And even though Joe, Matt, and Laird are his friends, they still insisted on getting paid when they took the tourists out during their student days. I'm pretty sure Travis never earned a nickel of profit."

"So he's quite the shrewd businessman, huh?"

Stephanie laughed. "Oh yeah. My brother. A budding Donald Trump, right? Actually, he doesn't much care about money and never has. I mean, sure, he earns a living and pays his own way, but anything left over goes to new boats or Jet Skis or trips here and there. It seems like he's been everywhere. Europe, Central and South America, Australia, Africa, Bali, China, Nepal . . ."

"Really?"

"You sound surprised."

"I guess I am."

"Why?"

"I'm not sure. I guess it's because . . ."

"Because he seems like such a goof-off? Like everything's a party?"

"No!"

"You sure about that?"

"Well . . ." Gabby trailed off, and Stephanie laughed again.

"He's a goof-off, *and* a worldly young man . . . but underneath, he's really just a small-town boy like the rest of them. Otherwise he wouldn't be living here, right?"

"Right," Gabby said, not sure whether an answer was even needed.

"Anyway, you'll love it. You're not afraid of heights, are you?"

"No. I mean, I'm not thrilled with them, but I'm sure I'll manage."

"It's no big deal. Just remember you have a parachute."

"I'll keep that in mind."

In the distance, a car door slammed, and Stephanie sat up straighter.

"Here come the Clampetts," Stephanie remarked. "Or, if you prefer, the Brady Bunch. Brace yourself. Our relaxing morning is about to end."

Gabby turned and spotted a rowdy group rounding the side of the house. Chatter and shouts rang out as the children ran in front of the adults, moving in that wobbly way that made them seem as if they were constantly on the verge of falling.

Stephanie leaned closer. "It's easy to distinguish them, believe it or not. Megan and Joe are the ones with blond hair. Laird and Allison are the tall ones. And Matt and Liz are . . . less thin than the others."

The corners of Gabby's mouth curled up slightly. "Less thin?"

"I didn't want to call them plump. But I was just trying to make it easy for you. In theory, I'd hate being introduced to a bunch of people and forgetting their names a minute later."

"In theory?"

"I don't forget names. It's kind of strange, but I never do."

"What makes you think I'd forget their names?"

Stephanie shrugged. "You're not me."

Gabby laughed again, liking her more by the minute. "How about the kids?"

"Tina, Josie, and Ben. Ben's easy to figure out. Just remember that Josie has the pigtails."

"What if she's not in pigtails the next time I see her?"

Stephanie grinned. "Why? Do you think you'll be coming over regularly? What about your boyfriend?"

Gabby shook her head. "No, you misunderstood what I meant—"

"I was teasing! My, you're touchy."

"I'm not sure I can keep them straight."

"All right. Try these memory association tricks. For Tina, think of Tina Louise from *Gilligan's Island*. Ginger? The movie star? She has red hair, too."

Gabby nodded.

"Okay, for Josie, think of Josie and the Pussycats. And for Ben—who's kind of big and square for his age, think of Big Ben, the giant clock in England."

"Okaaay . . ."

"I'm serious. This'll really help. Now, for Joe and Megan—the blonds, imagine blond GI Joe fighting a megalodon—you know, one of those giant prehistoric sharks. Really picture it, okay?"

Gabby nodded again.

"For Laird and Allison, imagine a supertall allosaurus stuck in his lair. And finally, for Matt and Liz . . ." Stephanie paused. "Oh, I know . . . imagine Elizabeth Taylor lying on a porch mat, eating fried pork rinds. Are you really picturing it?"

It took Gabby a minute—and Stephanie had to repeat the descriptions more than once—but when she was ready, she quizzed Gabby on the names. Amazingly, the names stuck, and Gabby couldn't hide her surprise.

"Neat, huh?"

"Very," Gabby admitted.

"It's one of the areas I study at UNC."

"Do you do this with everyone you meet?"

"Not specifically. Or rather, not consciously. For me, it comes almost naturally. But now you'll really impress them."

"Do I need to impress them?"

"No. But it's fun to impress people anyway." Stephanie shrugged. "Think about what I just did for you. But I've got one more question."

"Go ahead."

"What's my name?"

"I know your name."

"What is it, then?"

"It's . . ." Gabby's mouth opened soundlessly while her mind froze.

"Stephanie. Just Stephanie."

"What? No memory tricks?"

"No. That one, you'll have to remember." She rose from her seat. "Come on, now that you know their names, let me go ahead and introduce you to them. And pretend you don't already know who they are, so that way you can impress them, too."

Introductions were made to Megan, Allison, and Liz while they watched the kids chasing one another; Joe, Laird, and Matt, meanwhile, had strolled down to the dock, loaded up with towels and coolers to greet Travis.

Stephanie hugged each of them, and the conversation turned to her progress at school. Amazingly, the memory tricks continued to work. Gabby wondered whether she should try it with some patients before she remembered she could read their names on the charts beforehand.

With some of Kevin's co-workers, though . . .

"Hey! Y'all ready?" Travis called out. "We're good to go, here."

Gabby trailed a step behind the group, adjusting the T-shirt she'd worn over her bikini. In the end, she'd decided that, depending on what the other women wore, she could either take off her shirt or shorts—or maybe neither—and convince herself she hadn't been listening to her mother.

The men were already in the boat when they got to the dock.

The kids were dressed in life jackets and were handed to Joe; Laird held out his hand to help the women into the boat. Gabby stepped in, concentrating on keeping her balance amid the rocking, surprised at the size of the boat. It was longer than Travis's ski boat by a good five feet, with bench seats that ran along both sides, which was where most of the kids and adults seemed to congregate. Stephanie and Allison (the *supertall allosaurus*) had made themselves comfortable at the front of the boat. At the . . . bow? The stern? . . . Gabby wondered, then shook her head. Whatever. At the *back* of the boat was a large platform and crank, along with Travis, who stood behind the wheel. (*Blond, GI*) Joe was untying the line that held the boat in place, while Laird (*lair*) rolled it up. A moment later, Joe moved to a spot near Travis, while Laird approached Josie (*and the Pussycats*).

Gabby shook her head, thinking it amazing.

"Sit by me," Stephanie commanded, patting a spot beside her.

Gabby sat, and from the corner of her eye, she saw Travis grab a baseball hat he had tucked into a corner compartment. The cap, which she always believed looked goofy on grown men, somehow suited his carefree demeanor.

"Everyone ready?" he called.

He didn't wait for an answer, and the boat rumbled forward, working through the gentle swell. They reached the mouth of the creek and turned south, into the waters of Back Sound. Shackleford Banks loomed ahead, grass threaded along the dunes.

Gabby leaned toward Stephanie. "Where are we going?"

"Most likely Cape Lookout. Unless the sound is relatively clear of boats, we'll probably make for the inlet, then out into Onslow Bay. Afterward, we'll either picnic on the boat, on Shackleford Banks, or at Cape Lookout. Kind of depends on where we end up and what everyone's in the mood for. A lot of it depends on the kids. Hold on for a second. . . ." She turned toward Travis. "Hey, Trav! Can I drive?"

He raised his head. "Since when do you want to drive?"

"Now. It's been a while."

"Later."

"I think I should drive."

"Why?"

Stephanie shook her head, as if marveling at the stupidity of men. She rose from her spot and whipped off her T-shirt without a shred of self-consciousness. "I'll be back in a little while, okay? I have to talk to my idiot brother."

As Stephanie made her way toward the rear of the boat, Allison nodded toward her.

"Don't let her scare you. She and Travis always talk to each other that way."

"I take it they're close."

"They're best friends, even if both would deny it. Travis would probably say that Laird was his best friend. Or Joe or Matt. Anyone but Stephanie. But I know better."

"Laird's your husband, right? The one holding Josie?"

Allison couldn't hide her surprise. "You remembered? You just met us for a second."

"I'm good with names."

"You must be. You know everyone already?"

"Uh-huh." Gabby rattled off each of the passengers' names, feeling smug.

"Wow. You're just like Stephanie. No wonder you two hit it off."

"She's great."

"Sure, once you get to know her. But she takes a little getting used to." She watched Stephanie lecturing Travis, one hand on the boat to steady herself, the other hand gesturing.

"How did you and Travis meet? Stephanie mentioned you live in the neighborhood."

"We live next door to each other, actually."

"And?"

"And . . . well, it's kind of a long story. But to make it short, my dog, Molly, had some trouble when she had her puppies, and Travis was kind enough to come over and treat her. After that, he invited me to come."

"He's got a way with animals. Kids, too."

"How long have you known him?"

"A long time. Laird and I met in college, and Laird introduced me to him. They've been friends since they were kids. Actually, he was the best man at our wedding. And speak of the devil . . . Hey, Travis."

"Hey," he said. "Should be fun today, huh?" Behind him, Stephanie was perched behind the wheel, pretending not to watch them.

"Hopefully it won't get too windy."

Allison looked around. "I don't think it will."

"Why?" Gabby pressed. "What happens if it's windy?"

"Nothing good when you're parasailing," Travis answered. "Basically, the chute could collapse in places, the lines could get tangled, and that's the last thing you want in a parachute."

Gabby had an image of herself spinning out of control as she rushed toward the water.

"Don't worry," Travis reassured her. "If I even suspect a problem, no one goes up."

"I hope not," Allison chimed in. "But I'd like to volunteer Laird to be the first."

"Why?"

"Because he was supposed to paint Josie's room this week—he promised me over and over—but is it painted? Of course not. It'll serve him right."

"He'll have to stand in line. Megan already volunteered Joe to go first. Something about not spending enough time with the family after work."

Listening to their familiar banter, Gabby felt like a spectator. She wished that Stephanie hadn't left her side; oddly, she realized,

Stephanie already felt like the closest thing she had to a friend in Beaufort.

"Hold on!" Stephanie shouted, rotating the wheel.

Travis instinctively grabbed the side of the boat as it hit a large wake and the bow rose and fell with a thud. Allison's attention was diverted to the kids, and she rushed toward Josie, who'd fallen and was already beginning to cry. Laird pulled her to her feet with one arm.

"You were supposed to be holding her!" Allison reproached him while reaching for Josie. "Come here, baby. Mommy's got you. . . ."

"I was holding her!" Laird protested. "Maybe if Dale Earnhardt here was watching where she was going . . ."

"Don't bring me into this," Stephanie said, tossing her head. "I said to hold on, but I guess you didn't listen. It's not like I can control the swells out here."

"But you could go a little slower. . . ."

Travis shook his head and took a seat beside Gabby.

"Is it always like this?" she asked.

"Pretty much," he said. "At least since the kids have been around. Rest assured that each of the kids will have a few tearful moments today. But that's what keeps it interesting." He leaned back, planting his feet wide. "How'd you like my sister?"

With the sun behind him, his features were difficult to discern. "I like her. She's . . . unique."

"She seems taken with you, too. If she didn't like you, believe me—she would have let me know. As smart as she is, she doesn't always know when to keep her opinions to herself. If you ask me, I think she was secretly adopted by my parents."

"I don't think so. If you let your hair grow a little longer, you two could pass for sisters."

He laughed. "You sound like her now."

"I guess she rubbed off on me."

"Did you get a chance to meet everyone else?"

"Briefly. I visited with Allison for a bit, but that's all."

"They're the nicest bunch of people you'll ever meet," Travis said. "More like family than friends."

She studied Travis as he pulled the baseball cap from his head, suddenly grasping what had happened. "Stephanie sent you back here to talk to me, didn't she."

"Yeah," he admitted. "She reminded me that you were my guest and that I'd be rude if I didn't make sure you were comfortable."

"I'm fine." She waved a hand. "If you want to go drive the boat again, feel free. I'm perfectly happy enjoying the view."

"Have you ever been over to Cape Lookout?" Travis asked.

"No."

"It's a national park, and there's a cove that's great for little kids because the waves don't break there. And on the far side— the Atlantic side—there's a white-sand beach that's unspoiled, which is almost impossible to find anymore."

When he was finished, Gabby watched as he turned his attention to Beaufort. The profile of the town was visible; just beyond the marina where the masts of sailboats pointed toward the sky like upraised fingers, she could see the restaurants lining the waterfront. In every direction, there were boats and Jet Skis zipping past, leaving whitewashed curls of water behind them. Despite herself, she was conscious of the gentle way his body leaned against hers as the boat glided through the water.

"It's a pretty town," she finally said.

"I've always loved it," he agreed. "Growing up, I used to dream about moving to a big city, but in the end, this is home for me."

They turned toward the inlet. Behind them, Beaufort grew smaller; up ahead, the waters of Onslow Bay embraced the Atlantic. A solitary cloud drifted overhead, puffy and full, as if molded from snow. The gentle blue sky spread over water speckled with golden prisms of sunlight. In time, the hectic activity of Back Sound gave way to a sense of isolation, broken only by the sight of an occasional boat pulling into the shallows of Shackleford Banks. The three couples at the front of the boat were as transfixed by the view as she was, and even the kids seemed to have quieted. They sat contentedly on laps, their bodies relaxed, as if they were ready for a nap. Gabby could feel the wind whipping through her hair and the balm of the summer sun.

"Hey, Trav," Stephanie called out, "is this okay?"

Travis broke from his reverie and glanced around.

"Let's go a bit farther. I want to make sure we have enough room. We've got a rookie on board."

Stephanie nodded, and the boat accelerated again.

Gabby leaned toward him. "How does this work, by the way?"

"It's easy," he said. "First, I fill the parachute and get it ready to accept the harnesses by using that bar over there." He pointed toward the corner of the boat. "Then, you and your partner put the harnesses on, I clip those to the long bar, and you take a seat on the platform. I start the crank and you lift off. It takes a couple of minutes to reach the right height, and then . . . well, you float around. You get a great view of Beaufort and the lighthouse, and—because the weather's been so clear—you might get to see some dolphins, porpoises, rays, sharks, even turtles. I've seen whales on occasion. We might slow the boat, let you dunk your feet, and then go up again. It's a blast."

"Sharks?"

"Of course. It's the ocean."

"Do they bite?"

"Some do. Bull sharks can be pretty nasty."

"Then I'd rather not be dunked, thank you very much."

"There's nothing to be afraid of. They won't bother you."

"Easy for you to say."

"I've never, in all the years I've done this, heard of anyone getting bitten by a shark while parasailing. You're in the water for maybe two or three seconds at the most. And usually sharks feed at dusk."

"I don't know . . ."

"How about if I'm with you? Then would you try it? You shouldn't miss it."

She hesitated, then gave a quick nod. "I'll think about it," she offered. "I'm not promising anything."

"Fair enough."

"Of course, you're assuming that you and I will go up together."

He winked as he flashed that smile of his. "Of course."

Gabby tried to ignore the leaping sensation in her stomach. Instead, she reached for her bag and pulled out some lotion. After dabbing a bit on her hand, she began nervously to apply some to her face, trying to regain some distance.

"Stephanie tells me you're a world traveler."

"I've traveled a bit."

"She made it sound like more than that. Like you've pretty much been everywhere."

He shook his head. "I wish. Believe me, there are lots of places I haven't seen."

"What's been your favorite place?"

He took a while to answer, a wistful expression on his face. "I don't know."

"Well . . . where would you suggest I go?"

"It's not like that," he said.

"What do you mean?"

"Traveling has less to do with seeing things than experiencing them. . . ." He surveyed the water, gathering his thoughts. "Let me put it this way. When I graduated from college, I wasn't sure what I wanted to do, so I just decided to take a year to see the world. I had a bit of money saved—not as much as I thought I needed— but I packed some gear and my bike and caught a flight to Europe.

I spent the first three months there just . . . doing whatever I felt like, and it rarely had anything to do with what I was supposed to see. I didn't even have a planned itinerary. Don't get me wrong—I saw a lot. But when I think back on those months, I mostly remember the friends I made along the way and the good times we spent together. Like in Italy, I saw the Colosseum in Rome and the canals in Venice, but what I really remember was a weekend I spent in Bari—this out-of-the-way city in the southern part of the country that you've probably never heard of—with some Italian students I happened to meet. They took me to this little bar where a local band was playing, and even though most of them didn't speak a word of English and my Italian was limited to menu items, we ended up laughing all night long. After that, they showed me around Lecce and Matera, and little by little, we became good friends. Same type of thing in France and Norway and Germany. I stayed in hostels when I had to, but most of the time I'd just show up in a city and somehow meet someone who would offer to let me stay with them for a little while. I'd find odd jobs to pick up extra spending money, and when I was ready for someplace new, I'd just take off. At first, I thought it was easy because Europe and America are a lot alike. But the same thing happened when I went to Syria and Ethiopia and South Africa and Japan and China. At times, it almost felt like I was destined to take the trip, like all the people I met had somehow been waiting for me. But . . ."

He paused, looking directly at her.

"But I'm different now than I was then. Just like I was different at the end of the trip than I'd been at the beginning. And I'll be different tomorrow than I am today. And what that means is that I can never replicate that trip. Even if I went to the same places and met the same people, it wouldn't be the same. My *experience* wouldn't be the same. To me, that's what traveling should be about. Meeting people, learning to not only appreciate a different culture, but really enjoy it like a local, following whatever impulse strikes you. So how could I recommend a trip to someone else, if I don't even know what to expect? My advice would be to make a list of places on some index cards, shuffle them, and pick any five at random. Then just . . . go and see what happens. If you have the right mind-set, it doesn't matter where you end up or how much money you brought. It'll be something you'll remember forever."

Gabby was silent as she digested this. "Wow," she finally said.

"What?"

"You make it sound so . . . romantic."

In the ensuing quiet, Stephanie began to slow the boat and Travis sat up straighter. When his sister glanced at him, he nodded and stood up. Stephanie lowered the throttle, allowing the boat to slow even further.

"We're ready," he said, and moved to a storage box. Pulling out the parachute, he asked, "Are you up for a new experience?"

Gabby swallowed. "I can't wait."

Nine

Once the parachute was filled and harnesses strapped on, Joe and Megan lifted off first, followed by Allison and Laird, then Matt and Liz. One by one, the couples sat on the platform and were lifted into the air, the tow rope unwinding until they were a hundred feet up. From Gabby's spot on the boat, they looked small and inconsequential as they drifted over the water. Travis, who'd taken the wheel from Stephanie, kept the boat at a steady speed, making large, wide turns, then finally brought the boat to a gradual halt, allowing the riders to drift toward the sea. Just as their feet grazed the water, he'd gun the throttle, and the chute would rush skyward like a kite being pulled by a boy running in the park.

Everyone was chattering as they reached the platform, talking about the fish or dolphins they'd seen, but Gabby nonetheless felt herself growing nervous as her turn approached. Stephanie, splayed out in her bikini, was working on her tan and nursing a beer in the front of the boat. She raised the beer in salute.

"Here's getting to know you, kid."

Travis tossed aside his baseball cap. "C'mon," he said to Gabby, "I'll help you with your harness."

After stepping off the platform, Liz handed over the life preserver.

"It's so much fun," she said. "You're going to love it."

Travis led Gabby to the platform. After hopping up, he bent over, offering a hand. She could feel the warmth in it as he helped her up. The harness lay crumpled, and he pointed toward two open loops.

"Step in those and pull it up. I'll tighten it for you."

She held her body steady against the tugs of the canvas straps. "That's it?"

"Almost. When you sit on the platform, keep the wide strap under your thighs. You don't want it under your . . . backside, because that doesn't support your weight as well. And you might want to take off your shirt, unless you don't mind getting it wet."

She slipped off her shirt, trying not to feel nervous.

If Travis noticed her self-consciousness, he gave no sign. Instead, he hooked up the straps of her harness to the bar, then his own, then motioned for her to sit.

"It's under your thighs, right?" Travis asked. When she nodded, he smiled. "Just relax and enjoy, okay?"

A second later, Joe pushed the throttle, the chute filled, and Gabby and Travis were lifted from the deck. In the boat, she felt everyone's eyes on them as they rose diagonally toward the sky. Gabby gripped the canvas straps so hard that her knuckles turned white while the boat grew smaller. In time, the tow rope to the boat captured her attention like a hypnotic decoy. It quickly felt as if she were a whole lot higher than anyone else had been, and she was about to say something when she felt Travis touch her shoulder.

"Look over there!" he said, pointing. "There's a ray! Can you see it?"

She saw it, black and sleek, moving beneath the surface like a slow-motion butterfly.

"And a pod of dolphins! Over there! Near the banks!"

As she marveled at the sight, her nervousness started to subside. Instead, she began to soak in the view of everything below—the town, the families sprawled on the beaches, the boats, the water. As she relaxed, she found herself thinking that she could probably spend an hour up here without ever growing tired of it. It was extraordinary to drift along at this elevation, coasting effortlessly on a wind current, as if she were a bird. Despite the heat, the breeze kept her cool, and as she rocked her feet back and forth, she felt the harness sway.

"Are you willing to be dipped?" he asked. "I promise it'll be fun."

"Let's do it," she agreed. To her ears, her voice sounded strangely confident.

Travis engaged Joe in a quick series of hand signals, and beneath her, the whine of the boat suddenly diminished. The parachute began to descend. Staring at the rapidly approaching water, she scanned the surface to make sure nothing was lurking below.

The parachute dipped lower and lower, and though she lifted her legs, she felt cold water splash on her lower body. Just when she thought she was going to have to start treading water, the boat accelerated and they shot skyward again. Gabby felt adrenaline surge through her body and didn't bother trying to hide her grin.

Travis nudged her. "See? It wasn't bad at all."

"Can we do that again?" she asked.

Travis and Gabby rode for another quarter hour, dipping two or three more times; once they were brought back to the boat, each couple rode once more. By then, the sun was high in the sky and the kids were getting fussy. Travis steered the boat toward the cove at Cape Lookout. The water grew shallow, and Travis stopped the boat; Joe tossed the anchor overboard, removed his shirt, and followed the anchor into the water. The water was waist-deep, and with practiced ease, Matt handed him a cooler. Matt took off his shirt and jumped in; Joe handed him a cooler, then followed him into the water while Travis took his place. When Travis jumped in, he carried a small, portable grill and bag of charcoal briquettes. Simultaneously, the mothers hopped in the water and took hold of the kids. In minutes, only Stephanie and Gabby remained on board. Gabby stood in the back of the boat, thinking she should have helped, while Stephanie, seemingly oblivious to the commotion, lay sprawled on the seats at the front of the boat, continuing to collect the sun.

"I'm on vacation, so I feel no need to volunteer my services," Stephanie announced, her body as still as the boat itself. "And they're so good at it, I feel no guilt about being a slacker."

"You're not a slacker."

"Of course I am. Everyone should be a slacker now and then. As Confucius once said, 'He who does nothing is the one who does nothing.'"

Gabby pondered the words, then furrowed her brow. "Did Confucius really say that?"

Sunglasses in place, Stephanie managed the tiniest of shrugs. "No, but who cares? The point is, they had it handled, and most likely they found some sort of self-satisfaction in their industriousness. Who am I to deprive them of that?"

Gabby put her hands on her hips. "Or maybe you just wanted to be lazy."

Stephanie grinned. "Like Jesus said, 'Blessed are the lazy who lie in boats, for they shall inherit a suntan.'"

"Jesus didn't say that."

"True," Stephanie agreed, sitting up. She removed her glasses, stared through them, then wiped them on a towel. "But again, who cares?" She squinted up at Gabby. "Did you really want to carry coolers or tents all the way to the beach? Trust me, the experience is overrated." After adjusting her top, she rose from her spot. "Okay, the coast is clear. We're good to go." She slung her beach bag over her shoulder. "You gotta know when to be lazy. Done correctly, it's an art form that benefits everyone."

Gabby hesitated. "I don't know why, but I think I like the way you think."

Stephanie laughed. "Of course you do," she said. "It's human nature to be lazy. But it's good to know I'm not the only one who understands that essential truth."

As soon as Gabby started to deny it, Stephanie jumped overboard, the splash rising to the lip of the boat. "C'mon," she said, not letting Gabby finish, "I'm just kidding. And by the way, don't think twice about anything you did or didn't do. Like I said, these people draw meaning from doing these little things. It makes them feel manly and motherly, which is just the way the world *should* work. As single women, all we have to do is make sure to enjoy it."

Setting up the camp—like getting off and unloading the boat—was informally ritualized, with everyone apparently knowing exactly what to do. A pop-up tent was set in place, blankets spread, and the charcoal lit. In keeping with her inactivity on the boat, Stephanie simply grabbed a beer and a towel, picked a spot, and resumed sunbathing. Gabby, unsure of what else to do, spread her towel and did exactly the same thing. She felt the effects of the sun almost immediately and lay there trying to ignore the fact that everyone else—aside from Stephanie—seemed to be doing something.

"You need lotion," Stephanie instructed her. Without raising her head, she pointed to the bag she'd carried with her. "Grab the tube with fifty SPF. With that pale skin of yours, you'll be a lobster in half an hour if you don't. It's got zinc in it."

Gabby reached for Stephanie's bag. She took a few moments to spread the lotion; the sun did have a terrible way of punishing her if she missed a spot. Unlike her sisters or her mother, she'd taken after her Irish-skinned father. It was one of the middling curses of her life.

When she was ready, she lay down on her towel, still feeling guilty about the fact that she wasn't doing anything to help set up or get the lunch ready to go.

"How was it with Travis?"

"Fine," Gabby said.

"Just to remind you, he's my brother, you know."

Gabby turned her head to shoot Stephanie a questioning look.

"Hey," said Stephanie, "I was only reminding you so that you'd realize how well I know him."

"What does that matter?"

"I think he likes you."

"And I think you believe we're still in seventh grade."

"What? You don't care?"

"No."

"Because you have a boyfriend?"

"Among other reasons."

Stephanie laughed. "Oh, that's good. If I didn't know you, I might have even believed you."

"You don't know me!"

"Oh . . . I know you. Believe it or not, I know exactly who you are."

"Oh yeah? Where am I from?"

"I don't know."

"Tell me about my family."

"I can't."

"Then you really don't know me, do you?"

After a moment, Stephanie rolled over to face her. "Yes," she said, "I do." She couldn't hide the challenge in her tone. "Okay, how about this? You're a good girl and always have been, but deep down, you think there's more to life than always following the rules, and there's a part of you that craves the unknown. If you're honest with yourself, Travis is part of that. You're selective when it comes to sex, but once you commit to someone, the standards you would normally hold yourself to go out the window. You think you'll marry your boyfriend, but can't help but wonder why you don't have a ring on your finger yet. You love your family, but you wanted to make your own decisions about who you become, which is why you live here. Even so, you worry your choices will earn your family's disapproval. How am I doing so far?"

As she'd spoken, Gabby had grown pale. Interpreting a direct hit, Stephanie propped herself on an elbow. "You want me to go on?"

"No," Gabby said.

"I was right, wasn't I?"

Gabby exhaled sharply. "Not about everything."

"No?"

"No."

"Where was I wrong?"

Instead of answering, Gabby shook her head and rolled back onto her towel. "I don't want to talk about it."

Gabby expected Stephanie to persist, but instead, Stephanie simply shrugged and lay back on her towel, as if she'd never said anything at all.

Gabby could hear the sounds of children frolicking in the surf and distant, indistinguishable strains of conversation. Her head spun at Stephanie's assessment; it was as if the woman had known her all her life and were privy to her darkest secrets.

"By the way, in case you're freaking out, I should probably let you know I'm psychic," Stephanie remarked. "Weird, but true. Came from my grandmother, as far as I could tell. The woman was famous for predicting the weather."

Gabby sat up as a wave of relief washed over her, even though she knew the concept was preposterous. "Really?"

Stephanie laughed again. "No, of course not! My grandmother watched Let's Make a Deal for years and never once beat the contestants. But be honest. I was right on the money, wasn't I?"

Gabby's thoughts went full circle once more, leaving her almost dizzy. "But how . . . ?"

"Easy," Stephanie said, lying back down. "I just inserted your 'amazingly personal experiences' into pretty much every woman who ever lived. Well, except for the part about Travis. I guessed about that. But it's pretty amazing, huh? I study that, too, by the way. I've been part of half a dozen studies, and it always amazes me that once you cut through the clutter, people are pretty much the same. Especially through adolescence and early adulthood. For the most part, people go through the same experiences and think the same things, but somehow no one ever escapes the belief that his experience is unique in every conceivable way."

Gabby lay back on her towel, deciding it might be best if she simply ignored Stephanie for a while. As much as she liked her, the woman made her head spin way too frequently.

"Oh, in case you were curious," Stephanie remarked, "Travis isn't seeing anyone. He's not only single, but he's eligible."

"I wasn't curious."

"Since you have a boyfriend, right?"

"Right. But even if I didn't have a boyfriend, I wouldn't have been curious."

Stephanie laughed. "Yes, of course. How could I have been so wrong? I guess I must have been fooled by the way you keep staring at him."

"I haven't been staring."

"Oh, don't be so touchy. After all, he's been staring at you, too."

Ten

From her spot on her towel, Gabby inhaled the scent of charcoal, hot dogs, burgers, and chicken wafting on a gentle breeze. Despite the breeze—and the lotion—Gabby's skin felt as if it were beginning to sizzle. It sometimes struck her as ironic that her ancestors from Scotland and Ireland had bypassed northern climates with similar cloudy weather to move to a place where prolonged exposure to the sun practically guaranteed melanoma in people like them—or, at the very least, wrinkles, which was the reason her mother wore hats even if her time outside was limited to walking to and from the car. The fact that Gabby was subjecting herself to sun damage was something she didn't want to think about, because the truth was she liked having a tan, and getting a tan felt sort of good. Besides, in just a little while she'd put on her shirt again and force herself to sit in the shade.

Stephanie had been uncharacteristically quiet since her last comment. In some people, that would have struck Gabby as discomfort or shyness; in Stephanie, it came across as the kind of confidence Gabby had always secretly coveted. Because Stephanie was so comfortable with herself, she made Gabby feel comfortable around her, which, she had to admit, was a feeling she had been missing lately. For a long time, she hadn't been comfortable at home; she still wasn't comfortable at work; and she was less than confident about where things were going with Kevin.

As for Travis—the man definitely made her uncomfortable. Well, when he wasn't wearing his shirt, anyway. Sneaking a peek, she spotted him sitting in the sand near the water's edge, building drip castles with the three toddlers. When their attention seemed to waver, he rose from his spot and chased them into the shallow surf, the sound of their joyous screams echoing through the air. Travis seemed to be having as much fun as they were, and the sight of him made her want to smile. She forced herself not to, on the off chance he might see it and get the wrong idea.

The aroma finally forced Gabby to sit up. She couldn't shake the feeling of being on some exotic island vacation instead of only minutes from Beaufort. The gentle waves lapped in steady rhythm, and the few vacant beach houses behind them looked as if they'd been dropped from the sky. Over her shoulder, a path cut through the dunes, angling toward the black-and-white lighthouse that had weathered thousands of rainstorms.

Surprisingly, no one else had joined them at the cove, which only added to its appeal. Off to the side, she saw Laird standing over the portable grill, wielding a pair of tongs. Megan was lining up bags of potato chips and buns and opening Tupperware containers on a small fold-up table, while Liz was setting out condiments along with paper plates and plastic utensils. Joe and Matt were behind them, tossing a football back and forth. She couldn't remember a weekend from her childhood where a group of families got together to enjoy one another's company in a gorgeous spot simply because it was . . . Saturday. She wondered if this was the way most people lived, or whether it had more do with life in a small town, or whether it was simply a habit that these friends had formed long ago. Whatever it was, she suspected she could get used to it.

"Food's ready!" Laird shouted.

Gabby slipped on her shirt and wandered toward the food, surprised by how hungry she was until she remembered that she hadn't had a chance to eat breakfast. Over her shoulder, she saw Travis doing his best to herd the kids forward, scurrying around them like a cattle dog. The three of them rushed toward the grill, where Megan stood guard.

"Line up on the blanket," she ordered, and the toddlers—obviously out of well-trained habit—did exactly as they were told.

"Megan has magic powers with kids," Travis observed over her shoulder. He was breathing heavily, his hands on his hips. "I wish they listened to me like that. I have to resort to chasing them until I'm about to pass out."

"But you seem like such a natural."

"I love playing with them, not herding." He leaned toward her conspiratorially. "But between you and me? This is what I've learned about parents: The more you play with their kids, the more they love you. When they watch someone who adores their kids—genuinely delighting in them the same way they do—well, he just becomes the cat's meow in the parents' eyes."

"Cat's meow?"

"I'm a vet. I like animal clichés."

She couldn't suppress a smile. "You're probably right about playing with the kids. My favorite relative was an aunt who would climb trees with me and my sisters while all the other grown-ups sat in the living room talking."

"And yet . . . ," he said, motioning toward Stephanie, "there you were, just lounging on the towel with my sister, instead of taking the chance to show these people that you find their kids irresistible."

"I . . ."

"I was kidding." He winked. "The fact is, I wanted to spend time with them. And in a little while, they'll start getting cranky. That's when I finally collapse in a beach chair, wipe my brow, and let their parents take over."

"In other words, when the going gets tough, the tough get going."

"I think . . . that when the time comes, I just might volunteer your services."

"Gee, thanks."

"No problem. Hey—you hungry?"

"Starved."

By the time they reached the food, the kids were seated on the blanket with hot dogs, potato salad, and some diced fruit. Liz, Megan, and Allison sat near enough to monitor, but far enough away to converse. All three, Gabby noticed, ate chicken, along with various side dishes. Joe, Matt, and Laird had taken seats on the coolers and sat with their plates on their knees, bottles of beer propped up in the sand.

"Burgers or chicken?" Gabby inquired.

"I like chicken. But the burgers are supposed to be terrific. I just never really acquired the taste for red meat."

"I thought all men ate burgers."

"Then I guess I'm not a man." He straightened up. "Which, I must say, is really going to surprise and disappoint my parents. Being that they gave me a masculine name and all."

She laughed. "Well . . ." She nodded toward the grill. "They clearly saved the last piece of chicken for you."

"That's only because we got here before Stephanie. She would have taken it, even though she'd rather have a burger, just because she knows I'd end up not eating."

"I knew there was a reason I liked her."

They reached for some plates as they eyed the appetizing variety of side dishes spread out on the table—beans, casseroles, potato, cucumber, and fruit salads—all of which smelled delicious. Gabby grabbed a bun, added some ketchup, mustard, and pickles, and held out her plate. Travis dropped the chicken onto his plate, then lifted a burger from the side of the grill and added it to her bun.

He scooped some fruit salad onto his plate; Gabby added a taste of pretty much everything. When she was finished, she looked at both their plates with an almost guilty expression, which Travis thankfully didn't seem to notice.

"Would you like a beer?" he asked.

"Sounds great."

He reached into the cooler and fished out a Coors Light, then grabbed a bottle of water for himself.

"Gotta drive the boat," he explained. He lifted his plate in the direction of the dunes. "How about over there?"

"Don't you want to eat near your friends?"

"They'll be all right," he said.

"Lead the way."

They trudged toward the low dune, a spot shaded by a sickly, salt-poisoned tree, with branches all pointing in the same direction, bent by years of ocean breezes. Gabby could feel the sand slipping beneath her feet. Travis took a seat near the dune, lowering himself to the sand Indian style in a single movement. Gabby sat next to him with considerably less grace, making sure to leave enough distance between them so they wouldn't accidentally touch. Even in the shade, the sand and water beyond were so bright that she had to squint.

Travis began to cut his piece of chicken, the plastic utensils bending under the pressure.

"Coming out here reminds me of high school," he remarked. "I can't tell you how many weekends we spent here back then." He shrugged. "Different girls and no kids, of course."

"I'll bet that was fun."

"It was," he said. "I remember one night, Joe and Matt and Laird and I were out here with a few girls we were trying to impress. We were sitting around a bonfire, drinking beer, telling jokes, and laughing. . . and I remember thinking that life couldn't get any better."

"Sounds like a Budweiser commercial. Aside from the fact that you were underage and the whole thing was illegal."

"And you never did anything like that, right?"

"Actually, no," she said. "I didn't."

"Really? Never?"

"Why do you look so surprised?"

"I don't know. I guess . . . I just don't see you as someone who grew up following all the rules." When he saw her expression, he backtracked. "Don't get me wrong. I didn't mean it in a bad way. I just meant that you strike me as independent and someone who's always up for new adventures."

"You don't know anything about me."

As soon as she said it, she remembered saying the same thing to Stephanie. She braced herself for what might come next.

He absently moved his fruit with his fork. "I know that you moved away from your home, that you bought your own house, that you're making it on your own. To me, that means independence. And as for adventurous—you're here with a bunch of strangers, aren't you? You went parasailing and even overcame the thought of sharks to get dipped in the water. Those were new challenges. I think that's admirable."

She blushed, liking Travis's answer much better than his sister's. "Maybe," she conceded. "But it's not like traveling around the world without an itinerary."

"Don't let that fool you. You think I wasn't nervous when I left? I was terrified. I mean, it's one thing to tell your friends what you're going to do, and it's another thing entirely to actually get on the plane and land in a country where barely anyone speaks English. Have you traveled?"

"Not much. Aside from a spring break I spent in the Bahamas, I've never been out of the country. And if you get right down to it, if you stay close to the resort like I did—surrounded by American college kids—it could have passed for Florida."

She paused. "Where are you going next? Your next big adventure?"

"Nothing too far-flung this time. I'm going to the Grand Tetons. Do some camping, hiking, canoeing, the works. I've heard it's breathtaking, and I've never been there."

"Are you going alone?"

"No," he said. "I'm going with my dad. I can't wait."

Gabby made a face. "I can't imagine going off on a trip with either one of my parents."

"Why not?"

"My parents? You'd have to know them to understand."

He waited. In the silence, she set aside her plate and brushed off her hands.

"All right," she said with a sigh. "First off, my mom is the kind of lady who believes that staying in anything less than a five-star hotel is roughing it. And my dad? I suppose I could imagine him doing something more exciting, except for the fact that he's never shown interest in anything other than fishing. And besides, he wouldn't go anywhere without Mom, and since she has her standards, that means the only time spent outdoors is patio dining. With a fancy wine list and waiters in black and white, of course."

"Sounds like they really love each other."

"You inferred *that* from what I was saying?"

"That, and the idea that your mom isn't a fan of the great outdoors." That elicited a laugh. "They must be very proud of you," he added.

"What makes you say that?"

"Why wouldn't they be?"

Why indeed, she wondered. Let me count the ways. "Let's just say that I'm pretty sure my mom prefers my sisters. And trust me—my sisters are nothing like Stephanie."

"You mean they always say appropriate things?"

"No. I mean they're just like my mom."

"And that means she can't be proud of you?"

She took a bite of her burger, taking her time before responding. "It's complicated," she demurred.

"How so?" he persisted.

"For one thing, I have red hair. My sisters are all blond, like Mom."

"So?"

"And I'm twenty-six and still single."

"So?"

"I want a career."

"So?"

"None of that fits the image of the daughter my mother wants. She has definite ideas about the role of women, especially southern women of proper social standing."

"I'm getting the sense that you and your mother don't get along."

"Ya think?"

Just over his shoulder, Gabby saw Allison and Laird strolling down the path toward the lighthouse, hand in hand.

"Maybe she's jealous," he said. "Here you are, making your own life with your own goals and dreams, dreams independent of the world you grew up in, the world she expected you to inhabit— simply because she did. It takes courage to do something different, and maybe what you think is disappointment in you is actually, on some deeper level, disappointment in herself."

He took a bite of chicken and waited for her reaction. Gabby was flummoxed. It was something she'd never considered.

"That's not it," she finally forced out.

"Maybe not. Have you ever asked her?"

"Whether she felt disappointed in herself? I don't think so. And don't tell me that you'd confront your parents that way, either. Because . . ."

"I wouldn't," he said, shaking his head. "Not a chance. But I have a feeling that both of them are probably extremely proud of you, even if they don't know how to show it."

His comment was unexpected and strangely affecting. She leaned toward him slightly. "I don't know whether you're right, but thanks anyway. And I don't want you to get the wrong impression. I mean, we talk on the phone every week and we're civil. It's just that I sometimes wish things were different. I'd love to have the kind of relationship where we really enjoyed spending time together."

Travis said nothing in response, and Gabby found herself relieved that he didn't try to offer a solution or advice. When she'd related similar feelings to Kevin, his first instinct had been to come up with a game plan to change things. Pulling up her legs, she wrapped her arms around her knees. "Tell me—what's the best thing about being a vet?"

"The animals," he said. "And the people. But that's probably what you expected me to say, right?"

She thought about Eva Bronson. "The animals I can understand. . . ."

He held up his hands. "Don't get me wrong. I'm sure that some of the people I deal with are a lot like some of the people you have to deal with."

"You mean pushy? Neurotic? With tendencies toward hypochondria? In other words, crazy?"

"Of course. People are people, and a lot of them consider their pets members of the family. Which, of course, means that if they even suspect anything is wrong with their pet, they demand a full exam—which means they bring them in at least once a week, sometimes more. Almost always it's nothing, but my dad and I have a system in place to deal with it."

"What do you do?"

"We put a yellow sticker on the inside flap of the pet's file. So if Mrs. Worried comes in with Pokie or Whiskers, we see the sticker, do a cursory exam, and tell them that we don't currently see any-thing wrong, but we'd like to see the dog or cat in a week just to make sure. Since they were going to bring their pet in anyway, it helps get them in and out of the office quickly. And everyone is happy. We're the caring veterinarians, and the owners are assured that their pets are okay, but that they'd been right to worry, since we wanted to see them again."

"I wonder how the doctors in my office would react if I started putting yellow stickers on a few files."

"That bad?"

"Sometimes. Every time there's a new issue of *Reader's Digest*, or some news show that identifies a rare disease with specific symp-toms, the waiting room fills up with kids who naturally have exactly those symptoms."

"I'd probably be the same way with my kid."

She shook her head. "I doubt that. You strike me more as the walk-it-off or sleep-it-off kind of guy. And as a parent, I don't think you'll be any different."

"Maybe you're right," he admitted.

"Oh, I'm right."

"Because you know me?"

"Hey," she said, "you and your sister started it."

For the next half hour, they sat together, talking in a way that felt remarkably familiar. She talked more about her mother and father and their polar personalities; she told him a bit about her sisters and what it was like to grow up with so much pressure to conform. She filled him in on college and PA school and shared some of her memories of the evenings she'd spent in Beaufort be-fore moving to town. She mentioned Kevin only in passing, which surprised her until she realized that even though he was a major part of her life now, that hadn't always been the case. Somehow, talking to Travis reminded her that she'd become the woman she was going to be long before meeting Kevin.

As the conversation wound down, she found herself confessing to her occasional frustration at work, the words sometimes spilling out in a way she didn't quite intend. Though she didn't mention Dr. Melton, she did relate stories about some of the parents she'd met in her practice. She didn't give any names, but occasionally Travis would smile in a way that suggested he knew exactly whom she was talking about.

By then, Megan and Liz had packed most of the food back inside the coolers. Laird and Allison had gone for a walk. Matt, on the other hand, had half his body buried in sand by the toddlers, who didn't quite possess the coordination to prevent their shovels from raining sand into his eyes, nose, mouth, and ears.

Just then, a Frisbee landed near Gabby's feet, and she saw Joe approaching.

"I think it's time we rescued Matt," he called out. He pointed toward the Frisbee. "You up for it?"

"Are you saying they need some entertainment?"

Joe grinned. "I don't think we have a choice."

Travis looked at her. "Do you mind?"

"No, go ahead."

"I have to warn you—it's not going to be pretty." He stood up and shouted in the toddlers' direction, "Hey, kids? Are you guys ready to see the World Champion Frisbee expert in action?"

"Yay!!!" came the chorus. They dropped their shovels and dashed toward the water.

"Gotta go," Travis said. "My audience awaits."

As he jogged down to the waterline and sloshed in, Gabby found herself following his movements and feeling something oddly like affection.

Spending time with Travis wasn't at all the way she'd imagined it would be. There was no pretension, few attempts to impress, and he seemed to have an intuitive feel for when to stay silent or when to respond. It was that feeling of engagement, she realized, that led her to embark on a relationship with Kevin in the first place. It wasn't only the physical excitement she felt on the nights they spent together; more than that, she craved the comfort she experienced during those quiet moments they spent talking or when he gently took her hand as they walked through a parking lot on the way to dinner. Those were the moments in which it was easy to think he was the one she was meant to spend her life with, moments that lately had been fewer and farther between.

Gabby reflected on this as she watched Travis dive for the Frisbee. He bungled the catch, allowing the Frisbee to hit him in the chest, and landed in the surf with a dramatic cascade of water. The toddlers squealed with delight, as if it were the funniest thing they'd ever seen. When they shouted, "Do it again, Uncle Travis!" he jumped to his feet with equal flamboyance. He took three long, slow-motion strides and sent the Frisbee flying back to Joe. Putting on his game face, he assumed the exaggerated crouch of a baseball player, readying for the next catch in the infield. With a wink toward the kids, he promised, "The next time, I won't even get wet!" and followed his comment with a splashing, seizurelike miss that elicited even more squeals of delight. He seemed genuinely to enjoy performing for the kids, which only increased her feelings of warmth toward him. She was still trying to make sense of her reaction to Travis when he finally emerged from the ocean and started toward her, shaking the water from his hair. A moment later, he plopped down on the sand beside her, and when they accidentally touched, Gabby had the briefest flash of them sitting together just like this on a hundred different weekends in the future.

Eleven

The rest of the afternoon seemed to replay the events of the morning in reverse. They spent another hour at the beach before reloading the boat; on their way back, each couple rode once more in the parasail, though on her second trip Gabby rode with Stephanie. By late afternoon, the boat was cruising through the inlet, and Travis stopped to buy some shrimp from a local fisherman he obviously knew well. By the time they finally docked back at the house, all three toddlers were sound asleep. The adults were windblown and content, their faces darkened by the hours in the sun.

Once the boat was unloaded, the couples departed one by one, until only Gabby, Stephanie, and Travis remained. Travis was on the dock with Moby; he'd already spread the parachute on the dock so it could dry and was currently rinsing off the boat with a garden hose.

Stephanie stretched her arms overhead. "I guess I should be on my way, too. Dinner with the folks tonight. They get hurt feelings if I come down here and don't spend enough time with them. You know how it goes. Let me say good-bye to Travis."

Gabby nodded, watching lethargically as Stephanie leaned over the deck railing.

"Hey, Trav!" Stephanie shouted. "I'm outta here. Thanks for today!"

"Glad you could come," he shouted with a wave.

"You might want to toss something on the grill. Gabby just said she's starving!"

Gabby's lethargy vanished immediately, but before she could say anything, she saw Travis give a thumbs-up.

"I'll be up in a minute to start the grill!" he shouted. "Just let me finish up here."

Stephanie sauntered by Gabby, obviously pleased with her social engineering.

"Why'd you say that?" Gabby hissed.

"Because I'm going to be with my parents. I don't want my poor brother to have to spend the rest of the evening alone. He likes to have people around."

"Well, what if I wanted to go home?"

"Then tell him when he gets up here that you've changed your mind. He won't care. All I did was buy you a couple of minutes to think about it, since I guarantee that he would have asked you anyway, and then—if you'd said no—would have asked a second time." She slung her bag over her shoulder. "Hey, it was great getting to know you. I'm glad we had the chance to meet. Do you ever get up to the Raleigh area?"

"Sometimes," Gabby said, still thrown by what had just happened and unsure whether to be pleased or angry with Stephanie.

"Good. We can do lunch. I'd say we could do brunch tomorrow, but I really have to get back." She removed her sunglasses and wiped them with her shirt. "See you again?"

"Sure," Gabby said.

Stephanie went to the patio door, slid it open, then vanished inside, cutting through the house on the way to the door. By that point, Travis was already strolling up the dock, Moby trotting happily by his side. For the first time today, he'd put on a short-sleeved shirt, though he left it unbuttoned.

"Just give me a second to get the coals going. Shrimp kabobs okay?"

She debated only an instant before realizing that it was either this or head home to a microwave dinner and some awful show on television, and she couldn't help but remember the feeling she'd had when watching Travis frolic in the surf with the toddlers.

"Just give me a few minutes to change?"

While Travis got the coals going, Gabby checked on Molly, finding her sleeping soundly along with the puppies.

She took a quick shower before changing into a light cotton skirt and blouse. After drying her hair, she debated whether to put on makeup, then decided on just a bit of mascara. The sun had given her face some color, and when she stepped back from the mirror, it occurred to her that it had been years since she'd last had dinner with a man other than Kevin.

A case could be made that it was simply a continuation of the day, or that she'd been tricked into dinner by Stephanie, but she knew that neither was completely true.

Still, was her decision to have dinner with Travis something she should feel guilty about, perhaps even conceal from Kevin? Her first impulse was to insist that she'd have no reason *not* to tell Kevin. The day had been harmless—technically, she'd spent more time with Stephanie than she had with Travis. So what was the big deal?

You're dining alone tonight, of course, a little voice whispered.

But was that really a problem? Stephanie had been right: She was hungry again, and her neighbor had food. Human Necessity 101. It wasn't as though she were going to sleep with him. She had no intention of even kissing him. They were friends, that's all. And if Kevin were here, she was sure that Travis would have invited him along, too.

But he's not here, the voice insisted. *Will you tell Kevin about your little dinner for two?*

"Definitely. I'll definitely tell him," she muttered, trying to quiet the little voice. There were times when she absolutely hated the little voice. The little voice sounded like her mother.

Thus decided, she looked at herself one last time in the mirror and, pleased with what she saw, slipped out the patio door and started across the lawn.

As Gabby weaved her way between the hedges and appeared at the edge of the lawn, Travis caught the movement from the corner of his eye and found himself staring unabashedly as she approached. When she stepped onto the deck, he felt a strange shift in the atmosphere, catching him off guard.

"Hey," she said simply. "How long until dinner?"

"A couple of minutes," he answered. "Your timing is perfect."

She peeked at the skewered shrimp and brightly colored peppers and onions. As if on cue, her stomach grumbled. "Wow," she murmured, hoping he didn't hear it. "They look great."

"Do you want anything to drink?" He gestured toward the opposite end of the deck. "I think there's some beer and soda left over in the cooler."

As she crossed the deck, Travis tried to ignore the gentle sway of her hips, wondering what had gotten into him. He watched as she flipped open the lid, rummaged through the cooler, and pulled out two beers. When she returned to hand him one, he felt her fingers graze his. He twisted open the cap and took a long pull, looking down the line of the bottle at her. In the silence, she stared at the water. The sun, hovering over the tree line, was still bright, but its heat had diminished and shadows were gradually stretching across the lawn.

"This is why I bought my place," she finally said. "For views like this."

"It's gorgeous, isn't it?" He realized that he was watching her as he said it and forced away the subconscious implications. He cleared his throat. "How's Molly?"

"She seems fine. She was sleeping when I checked on her." She looked around. "Where's Moby?"

"I think he wandered around the front. He got bored with my cooking once he realized I wasn't about to offer him any scraps."

"He eats shrimp?"

"He eats anything."

"Discriminating," she said with a wink. "Is there anything I can do to help?"

"Not really. Unless you want to grab some plates from the kitchen."

"Be happy to." She nodded. "Where are they, exactly?"

"In the cupboard to the left of the sink. Oh, and the pineapple, too. It's on the counter. And the knife. It should be right there."

"Be back in a minute."

"And would you mind bringing some silverware, too? It's in the drawer near the dishwasher."

As soon as she turned to enter the house, Travis found himself studying her. There was definitely something about Gabby that interested him. It wasn't simply that she was attractive; there were pretty women everywhere. There was something about her straightforward intelligence and unforced humor that suggested a grounded sense of right and wrong. Beauty and earthy common sense were a rare combination, yet he doubted she was even aware she possessed it.

By the time she emerged, the kabobs were ready. He loaded a couple on each plate along with some slices of pineapple, and they took their seats at the table. Beyond them, the slow-moving creek reflected the sky like a mirror, the stillness broken only by a flock of starlings passing overhead.

"This is delicious," she said.

"Thank you."

She took a sip of her beer and motioned to the boat. "Are you going out again tomorrow?"

"I don't think so. Tomorrow I'll probably go riding."

"Horseback riding?"

He shook his head. "Motorcycle. When I was in college, I bought a beat-up 1983 Honda Shadow with the goal of restoring it and turning it around for a quick profit. Let's just say it wasn't quick, and I doubt I'll ever make a profit. But I can say I did all the work myself."

"That must be rewarding."

"*Pointless* is probably a better word. It's not very practical, since it has a tendency to break down and genuine parts are almost impossible to find. But isn't that the price of owning a classic?"

The beer was going down easy, and she took another drink. "I have no idea. I don't even change my own oil."

"Have you ever gone riding?"

"No. Too dangerous."

"Danger depends more on the rider and the conditions than the bike."

"But yours breaks down."

"True. But I like to live life on the edge."

"I've noticed that about your personality."

"Is that good or bad?"

"Neither. But it's definitely unpredictable. Especially when I try to reconcile it with the fact that you're a veterinarian. It's such a stable-sounding profession. When I think of veterinarians, I automatically think family man, complete with an apron-wearing wife and kids visiting the orthodontist."

"In other words, boring. Like the most exciting thing I should do is golf."

She thought of Kevin. "There are worse things."

"Just to let you know, I am a family man." Travis shrugged. "Except for the family part."

"That's kind of a prerequisite, don't you think?"

"I think that being a family man is more about having the proper worldview than the actual condition of having a family."

"Nice try." She squinted at him, feeling the effects of the beer.

"I'm not sure I could ever imagine you being married. Somehow, it just doesn't seem to fit you. You seem more like the dating lots of women, perpetual bachelor kind of guy."

"You're not the first person to say that to me. In fact, if I didn't know better, I'd say you spent too much time listening to my friends today."

"They were very flattering."

"That's why I take them on the boat."

"And Stephanie?"

"She's an enigma. But she's also my sister, so what can I do? Like I said, I'm a family-oriented guy."

"Why do I get the feeling you're trying to impress me?"

"Maybe I am. Tell me about your boyfriend. Is he a family man, too?"

"None of your business," she said.

"Okay, don't tell me. At least not yet. Tell me about growing up in Savannah instead."

"I already told you about my family. What else is there to tell?"

"Tell me anything."

She hesitated. "It was hot in the summer. Very hot. And humid, too."

"Are you always this vague?"

"I think a little mystery keeps things interesting."

"Does your boyfriend think that, too?"

"My boyfriend knows me."

"Is he tall?"

"What does that matter?"

"It doesn't. I'm just making conversation."

"Then let's talk about something else."

"All right. Have you ever been surfing?"

"Nope."

"Scuba diving?"

"Nope."

"Bummer."

"Why? Because I don't know what I'm missing?"

"No," he said. "Because now that my friends are married with children, I need to find someone who's up for things like that on a regular basis."

"As far as I can tell, you seem to find ways to keep yourself entertained. You're wakeboarding or Jet Skiing as soon as you get off work."

"There's more to life than just those two things. Like parasailing."

She laughed and he joined in, and she realized she liked the sound of it.

"I have a question about vet school," she said apropos of nothing, but no longer caring about the direction of their conversation. It felt good just to relax, to bask in the pleasure of Travis's company. It made her feel at ease. "I know it's dumb, but I've always wondered how much anatomy you had to study. As in, how many different kinds of animals?"

"Just the major ones," he said. "Cow, horse, pig, dog, cat, and chicken."

"And you had to know pretty much everything about each one?"

"As far as anatomy goes, yes."

She considered that. "Wow. I thought it was hard just doing people."

"Yeah, but remember: Most people won't sue me if their chicken dies. Your responsibility is much greater, especially since you're dealing with kids." He paused. "And I'll bet you're great with them."

"Why would you say that?"

"You have an aura of kindness and patience."

"Uh-huh. I think you got too much sun today."

"Probably," he said. He motioned to her bottle as he stood. "Want another?"

She hadn't even realized she'd finished. "I'd better not."

"I won't tell anyone."

"That's not the point. I don't want to give you the wrong impression about me."

"I doubt that's possible."

"I don't think my boyfriend would appreciate it."

"Then it's a good thing he's not here, isn't it? Besides, we're just getting to know each other. What harm is there in that?"

"Fine." She sighed. "Last one, though."

He brought two more over and opened hers. As soon as she took a drink and felt the corresponding buzz as it went down, she heard a voice inside her whisper, *You shouldn't be doing this.*

"You'd like him," she said, trying to reestablish some boundaries between them. "He's a great guy."

"I'm sure he is."

"And yes, to answer your earlier question, he's tall."

"I thought you didn't want to talk about him."

"I don't. I just want you to know I love him."

"Love is a wonderful thing. It makes life worthwhile. I love being in love."

"Spoken like a man with plenty of experience. But keep in mind that true love lasts forever."

"Poets would say that true love always ends in tragedy."

"And you're a poet?"

"No. I'm just telling you what they say. I'm not saying I agree. Like you, I'm more of a happy-ending romantic. My parents have been married forever, and that's what I want to have one day, too."

Gabby couldn't help thinking that he was very good at this sort of flirty banter—and then reminded herself that it was because he'd had a lot of practice. Still, she had to admit there was something flattering about his attention, even if she knew Kevin wouldn't approve.

"Did you know that I almost bought your house?" he asked.

She shook her head, surprised.

"It was for sale at the same time this one was. I liked the floor plan better than this one, but this one already had the deck and the boathouse and a lift. It was a tough choice."

"And now you've even got a hot tub."

"You like that?" He cocked an eyebrow. "We could get in later, once the sun goes down."

"I don't have my suit."

"Bathing suits are optional, of course."

She rolled her eyes, pointedly ignoring the shiver that had gone through her. "I don't think so."

He stretched, looking pleased with himself. "How about just our feet, then."

"I could probably handle that."

"It's a start."

"And a finish."

"That goes without saying."

On the other side of the creek, the setting sun was changing the sky to a golden palette of colors that stretched across the horizon. Travis pulled another chair closer and propped his feet on it. Gabby stared across the water, feeling a sense of well-being she hadn't experienced in a long time.

"Tell me about Africa," she said. "Is it as otherwordly as it seems?"

"It was for me," he said. "I kept wanting to go back. Like something in my genes recognized it as home, even though there was so little there that I saw that reminded me of the world I came from."

"Did you see any lions or elephants?"

"Many."

"Was that amazing?"

"It's something I'll never forget."

She was quiet for a moment. "I'm envious."

"Then go. And if you do, make sure you visit Victoria Falls. It's the most amazing place I've ever seen. The rainbows, the mist, the incredible roar—it's like you're standing on the very edge of the world."

She smiled dreamily. "How long were you there?"

"Which time?"

"How many times have you been there?"

"Three."

She tried to imagine living a life so free but somehow failed. "Tell me about all of them."

They talked quietly for a long time, dusk giving way to darkness. His colorful descriptions of people and places were vivid and detailed, making her feel as if she'd been alongside him, and she found herself wondering how many times, and with how many other women, he'd shared these stories. Halfway through, he rose from the table and brought back two bottles of water, respecting her earlier comment, and the appreciation she felt added to her growing sense of affection for Travis. Though she knew it was wrong, she was somehow unable to stop it.

By the time they got up to bring the dishes into the house, stars were twinkling overhead. While Travis rinsed the dishes, Gabby toured Travis's living room, thinking it was less like a bachelor pad than she'd imagined it would be. The furniture was comfortable and stylish, brown leather couches, walnut end tables, and brass lamps, and while the room was clean, it wasn't obsessively so. Magazines were stacked haphazardly on the television, and she could see a thin layer of dust on the stereo, which somehow seemed just right. Instead of artwork lining the walls, there were movie posters that reflected Travis's eclectic taste: *Casablanca* on one wall, *Die Hard* on another, with *Home Alone* right next to that. Behind her, she heard the faucet stop, and a moment later, Travis stepped into the room.

She smiled. "You ready to go soak our feet?"

"As long as you don't show too much skin."

They wandered back outside to the hot tub. Travis flipped open the cover and set it aside while Gabby removed her sandals; a moment later, they were sitting beside each other, their feet swishing back and forth. Gabby stared upward, tracing images in the skies above her.

"What are you thinking about?" Travis asked.

"The stars," she said. "I bought an astronomy book, and I'm trying to see if I remember anything."

"Do you?"

"Just the big ones. The obvious ones." She pointed toward the house. "Go straight up from the chimney about two fists and you'll see Orion's belt. Betelgeuse is on Orion's left shoulder, and Rigel is the name of his foot. He has two hunting dogs. The bright star over there is Sirius, and that's part of Canis Major, and Procyon is part of Canis Minor."

Travis spotted Orion's belt, and though he tried to follow her direction, he couldn't make out the others. "I'm not sure I see the other two."

"I can't, either. I just know they're there."

He pointed over her shoulder. "I can see the Big Dipper. Right over there. That's the only one I can always find."

"It's also known as the Big Bear, or Ursa Major. Did you know that a bear figure has been associated with that constellation since the ice age?"

"I can't say that I did."

"I just love the names, even if I can't make out all the constellations yet. Canes Venatici, Coma Berenices, the Pleiades, Antinous, Cassiopeia . . . their names sound like music."

"I take it this is a new hobby of yours."

"It's more like good intentions buried in the detritus of daily life. But for a couple of days there, I was really into it."

He laughed. "At least you're honest."

"I know my limitations. Still, I wish I knew more. When I was in seventh grade, I had a teacher who loved astronomy. He had this way of talking about stars that made you remember them forever."

"What did he say?"

"That staring at the stars was like staring backward in time, since some stars are so far away that their light takes millions of years just to reach us. That we see stars not as they look now, but as they were when dinosaurs roamed the earth. The whole concept just struck me as . . . amazing somehow."

"He sounds like a great teacher."

"He was. And we learned a lot, although I've forgotten most of it, as you can tell. But the feeling of wonder is still there. When I stare at the sky, I just know that someone was doing the exact same thing thousands of years ago."

Travis watched her, entranced by the sound of her voice in the darkness.

"And what's strange," she went on, "is that even though we know so much more about the universe, ordinary people today know less about the daily sky than our ancestors. Even without telescopes or mathematics or even the knowledge that the world was round, they used stars to navigate, they scanned the sky for specific constellations to know when to plant their crops, they used stars when constructing buildings, they learned to predict eclipses . . . it just makes me wonder what it was like to live so faithfully by the stars." Lost in thought, she was quiet for a long moment. "Sorry. I'm probably boring you."

"Not at all. In fact, I'll never think of stars in the same way again."

"You're teasing me."

"Absolutely not," he said seriously.

His gaze held hers. She had the sudden sense that he was about to kiss her, and she quickly turned away. In that moment, she was acutely aware of the sound of frogs calling from the marsh grass and crickets singing in the trees. The moon had reached its apex, casting a shimmery glow around them. Gabby moved her feet nervously in the water, knowing she should leave.

"I think my feet are getting wrinkled," she said.

"Do you want me to get a towel?"

"No, that's okay. But I should probably be going. It's getting late."

He stood and offered a hand. When she took it, she felt the warmth and strength in it. "I'll walk you back."

"I'm sure I can find my way."

"Just to the bushes, then."

At the table, she picked up her sandals and spotted Moby heading their way. He trotted up to them just as they stepped onto the grass, his tongue flapping happily. Moby circled them before charging toward the water, as if making sure nothing was hiding. He came to a stop with front paws slapping, then charged off in another direction.

"Moby is a dog with boundless curiosity and enthusiasm," Travis observed.

"Kind of like you."

"Kind of. Except I don't roll in fish guts."

She smiled. The grass was soft underfoot, and they reached the hedge a moment later. "I had a wonderful time today," she said. "And tonight, too."

"So did I. And thanks for the astronomy lesson."

"I'll do better next time. I'll impress you with my stellar knowledge."

He laughed. "Nice pun. Did you just think of that?"

"No, that was my teacher again. That's what he used to say when class was ending."

Travis shuffled his feet, then looked up at Gabby again. "What are you doing tomorrow?"

"Nothing really. I know I have to go to the grocery store. Why?"

"Do you want to come with me?"

"On your motorcycle?"

"I want to show you something. And it'll be fun—I promise. I'll even bring lunch."

She hesitated. It was a simple question, and she knew what the answer should be, especially if she wanted to keep her life from getting complicated. "I don't think that's a good idea" was all she had to say, and it would be over.

She thought about Kevin and the guilt she'd felt minutes earlier, about the choice she'd made by moving here in the first place. Yet despite those things, or maybe even because of them, she found herself beginning to smile.

"Sure," she said. "What time?"

If he seemed surprised by her answer, he didn't show it. "How about eleven? I'll give you a chance to sleep in."

She raised a hand to her hair. "Well, listen, thanks again. . . ."

"Yeah, you too. See you tomorrow."

For an instant, she thought she'd simply turn and leave. But again their eyes met and held for just a beat too long, and before she realized what was happening, Travis placed a hand on her hip and pulled her toward him. He kissed her, his lips neither soft nor hard against hers. It took an instant for her brain to register what was happening, and then she pushed him back.

"What are you doing?" she gasped.

"I couldn't help it." He shrugged, seeming not the least bit apologetic. "It just seemed like the right thing to do."

"You know I have a boyfriend," she repeated, knowing that deep down she hadn't minded the kiss at all and hating herself for it.

"I'm sorry if I made you uncomfortable," he said.

"It's fine," she said, holding up her hands, keeping him at a distance. "Just forget about it. But it's not going to happen again, okay?"

"Right."

"Right," she repeated, suddenly wanting to go home. She

shouldn't have put herself in this position. She'd known what was going to happen, she'd even warned herself about it, and sure enough, she'd been right.

She turned and started through the hedge, breathing fast. He'd kissed her! She still couldn't believe it. Though she intended to march straight to her door, making sure he realized how adamant she'd been about not wanting it to happen again, she snuck a peek over her shoulder and was mortified to realize he'd seen her. He raised a hand in a relaxed wave.

"See you tomorrow," he called out.

She didn't bother to respond, since there was really no reason to. The thought of what might happen tomorrow left her with a sense of dread. Why did he have to ruin things? Why couldn't they just be neighbors and friends? Why had it ended like this?

She pulled the slider closed behind her and marched to her bedroom, doing her best to work up the anger she felt the situation merited. It should have worked, but for the shaky legs and hammering heart, and the lingering realization that Travis Parker found her desirable enough to want to kiss her.

Twelve

After Gabby had left, Travis emptied the cooler. Wanting to spend some time with Moby, he grabbed the tennis ball, but even as he began their familiar game of fetch, his thoughts kept returning to Gabby. As Moby bounded through the yard, he couldn't shake the memory of the way Gabby's eyes crinkled when she smiled or the awe in her voice as she'd named the stars. He found himself wondering about her relationship with her boyfriend. Curiously, she hadn't said much about him—whatever her reasons, it struck him as an effective way to keep him guessing.

No question, he was definitely interested in her. It was odd, though. If history was any guide, she really wasn't his type. She didn't strike him as particularly delicate or touchy, a hothouse flower—he seemed to attract those types of women in droves. When he teased her, she teased him right back; when he pushed the boundaries, she had no qualms about putting him in his place. He liked her spirited nature, her self-control and confidence, and he especially liked the fact that she didn't seem conscious of possessing those qualities. The whole day struck him as a tantalizing dance, in which each of them had taken turns leading, one pushing, the other pulling, and vice versa. He wondered if a dance like that could go on forever.

That had been one of the downfalls of his past relationships. Even in the early stages, they had always been one-sided. Usually he'd ended up making most of the decisions about what to do or where to eat or whose house to go to or what movie to see. That part didn't bother him; what bothered him was that over time, the one-sidedness began to define everything about the relationship, which inevitably left him feeling as if he were dating an employee instead of a partner. Frankly, it bored him.

It was strange, he hadn't really thought of his previous relationships in this light. He usually didn't think about them at all. Somehow, spending time with Gabby made him think about what he'd been missing. He replayed their conversations in his head, realizing that he wanted more of them, more of her. He shouldn't have kissed her, he thought with a burst of uncharacteristic anxiety—he had gone too far. But now, all he could do was wait and see, and hope she didn't change her mind about coming with him tomorrow. What could he do? Nothing, he realized. Nothing at all.

"How'd it go?" Stephanie asked.

Feeling foggy the following morning, Travis could barely open his eyes. "What time is it?"

"I don't know. It's early, though."

"Why are you calling me?"

"Because I want to know how dinner went with Gabby."

"Is the sun even up?"

"Don't change the subject. Spill it."

"You're being awfully nosy about this."

"I'm a nosy gal. But don't worry. You already told me the answer."

"I didn't say anything."

"Exactly. I assume you're seeing her today, too?"

Travis pulled the phone away and stared at it, wondering how his sister always seemed to know everything.

"Steph—"

"Tell her I said hey. But listen, I gotta go. Thanks for keeping me informed."

She hung up before he had a chance to respond.

Gabby's first thought upon waking the next morning was that she liked to think of herself as a good person. Growing up, she'd always tried to follow the rules. She kept her room clean, studied for exams, did her best to mind her manners around her parents.

It wasn't last night's kiss that had her doubting her integrity. She hadn't had anything to do with that—that was all Travis. And the day had been innocent enough—she'd be perfectly happy telling Kevin all about it. No, her guilt had more to do with the fact that she'd willingly returned for dinner with Travis. If she had been honest with herself, she could have anticipated Travis's agenda and headed off the situation. Especially at the end. What had she been thinking?

As for Kevin . . . talking to him hadn't done much to erase the memory.

She'd called him last night after she'd gotten back to her house. As his cell phone rang, she'd prayed he wouldn't detect the guilt in her tone. No problem there, she'd quickly realized; they could barely hear each other at all, since he'd answered the phone while in a nightclub.

"Hey, sweetie," she said, "I just wanted to call—"

"Hey, Gabby!" he interrupted. "It's really loud in here, so speak up."

He shouted so loudly that she had to hold the phone away from her ear. "I can tell."

"What?"

"I said it sounds noisy!" she shouted back. "I take it you're having a good time?"

"I can barely hear you! What did you say?"

In the background, she heard a woman's voice asking if he

wanted another vodka tonic; Kevin's answer was lost in the cacophony.

"Where are you?"

"I'm not sure of the name. Just some club!"

"What kind of club?"

"Just someplace these other guys wanted to go! No big deal!"

"I'm glad you're having a good time."

"Speak up!"

She brought her fingers to the bridge of her nose and squeezed. "I just wanted to talk. I miss you."

"Yeah, miss you, too, but I'll be home in a few days! Listen, though . . ."

"I know, I know—you've got to go."

"Let me call you back tomorrow, okay?"

"Sure."

"Love you!"

"Love you, too."

Gabby hung up, annoyed. She'd just wanted to talk to him, but she supposed she should have known better. Conventions had a way of turning grown men back into adolescents—she'd witnessed that firsthand at a medical convention she'd attended in Birmingham a few months ago. By day, meetings were packed with earnest, serious-minded doctors; at night, she'd watched from her hotel window as they'd traveled in packs, drunk too much, and generally made fools of themselves. No harm in that. She didn't believe for a moment that he had gotten himself into trouble or done anything he'd regret.

Like kiss someone else?

She threw back the covers, really wishing she could stop thinking about that. She didn't want to think about the weight of Travis's hand on her hip as he'd pulled her toward him, and she definitely didn't want to think about the way his lips felt against hers or the electric spark she'd felt because of it. Still, as she headed for the shower, something else was bugging her, something she couldn't quite put her finger on. Turning on the water, she found herself wondering if—in the brief instant it had happened—she'd also kissed him back.

Unable to go back to sleep after Stephanie's call, Travis went jogging. Afterward, he'd tossed his surfboard in the back of his truck and driven across the bridge to Bogue Banks. After parking in the Sheraton Hotel lot, he hefted his board and made for the water. He wasn't alone; there were a dozen others who'd had the same idea, and he waved at a few he recognized. Like Travis, most wouldn't stay long; the best waves came early and would be gone as soon as the tide shifted. But it was still the perfect way to start the day.

The water was brisk—in another month, it would be nearly perfect—and he paddled over the swells, trying to get into rhythm. He wasn't a great surfer—in Bali, he'd studied some of the monster waves and shook his head, knowing that if he even attempted to ride them, he'd probably be killed—but he was good enough to enjoy himself.

He was used to being alone. Laird was the other surfer in his group of friends, but he hadn't gone with Travis in years. Ashley and Melinda, two former girlfriends, had gone surfing with him a few times in the past—but neither ever seemed able to meet him on the spur of the moment, and typically, by the time they arrived, he was just finishing up, which threw the morning out of whack. And as usual, it had been up to him to suggest the activity in the first place.

He was, he realized, a little disappointed in himself for choosing the same type of woman over and over. No wonder Allison and Megan liked to give him such a hard time. It must have been like watching the same play with different actors, the outcome always the same. As he lay on the surfboard, watching the swells approach, he realized that the same thing that made women initially attractive to him—their need to be taken care of—was the very thing that eventually signaled the end of the relationship. How did that old saying go? If you've been divorced once, you might be right in thinking your ex was the problem. If you've been divorced three times? Well, folks, the problem is most definitely you. Granted, he hadn't been divorced, but the point was well taken.

It amazed him that all this soul-searching seemed prompted by his day with Gabby. Gabby, the woman who'd falsely accused him, consistently avoided him, overtly antagonized him, and then made a point of repeatedly mentioning that she was in love with someone else. Go figure.

Behind him a swell seemed promising, and Travis began to paddle hard, maneuvering himself into the best possible position. Despite the glory of the day and the pleasures of the ocean, he couldn't escape the truth: What he really wanted to do was to spend as much time as possible with Gabby, for as long as he possibly could.

"Good morning," Kevin said into the phone, just as Gabby was getting ready to leave. Gabby moved the receiver to her other shoulder.

"Oh, hey," she answered. "How are you?"

"Good. Listen, I just wanted to tell you that I'm sorry about the call last night. I wanted to call you when I got back to the room to apologize, but by then it was pretty late."

"It's okay. You sounded like you were having fun."

"It was less thrilling than you probably think. The music was so loud that my ears are still ringing. I don't know why I went with those guys in the first place. I should have known I was in trouble when they started doing shots right after dinner, but someone had to keep an eye on them."

"And I'm sure you were the model of sobriety."

"Of course," he said. "You know I don't drink much. Which means, of course, that I'll probably crush them in the golf tournament today. They'll be too hung over to even hit the ball."

"Who were they?"

"Just some other brokers from Charlotte and Columbia. By the way they were acting, you'd have thought they hadn't been out in years."

"Maybe they haven't."

"Yeah, well . . ." She could hear him rustling and assumed he was getting dressed. "How about you? What did you end up doing?"

She hesitated. "Not too much."

"I wish you could have come down. It would have been a lot more fun if you'd been here."

"You know I couldn't get off work."

"I know. But I wanted to say it anyway. I'll try to give you a call later, okay?"

"Sure. I might be out and about."

"Oh, how's Molly doing?"

"She's doing well."

"I think I might want one of those puppies. They were cute."

"You're just trying to get on my good side."

"That's the only side to be on. Hey, I was thinking, though. Maybe you and I could head down to Miami this fall for a long weekend. One of the guys I was talking to just got back from South Beach, and he said there were a couple of great golf courses nearby."

She paused. "Have you ever thought about going to Africa?"

"Africa?"

"Yeah. Just taking off for a while, going on safari, seeing Victoria Falls? Or if not Africa, someplace in Europe? Like Greece?"

"Not really. And even if I wanted to, it's not like I could get the time off. What made you think of that?"

"No reason," she said.

While Gabby was on the phone, Travis walked up onto Gabby's porch and knocked. A moment later, she appeared in the doorway, the phone to her ear. Motioning to the phone, she waved him inside. He stepped into the living room, expecting her to make some excuse on the phone, but instead she pointed to the couch and vanished into the kitchen, the swinging doors swaying behind her.

He took a seat and waited. And waited. And waited. He felt ridiculous, as if she were treating him like a child. He could hear her speaking in hushed tones and had no idea whom she was talking to, and he contemplated getting up and walking out the door. Still, he remained on the couch, wondering why she seemed to have such a hold over him.

Finally, with the doors swinging behind her again, she stepped into the living room.

"I'm sorry. I know I'm a little late, but the phone's been ringing off the hook all morning."

Travis stood, thinking that Gabby had grown even prettier overnight, which made no sense at all. "No big deal," he answered.

The call with Kevin left her wondering again what she was doing, and she willed herself to stop thinking about it. "Let me just get my things, and we'll be good to go." She took a step toward the door. "Oh, and I want to check on Molly—she was fine this morning, but I want to make sure she has plenty of water."

A moment later, with her bag flung over her shoulder, they moved into the garage and filled the water bowl to the brim.

"Where are we going, by the way?" she asked on their way back out. "Not to some biker bar out in the sticks, I hope?"

"What's wrong with biker bars?"

"I wouldn't fit in. Not enough tattoos."

"You're generalizing, don't you think?"

"Probably. But you still haven't answered my question."

"Just a ride," he said. "Over the bridge, all the way down Bogue Banks to Emerald Isle, back over the bridge, and then we'll wind our way back to this place I want to show you."

"Where?"

"It's a surprise."

"Is it a fancy place?"

"Hardly."

"Can we eat there?"

He thought about it. "Sort of."

"Is it inside or outside?"

"It's a surprise," he said. "I don't want to ruin it for you."

"It sounds exciting."

"Don't build it up too much. It's just this place I like to go—nothing spectacular."

By that time, they'd reached the drive. Travis motioned toward the bike. "This is it."

The chrome on the bike made Gabby squint, and she put on a pair of sunglasses.

"Your pride and joy?"

"Frustration and angst."

"You're not going to start whining about how hard it is to get parts again, are you?"

He made a face, then chuckled. "I'll try to keep it to myself."

She motioned toward the basket he'd attached to the back of the bike with bungee cords. "What's for lunch?"

"The usual."

"Filet mignon, baked Alaska, roast lamb, Dover sole?"

"Not quite."

"Pop-Tarts?"

He ignored her gibe. "If you're ready, we can go. I'm pretty sure the helmet will fit you, but if it doesn't, I've got more in the garage."

She raised a sardonic eyebrow. "What about this special place? Have you taken a lot of different women there?"

"No," he said. "Actually, you'll be the first."

She waited to see if he would add anything else, but for once he seemed serious. She nodded slightly and walked to the motorcycle. She put on her helmet, fastened it beneath her chin, and threw her leg over the back of the seat. "Where do I put my feet?"

Travis unfolded the rear pegs. "There's one on each side. And try not to touch the exhaust with your leg. It gets very hot and you could get a nasty burn."

"Good to know. What about my hands?"

"They'll be around me, of course."

"Such a ladies' man," she said. "Why, if you were any smoother, I probably wouldn't even be able to hold on, would I?"

He put on his helmet and in a single, smooth motion climbed on and started the bike, allowing it to idle. It was quieter than some motorcycles, but she could feel the slight vibration through her seat. She felt a distinct anticipatory thrill, as if she were seated on a roller coaster as it was about to start, only this time without a seat belt.

Travis eased the motorcycle forward, out of the drive, and onto the street. Gabby reached for his hips, but as soon as she touched him, she thought about his hip flexors, which made her stomach do a flip-flop. It was either that or wrap her arms around him, and she didn't feel ready for *that*. As the motorcycle began to accelerate, she told herself not to squeeze, not to move her hands at all, just to keep her hands steady, like a statue.

"What's that?" Travis asked, craning his neck.

"What?"

"You said something about hands and a statue?"

Unaware she'd spoken aloud, she squeezed his hips, telling herself that she was doing it only to provide cover. "I said keep your hands steady, like a statue. I don't want to crash."

"We're not going to crash. I don't like crashing."

"Have you ever crashed before?"

Continuing to crane his neck and making her nervous by doing so, he nodded. "A couple of times. Spent two nights in the hospital once."

"And you didn't think this was important to mention before you invited me?"

"I didn't want you to get scared."

"Just keep your eyes on the road, okay? And don't do anything fancy."

"You want me to do something fancy?"

"*No!*"

"Good, because I'd rather just enjoy the ride." He craned his neck again; despite the helmet, she could swear she saw him wink. "The most important thing is to keep you safe, so just keep your hands steady like a statue, okay?"

On the back of the seat, Gabby felt herself shrink, just as she had in his office, aghast that she'd said those words aloud. And that despite the wind in their faces and the roar of the engine, Travis had actually heard them. There were moments when it honestly seemed as if the world were conspiring against her.

That he didn't bring it up again over the next few minutes made her feel slightly better. With the motorcycle zipping along, they left the quiet confines of their neighborhood. Gabby slowly got the hang of leaning when Travis leaned, and a few turns later, they were making their way through Beaufort and over the small bridge that separated them from the Morehead City limits. The road widened to two lanes and was clogged with weekend beach traffic. Gabby tried to ignore the feeling of vulnerability as they rode alongside a gigantic dump truck.

They veered toward the bridge that crossed the Intracoastal Waterway, and the traffic slowed to a crawl. When they reached the highway that bisected Bogue Banks, the traffic headed for Atlantic Beach evaporated and Travis gradually began to pick up speed. Sandwiched between two minivans, one in front and the other behind them, Gabby felt herself relaxing. As they sped past condominiums and houses hidden amid the Maritime Forest, she could feel the heat of the sun beginning to soak through her clothing.

She held Travis to keep herself steady, intensely conscious of the outline of his back muscles through the thin fabric of his shirt. Despite her best intentions, she was beginning to accept the reality of the attraction she felt for him. He was so different from her, yet in his presence she felt the possibility of another kind of life, a life she had never imagined could be hers. A life without the rigid limitations others had always set for her.

They drifted in an almost dreamlike silence past one town, then another: Atlantic Beach, Pine Knoll Shores, and Salter Path. On her left, largely hidden from view by oaks bent by the never-ending wind, lay some of the most desirable oceanfront property in the state. A few minutes earlier, they'd bypassed the Iron Steamer Pier. Though warped from years of storms, today it was home to scores of people fishing.

At Emerald Isle, the most westerly town on the island, Travis applied the brakes to slow for a turning car, and Gabby felt herself lean into him. Her hands inadvertently slid from his hips to his stomach, and she wondered if he noticed the way their bodies were pressed together. Though she willed herself to pull away, she didn't.

There was something happening here, something she didn't quite understand. She loved Kevin and wanted to marry him; in the past couple of days, that feeling hadn't changed at all. And yet . . . she couldn't deny that spending time with Travis seemed . . . right, somehow. Natural and easy, the way things were supposed to be. It seemed an impossible contradiction, and as they crossed the bridge at the far end of the island, heading toward home, she gave up trying to resolve it.

Surprising her, Travis slowed the bike before turning onto a partially hidden one-lane road perpendicular to the highway that stretched into the forest. When he brought the bike to a halt, Gabby turned from side to side, puzzled.

"Why are we stopping?" she asked. "Is this the place you wanted to show me?"

Travis got off the bike and removed his helmet. He shook his head.

"No, that's back in Beaufort," he said. "I wanted to see if you'd like to try driving for a bit."

"I've never driven a motorcycle." Gabby crossed her arms, remaining on the bike.

"I know. That's why I asked."

"I don't think so," she said, pushing up the helmet visor.

"C'mon, it'll be fun. I'll be right behind you on the bike, and I'm not going to let you crash. I'll have my hands right next to yours, I'll do all the shifting. All you'll have to do is steer until you get used to it."

"But it's illegal."

"A technicality. And besides, this is a private road. It leads to my uncle's place—a little way up, it turns into a dirt road, and he's the only one who lives that way. It's where I learned to ride."

She hesitated, torn between excitement and terror, amazed that she was actually considering it.

Travis raised his hands. "Trust me—there aren't any cars on the road, no one's going to stop us, and I'll be right there with you."

"Is it hard?"

"No, but it takes a little getting used to."

"Like riding a bike?"

"As far as the balance goes. But don't worry. I'll be right there, so nothing can go wrong." He smiled. "You up for this?"

"Not really. But—"

"Great!" he said. "First things first. Slide forward, okay? On your right handlebar is the throttle and the front brake. On the left is the clutch. The throttle governs your speed. Got it?"

She nodded.

"Your right foot controls the back brake. You use your left foot to shift the gears."

"Easy."

"Really?"

"No. Just making you feel better about your teaching skills."

She was beginning to sound like Stephanie, he thought. "After that, the shifting is kind of like driving a manual car. You let off the throttle, engage the clutch, shift, and then throttle up again.

But I'm going to show you, okay? But to do that, we're kind of going to be sandwiched together. My arms and legs aren't long enough to reach from the backseat."

"A convenient excuse," she said.

"Which just happens to be true. You ready for this?"

"I'm scared out of my wits."

"I'll take that as a yes. Now, scoot up a bit."

She slid forward, and Travis got on. After putting on his helmet, he wedged up against her, reaching for the handlebars, and despite his warning, she felt something jump inside, a light shock that started in her stomach and radiated outward.

"Now just put your hands on top of mine," he instructed. "And do the same with your feet. I just want you to feel what's happening. It's kind of a rhythm thing, but once you get the hang of it, you'll never forget."

"Is this how you learned?"

"No. My friend stood off to the side, yelling instructions. My first time out, I squeezed the clutch instead of the brake and ended up crashing into a tree. Which is why I want to be right here your first time out." He lifted the kickstand, engaged the clutch, and started the engine; as soon as it began to idle, she felt the same fluttery nerves she'd felt the moment before the parasail lifted her from the boat. She put her hands on his, relishing the feel of him against her.

"You ready?"

"As I'll ever be."

"Keep your hands light, okay?"

Travis turned the throttle and slowly eased out the clutch; in the instant the motorcycle began to move, he lifted his foot from the ground. Gabby allowed her foot to settle lightly on his.

They went slowly at first, Travis accelerating gradually, then easing off, accelerating again, and finally shifting to another gear before slowing again and coming to a stop. Then they started over again, Travis carefully explaining what he was doing—using the brake or getting ready to shift and reminding her never to squeeze the front brake in panic or she'd go flying over the handlebars. Little by little, as the process continued, Gabby got the hang of it. The choreographed movement of his hands and feet struck her as something akin to playing the piano, and after a few minutes, she could almost anticipate what he was going to do. Even so, he continued to guide her until the movements felt almost second nature.

With that, he had them switch places; her hands and feet were now on the controls, with his atop hers, and they repeated the process from the beginning. It wasn't as easy as he'd made it seem. At times the motorcycle jerked or she squeezed the hand brake too hard, but he was patient and encouraging. He never raised his voice, and she found herself recalling the way he'd been with the toddlers at the beach the day before. There was, she admitted, more to Travis than she had initially realized.

Over the next fifteen minutes, as she continued to practice driving, his touch became even lighter, until finally he let go entirely. Though she wasn't entirely comfortable, she began to accelerate faster and more smoothly, and braking came just as naturally. For the first time, she felt the power and freedom the motorcycle offered.

"You're doing fantastic," Travis said.

"This is great!" she cried, feeling almost giddy.

"Are you ready to try riding solo?"

"You're kidding."

"Not at all."

She debated only an instant. "Yeah," she said enthusiastically. "I think I am."

She brought the bike to a stop, and Travis hopped off. After watching him step back, she took a deep breath, ignored the pounding in her chest, and got the motorcycle going. A moment later, she was zipping along. On her own, she stopped and started a dozen times, gradually reducing the distances. Surprising Travis, she turned the bike around in a slow, wide arc and came racing back toward him. For a moment, he thought she was out of control, but she brought the bike to an elegant stop only steps from him. Unable to stop grinning, she ran her words together with kinetic energy.

"I can't believe I just did that!"

"You did great!"

"Did you see me turn around? I know I was going too slow, but I made it."

"I saw that."

"This is great! I can see why you love riding. It's a blast."

"I'm glad you enjoyed it."

"Can I try it again?"

He motioned to the road. "Feel free."

She rode back and forth along the road for a long while, Travis watching her confidence grow with every stop and start. Her turns were executed with greater ease as well—she even began driving in a circle—and by the time she stopped in front of him, her face was flushed. When she took off her helmet, Travis was sure he'd never seen anyone more alive and beautiful.

"I'm done," she announced. "You can drive now."

"You sure?"

"I learned a long time ago to quit while I'm ahead. I'd hate to crash and ruin this feeling."

Gabby scooted back and Travis got on the bike, only to feel her wrap her arms around him. As he wound his way back to the highway, Travis felt charged, as if his senses had been put on overdrive, and he was acutely aware of the curves of her body against his. They made their way up the highway, turned, and cut through Morehead City, passing by the Atlantic Beach bridge and completing the loop on their way back to Beaufort.

Minutes later, they were passing through the historic district, cruising past restaurants and the marina on their way down Front Street. Travis finally slowed the motorcycle, pulling onto a large

grassy lot near the end of the block. The empty lot bordered a
weathered Georgian that was at least a hundred years old on one
side and an equally aged Victorian on the other. He turned off the
engine and removed his helmet.

"Here we are," he said, ushering her off the bike. "This is what
I wanted to show you."

There was something in his voice that kept her from making
light of what seemed to be nothing more than a vacant lot, and
for a moment, she simply watched Travis as he walked a few steps
in silence. He was staring across the road, toward Shackleford
Banks, his hands in his pockets. Removing her helmet and running a hand through her matted hair, Gabby walked toward him.
Reaching his side, she sensed he would tell her what this was all
about when he was ready.

"In my opinion, this place has one of the most beautiful views
anywhere along the coast," he finally said. "It's not like an ocean
view, where all you see is waves and water stretching to the horizon. That's great, but after a while it gets boring, because the view
is always pretty much the same. But here, there's always something
to see. There are always sailboats and yachts streaming toward the
marina; if you come out here at night, you can see the crowds
along the waterfront and listen to the music. I've seen porpoises
and rays passing through the channel, and I especially love to see
the wild horses over on the island. I don't care how many times
I've seen them, I'm always amazed."

"You come out here a lot?"

"Twice a week, maybe. This is where I come to think."

"I'm sure the neighbors are thrilled about that."

"It's not like they can do anything about it. I own it."

"Really?"

"Why do you sound so surprised when you say that?"

"I'm not sure. I guess it just sounds so . . . domestic."

"I do own a house already. . . ."

"And I hear your neighbor is terrific."

"Yeah, yeah . . ."

"I just meant that buying a lot makes it sound like you're the kind of guy who has long-term plans."

"And you don't see me like that?"

"Well . . ."

"If you're trying to flatter me, you're not doing a very good job."

She laughed. "How about this, then: You continually surprise me."

"In a good way?"

"Every time."

"Like when you brought Molly to the clinic and realized I was a veterinarian?"

"I'd rather not talk about that."

He laughed. "Then let's eat."

She followed him back to the motorcycle, where he unpacked the basket and a blanket. After leading her up a small incline toward the rear of the property, he spread the blanket and motioned for her to sit. Once they were both comfortable, he started removing Tupperware containers.

"Tupperware?"

He winked. "My friends call me Mr. Domestic."

He pulled out two chilled cans of strawberry-flavored iced tea. After opening hers, he handed it to her.

"What's on the menu?" she asked.

He pointed to various containers as he spoke. "I've got three different kinds of cheese, crackers, Kalamata olives, and grapes— it's more a snack than a lunch."

"Sounds perfect." She reached for the crackers and then sliced herself some cheese. "There used to be a house here, right?" When she saw his surprise, she waved toward the houses on either side of the lot. "I can't imagine that this particular spot has been vacant for a hundred fifty years."

"You're right," he said. "It burned down when I was a kid. I know you think Beaufort is small now, but when I grew up here, it wasn't more than a blip on the map. Most of these historic homes had fallen into disrepair, and the one that had been here had been abandoned for years. It was a great big rambling kind of place with big holes in the roof, and it was rumored to be haunted, which made it that much more attractive to us when we were kids. We used to sneak over here at night. It was like our fort, and we'd play hide-and-seek for hours in the rooms. There were tons of great hiding places." He pulled absently at some grass, as if reaching for the memories. "Anyway, one winter night, I guess a couple of vagrants lit a fire inside to stay warm. The place went up in minutes, and the next day it was just this smoldering pile. But the thing was, no one knew how to contact the man who owned it. The original owner had died and left it to his son. The son died, and he'd left it to someone else, and so on, so that pile of rubble sat there for about a year until the town came in and bulldozed it away. The lot kind of got forgotten after that, until I finally tracked down the owner in New Mexico and made a lowball offer on it. He accepted it immediately. I doubt if he'd ever been here, and he didn't know what he was giving up."

"And you're going to build a house here?"

"That's part of my long-term plan, anyway, being that I'm so domestic and all." Travis grabbed an olive and popped it into his mouth. "You ready to tell me about your boyfriend yet?"

Her mind flashed to the conversation she'd had with Kevin earlier. "What's your interest?"

"I'm just making conversation."

Gabby reached for an olive as well. "Then let's talk about one of your previous girlfriends instead."

"Which one?"

"Any of them."

"All right. One of them gave me some movie posters."

"Was she pretty?"

He considered his answer. "Most people would say she was."

"And what would you say?"

"I would say . . . that you're right. Maybe we shouldn't talk about this."

She laughed, then pointed to the olives. "These are great, by the way. Everything you brought is perfect."

He added cheese to another cracker. "When does your boyfriend get back to town?"

"Are we back to this again?"

"I'm just thinking of you. I don't want to get you in trouble."

"I appreciate your concern, but I'm a big girl. And not that it matters, but he'll be coming home on Wednesday. Why?"

"Because I've enjoyed getting to know you these last couple of days."

"And I've enjoyed getting to know you."

"But are you bummed it's coming to an end?"

"It doesn't have to come to an end. We'll still be neighbors."

"And I'm sure your boyfriend wouldn't mind if I took you out for another motorcycle ride, or went for a picnic with you, or if you sat in the hot tub with me, right?"

The answer was obvious, and her expression became more serious. "He probably wouldn't be too happy about it."

"So it'll be ending."

"We can still be friends."

He stared at her for a moment, then suddenly grabbed at his chest as if he'd been shot. "You really know how to hurt a guy."

"What are you talking about?"

He shook his head. "There's no such thing as being friends. Not with single men and women our age. It just doesn't work like that, unless you're talking about someone you've known for a very long time. Certainly not when it comes to strangers."

Gabby opened her mouth to respond, but there was really nothing to say.

"And besides," he went on, "I'm not sure I want to be friends."

"Why not?"

"Because most likely I'd find myself wanting more than that."

Again, she said nothing. Travis watched her, unable to read her expression. Finally he shrugged.

"I don't think you'd want to be friends with me, either. It wouldn't be good for your relationship, since there's no doubt you'd probably end up falling for me, too, and in the end, you'd do something you'd regret. After that, you'd blame me for it, and then after a while, you'd probably end up moving, since the whole thing would be so uncomfortable for you."

"Is that so?"

"It's one of the curses of my life to be as charming as I am."

"It sounds like you've got the whole thing figured out."

"I do."

"Except for the part about me falling for you."

"You can't see that happening?"

"I have a boyfriend."

"And you're going to marry him?"

"As soon as he asks. That's why I moved here."

"Why hasn't he asked you yet?"

"That's none of your business."

"Do I know him?"

"Why are you so curious?"

"Because," he said, his eyes steady on hers, "if I was him, and you moved up here to be with me, I would've already asked you."

She heard something in his tone that made her realize he was telling the truth, and she looked away. When she spoke, her voice was soft. "Don't ruin this for me, okay?"

"Ruin what?"

"This. Today. Yesterday. Last night. All of it. Don't ruin it."

"I don't know what you mean."

She took a deep breath. "This weekend has meant a lot to me, if only because I finally felt I'd made a friend. A couple of them, actually. I didn't realize how much I'd missed having friends in my life. Spending time with you and your sister reminded me of how much I left behind when I moved here. I mean, I knew what I was doing, and I'm not sorry I made the decision I did. Believe it or not, I do love Kevin." She paused, struggling to order her thoughts. "But it's hard sometimes. Weekends like this most likely won't happen again, and I'm partly reconciled to that, because of Kevin. But there's a part of me that doesn't want to accept that it's a onetime thing, even though we both know it is." She hesitated. "When you say things like you just said, and I know you don't mean them, it just trivializes everything I'm going through."

Travis listened intently, recognizing an intensity in her voice she hadn't allowed him to hear before. And though he knew he should have simply nodded and apologized, he couldn't stop himself from responding.

"What makes you think I didn't mean what I said?" he countered. "I meant every word. But I understand that you don't want to hear it. Let me just say that I hope your boyfriend realizes how lucky he is to have someone like you in his life. He's a fool if he doesn't. I'm sorry if that makes you uncomfortable, and I won't say it again." He grinned. "But I had to say it once."

She looked away, liking what he had said despite herself. Travis turned toward the water, allowing her the silence she needed; unlike Kevin, he always seemed to know how to respond.

"We should probably be heading back, don't you think?" He motioned toward the bike. "And you should probably check on Molly."

"Yeah," she agreed. "That's probably a good idea."

They packed up the remains of the food and placed the containers back into the basket, then folded up the blanket and retraced their steps to the motorcycle. Over her shoulder, Gabby saw people beginning to crowd the restaurants for a late lunch, and she found herself envying the simplicity of their choices.

Travis refastened the blanket and basket, then put on his helmet. Gabby did the same, and they pulled out of the lot a moment later. Gabby clung to Travis's hips, trying and failing to convince

herself that he'd said similar things to dozens of different women
in the past.

They pulled into her drive, and Travis brought the motorcycle
to a halt. Gabby let go of him and dismounted, removing her
helmet. Standing before him, she felt an awkwardness she hadn't
experienced since high school, a notion that seemed ridiculous,
and she had the feeling he was about to kiss her again.

"Thanks for today," she said, wanting to preserve a little distance between them. "And thanks for the riding lesson, too."

"My pleasure. You're a natural. You should consider getting your
own bike."

"Maybe one day."

In the silence, Gabby could hear the engine ticking in the
heat. She handed Travis the helmet, watching as he placed it on
the seat.

"Okay, then," he said. "I guess I'll see you around?"

"Hard not to, us being neighbors and all."

"Do you want me to check on Molly for you?"

"No, that's okay. I'm sure she's doing fine."

He nodded. "Hey, listen, I'm sorry about what I said earlier. It
wasn't my place to pry like I did, or make you feel uncomfortable."

"It's okay," she said. "It didn't bother me at all."

"Sure it didn't."

She shrugged. "Well, since you were lying, I figured I'd lie."

Despite the tension, he laughed. "Do me a favor? If this whole
boyfriend thing doesn't work out, give me a call."

"I might just do that."

"And on that note, I think I'll take my leave." He turned the
handlebars and started walking the motorcycle backward, getting
into position to leave her drive. He was about to start the engine
when he looked at her again. "Would you have dinner with me
tomorrow night?"

She crossed her arms. "I can't believe you just asked me that."

"A man's got to seize the moment. It's kind of my motto."

"So I've learned."

"Is that a yes or a no?"

She took a step backward, but in spite of her reservations, she found herself smiling at his persistence. "How about if I make you dinner tonight instead? At my place. Seven o'clock."

"Sounds great," he said, and a moment later she was standing in the drive, wondering if she had taken temporary leave of her senses.

Thirteen

~·~

With the sun beating down mercilessly and the water from the hose icy cold, Travis had a hard time keeping Moby in one place. The short leash didn't seem to help much; Moby hated baths, which struck Travis as ironic, considering how much the dog loved to chase after tennis balls thrown into the ocean. On those occasions, Moby would bound through the waves, dog-paddling with fury, and showed no hesitation about shoving his head underwater for a better grip if the tennis ball bobbed away from him. But if he noticed Travis opening the drawer where his leash was kept, Moby would seize the opportunity to explore the neighborhood for hours, usually returning long after dark.

Travis had grown used to Moby's tricks, which was why he'd kept the leash out of sight until the last instant, then hooked it to Moby's collar before he could react. Moby, as usual, had given him his best "how could you do this to me?" expression as he was being walked around back, but Travis had shaken his head.

"Don't blame me. I didn't tell you to roll in dead fish, did I?"

Moby loved to roll in dead fish, the more foul-smelling the better, and while Travis was parking his motorcycle in the garage, Moby had trotted up happily with his tongue hanging out, acting proud of himself. Travis had smiled for only an instant before the stench hit and he noticed the disgusting chunks embedded in Moby's fur. After giving Moby a tentative pat on the head, he had sneaked inside to change into shorts, tucking the leash in his back pocket.

Now out back, with the leash secured to the deck railing, Moby danced from side to side, trying and failing to avoid getting even more wet than he already was.

"It's only water, you big baby," Travis scolded, although truthfully, he'd been spraying Moby for almost five minutes. As much as he loved animals, he didn't want to start shampooing until all the . . . *debris* had been rinsed away. Dead fish parts were disgusting.

Moby whined and continued to dance, tugging backward on the leash. When he was finally ready, Travis set aside the hose and poured a third of the bottle of shampoo on Moby's back. He scrubbed for a few minutes and rinsed, then sniffed the dog and winced. They went through the process two more times, at which point Moby was despondent. He fixed his eyes on Travis with a mournful expression that seemed to say, *Don't you realize I rolled in fish guts as my personal gift to you?*

Once Travis was satisfied, he brought Moby to another part of the deck and secured him again. He'd learned that if allowed to roam immediately after a bath, Moby would return to the scene of the crime as quickly as possible. His only hope was to keep him secured so long that he forgot about it. Moby shook away the excess water and—realizing he was stuck—finally lay down on the deck with a grunt.

Afterward, Travis mowed the lawn. Unlike most of his neighbors, who rode their lawn mowers, Travis still used a push mower. It took a little longer, but it was not only decent exercise, he found the repetitive back-and-forth nature of the activity relaxing. As he mowed, he kept glancing reflexively toward Gabby's house.

A few minutes earlier, he'd seen her leaving the garage and hop in her car. If she'd noticed him, she hadn't shown it. Instead, she'd simply backed out, then headed down the road toward town. He'd never met anyone quite like her. And now she'd invited him to dinner.

He didn't know what to make of that, and he'd been trying to figure it out ever since dropping her off. Most likely he'd simply worn her down. Lord knows he'd been oiling that wheel ever since they'd met, but as he mowed, he found himself wishing that he'd been a bit more subtle about the whole thing. It would have made him feel better about her dinner invitation, knowing that it hadn't been coerced somehow.

Wondering about all of this was new to him. But then again, he couldn't remember the last time he'd enjoyed himself so thoroughly with a woman. He'd laughed more with Gabby than he had with Monica or Joelyn or Sarah or anyone else he'd dated in the past. Finding a woman with a sense of humor had been the one piece of advice his father had given him when he'd first begun to get serious about dating, and he finally understood why his dad had considered it important. If conversation was the lyrics, laughter was the music, making time spent together a melody that could be replayed over and over without getting stale.

After finishing the lawn, he dragged the mower back to the garage, noting that Gabby still hadn't returned. She'd left the garage door cracked open, and Molly wandered out into the yard, then turned around and headed back inside.

Back in his kitchen, Travis downed a glass of iced tea in one long gulp. Knowing better but not caring, he let his thoughts drift to Gabby's boyfriend. He wondered if Kevin was someone he knew. He found it odd that she'd said so little about him and that it had taken her so long simply to tell him his name. It would be easy to attribute it to something like guilt, except for the fact that she had shied away from the topic from the beginning. He didn't know what to make of it, and he wondered what the guy was like or what he had done to make Gabby fall in love with him. In his mind's eye, images floated past—

athletic, bookish, somewhere in between—but none of them seemed exactly right.

Noting the time, he figured that he could get the parasail boat back to the marina before showering and getting ready. He retrieved the boat key and headed out the back slider, untied Moby, and watched as Moby raced past him down the steps. Stopping at the edge of the dock, Travis motioned to the boat.

"Yeah, go ahead. Get in."

Moby jumped into the boat, his tail darting to and fro. Travis followed him in. Minutes later they were cruising down the creek, the wake leaving a trail that pointed them in the right direction. Passing Gabby's house, he stole a look at her windows, thinking again about their upcoming dinner and wondering what would happen. He was, he realized for the first time in his dating life, nervous that he might do something wrong.

Gabby made the short drive to the grocery store and pulled into the crowded lot. It was always packed on Sundays, and she ended up parking in the far corner, making her wonder why she'd driven the car in the first place.

Slinging her purse over her shoulder, she got out of the car, located a cart, and entered the store.

She'd spotted Travis mowing the lawn earlier, but she'd ignored him, needing somehow to feel more in control than she actually was. The nice, orderly little world she'd created had been thrown out of whack, and she desperately needed some time to regain her composure.

Inside, Gabby made her way to the produce section, where she collected some fresh green beans and the makings for a salad. Moving quickly, she located a box of pasta and some croutons, then headed toward the rear of the store.

Knowing that Travis liked chicken, she put a packet of breasts in the cart, thinking that a bottle of Chardonnay would go well with them. She wasn't sure whether Travis liked wine—she somehow doubted it—but it sounded good to her, and she scanned the limited selection for a winery that she recognized. There were two offerings from Napa Valley, but she chose something from Australia, thinking it sounded a little more exotic.

The checkout lines were long and moving slowly, but at last she made it back to her car. Glancing in the rearview mirror, she caught an image of herself and paused for a moment, staring at herself as if through someone else's eyes.

How long had it been since someone besides Kevin had kissed her? As much as she'd tried to forget that little incident, she'd found herself returning to it over and over, like a forbidden secret.

She was drawn to Travis; she couldn't deny that. It wasn't just that he was handsome and that he made her feel desirable. It had something to do with his natural exuberance and the way he'd made her feel a part of it; it was the fact that he had lived a life that seemed so different from hers, yet they still spoke the same language, a familiarity that belied the short period they had known each other. She'd never met someone like him before. Most people she'd known, and certainly everyone in her PA class, seemed to live their lives as if marking off goals on a score sheet. Study hard, get a job, get married, buy a house, have kids—and until this weekend, she realized she'd been no different. Somehow, compared with the choices he'd made and the places he'd traveled, her life seemed so . . . banal.

But would she do it differently if she could? She doubted it. Her experiences growing up had formed her into the woman that she'd become, just as his experiences had formed him, and she didn't regret them. And yet, as she turned the key and started the engine, she knew that wasn't the question that mattered. As the car idled, she realized the choice before her was this: Where do I go from here?

It is never too late to change things. The thought frightened her even as it excited her. A few minutes later, she was heading toward

Morehead City, feeling as if somehow she'd been given the chance to start over.

The sun had drifted across the sky by the time Gabby got home, and she spotted Molly lying in the marsh grass, her ears perked up and tail thumping. She trotted toward Gabby as she opened the rear door, greeting her with a couple of sloppy licks.

"You seem almost back to normal," Gabby said. "Your babies doing okay?"

As if on cue, Molly began wandering that way.

Gabby reached for the bags and brought them inside, setting the groceries on the counter. It had taken her longer than she'd anticipated, but she still had enough time to get things started. She set a pot of water on the stove and set the burner on high for the pasta. While it was heating, she chopped the tomatoes and cucumbers for the salad. She cut up the lettuce and mixed the ingredients together with a bit of cheese and the olives Travis had introduced her to the day before.

She added the pasta to the water with a dash of salt, unwrapped the chicken, and began to sauté it in olive oil, wishing she could have done something a bit fancier. She added a bit of pepper and other seasonings, but by the end, it looked almost as boring as it had before she started. Never mind, it would have to do. She set the oven to warm, added some broth to the bowl along with the chicken, and set it inside, hoping that would be enough to keep it from drying out. She drained the pasta and put it in a bowl in the fridge, planning to add a little flavoring to it later.

In her bedroom, she laid out some clothes and headed into the shower. The warm water was luxurious. She shaved her legs, forcing herself not to rush so she wouldn't nick herself, washed and conditioned her hair, and finally stepped out and dried off.

On the bed were a new pair of jeans and a beaded, low-cut shirt. She'd chosen her outfit carefully, not wanting to dress too formally or casually, and these seemed just right. She dressed and then slipped on a new pair of sandals and a dangly pair of earrings. Stepping in front of the floor mirror, she turned from side to side, pleased with the way she looked.

With time running out, she set out some candles throughout the house and was adding the last of them to the table when she heard Travis knocking. She stood straight, trying to compose herself, then made her way to the door.

Molly had wandered up to Travis, and he was scratching her behind the ears when the door opened. He found himself unable to turn away. Nor could he find his voice. Instead, he stared wordlessly at Gabby, trying to sort through the jumble of emotions that began to crowd his heart.

Gabby smiled at his obvious discomfiture. "Come in," she said. "I've just about got everything ready."

Travis followed her inside, trying not to stare as she walked ahead of him.

"I was just about to open a bottle of wine. Would you like a glass?"

"Please."

In the kitchen, she reached for the bottle and opener as Travis stepped forward.

"I can get that for you."

"I'm glad you said that. I have a tendency to shred the cork, and I hate having pieces floating in my glass."

As he opened the bottle, Travis watched her retrieve two glasses from the cupboard. She set them on the counter, and Travis noted the label, feigning more interest than he felt, trying to steady his nerves.

"I've never had this kind before. Is it any good?"

"I have no idea."

"Then I guess it'll be new for the both of us." He poured and handed one glass to her, trying to read her expression.

"I wasn't sure what you wanted for dinner," she chatted on, "but I knew that you liked chicken. I have to warn you, though. I've never been the chef in my family."

"I'm sure whatever you made will be fine. I'm not that picky."

"As long as it's plain, right?"

"That goes without saying."

"Are you hungry?" She smiled. "It'll only take a few minutes to heat this up. . . ."

He debated for a moment before leaning against the counter. "Actually, could we wait for a little while? I'd like to enjoy my glass of wine first."

She nodded, and in the silence she stood before him, wondering what she was supposed to do next.

"Would you like to go sit outside?"

"Love to."

They took a seat in the rockers she'd placed near the door. Gabby took a sip of her wine, glad for something to take the edge off her nerves.

"I like your view," Travis said gamely, rocking back and forth with energy. "It reminds me of mine."

Gabby laughed, feeling a little burst of relief. "Unfortunately, I haven't learned to enjoy it the way you do."

"Very few people do. It's kind of a lost art these days, even in the South. Watching the creek flow by is a little like smelling the roses."

"Maybe it's a small-town thing," she speculated.

Travis eyed her with interest. "Tell me honestly, are you enjoying life in Beaufort?" he asked.

"It has its good points."

"I hear the neighbors are terrific."

"I've only met one."

"And?"

"He has a tendency to ask loaded questions."

Travis grinned. He loved her sense of play.

"But to answer your question," she went on, "yes, I do like it here. I like the fact that it takes only a few minutes to get anywhere, it's beautiful, and for the most part, I think I'm learning to love the slower pace of life."

"You make it sound like Savannah is as cosmopolitan as New York or Paris."

"It isn't." She looked over her glass at him. "But I will say that Savannah is definitely closer to New York than Beaufort. Have you ever been there?"

"I spent a week there one night."

"Ha-ha. You know, if you're going to make a joke, you could try coming up with something original."

"That's too much work."

"And you're averse to work, right?"

"Can't you tell?" He leaned back in his rocker, the picture of ease. "Tell me the truth, though. Do you think you'll ever move back?"

She took a swallow of wine before answering. "I don't think so," she said. "Don't get me wrong. I think it's a great place, and it's one of the most beautiful cities in the South. I love the way the city was laid out. It has the most beautiful squares—these lovely parks scattered every few blocks—and some of the houses that front them are stunning. When I was a little girl, I used to imagine myself living in one of them. For a long time, it was a dream of mine."

Travis stayed silent, waiting for her to continue. Gabby shrugged. "But as I grew older, I began to realize that it was more my mom's dream than my own. She always wanted to live in one of those homes, and I remember the way she used to badger my dad to put in an offer whenever one was for sale. My dad did well, don't get me wrong, but I could tell it always bothered him that he couldn't afford one of the really grand houses, and after a while, it just rubbed me the wrong way." She paused. "Anyway, I guess I wanted something different. Which led, of course, to college and PA school and Kevin. And here I am."

From a distance, they heard Moby begin barking frantically, the sound followed by the faint rustling of claws on bark. Glancing at the large oak tree near the hedges, Travis watched as a squirrel raced up the trunk. Though he couldn't see him, he knew that Moby was still circling the oak, thinking that somehow the critter would lose its grip. Noticing that Gabby had turned at the sound, Travis raised his glass in that direction.

"My dog is crazy about chasing squirrels. He seems to regard it as his life's purpose."

"Most dogs do."

"Does Molly?"

"No. Her owner has a bit more control over her, and she nipped that little problem in the bud before it got out of hand."

"I see," Travis said with mock seriousness.

Over the water, the first brilliant act of the sun's descent was beginning. In another hour the creek would turn golden, but for now there was something dark and mysterious about its brackish color. Beyond the cypress trees lining the bank, Travis could see an osprey floating on updrafts and watched as a small motorboat loaded with fishing gear puttered past. It was captained by some-one old enough to be Travis's grandfather, and the gentleman waved. Travis returned the greeting, then took another drink.

"With all you said, I'm curious as to whether you can imagine yourself staying in Beaufort."

She thought about her answer, sensing there was more to the question than it appeared.

"I suppose that depends," she finally hedged. "It's not exactly exciting, but on the other hand, it's not a bad place to raise a family."

"And that's important?"

She turned toward him with a faint air of challenge. "Is there anything more important?"

"No," he agreed evenly, "there isn't. I'm evidence of that belief because I lived it. Beaufort is the kind of place where Little League baseball generates more conversation than the Super Bowl, and I like thinking that I can raise my kids where the little world they live in is all they know. Growing up, I used to think that this was the most boring place in the world, but when I think back, I realize that the corollary to that was that anything exciting meant that much more to me. I never grew jaded, the way so many city kids do." He paused. "I remember going fishing with my dad every Saturday morning, and even though my dad was just about the worst fisherman who ever baited a hook, I found it thrilling. Now I understand that for my dad, at least, it was all about spending time with me, and I can't tell you how grateful I am for that. I like thinking that I can give my kids the same kinds of experiences someday."

"It's nice to hear you say something like that," Gabby said. "A lot of people don't think that way."

"I love this town."

"Not that," she said, smiling. "I was talking about the way you wanted to raise your kids. It seems like you've given it a lot of thought."

"I have," he conceded.

"You always have a way of surprising me, don't you."

"I don't know. Do I?"

"A little. The more I've gotten to know you, the more you've come to strike me as impossibly well-adjusted."

"I could say the same about you," he responded. "Maybe that's why we get along so well."

She stared at him, feeling the crackle of tension between them. "You ready for dinner yet?"

He swallowed, hoping she couldn't sense his feelings for her. "That sounds great," he forced out.

Taking their wineglasses, they returned to the kitchen. Gabby motioned for Travis to sit at the table while she got things ready, and as he watched her move around the kitchen, he felt a sense of contentment settle upon him.

At dinner, he ate two pieces of chicken, enjoyed the green beans and the pasta, and complimented Gabby extravagantly on her cooking, until she giggled, begging him to stop. He asked her repeatedly about her childhood in Savannah, and she finally relented, regaling him with a couple of girlhood stories that made them both chuckle. In time, the sky turned gray and blue and finally black. The candles burned lower, and they poured the last of the wine into their glasses, both aware that they were sitting across from a person who just might change the course of their lives forever if they weren't careful.

After dinner was over and Travis helped Gabby clean up, they retreated to the couch, nursing their wine and sharing stories from their pasts. Gabby tried to imagine Travis as a young boy, wondering also what she would have thought about him had they met during her high school or college years.

As the evening wore on, Travis inched closer, casually slipping his arm around her. Gabby leaned into him, feeling snug against him, content to watch the play of silver moonlight as it filtered through the clouds.

"What are you thinking about?" Travis asked at one point, breaking a particularly long yet comfortable silence.

"I was thinking how natural this whole weekend has seemed." Gabby looked at him. "Like we've known each other forever."

"I guess that means a couple of my stories were boring, huh?"

"Don't underestimate yourself," she teased. "Lots of your stories were boring."

He laughed, pulling her tighter. "The more I get to know you, the more you surprise me. I like that."

"What are neighbors for?"

"Is that still all I am to you? Just a neighbor?"

She glanced away without responding, and Travis went on. "I know it makes you uncomfortable, but I can't leave tonight without telling you that just being neighbors isn't enough for me."

"Travis . . ."

"Let me finish, okay?" he said. "Earlier today, when we talked, you told me how much you'd missed having friends around, and I've been thinking about that ever since, but not in the way that you probably imagine. It made me realize that even though I have friends, I've been missing something that all my friends do have. Laird and Allison, Joe and Megan, Matt and Liz, all have each other. I don't have that in my life, and until you came along, I wasn't sure I even wanted it. But now . . ."

She picked at the beadwork on her shirt, resisting his words and yet welcoming them, too.

"I don't want to lose you, Gabby. I can't imagine seeing you walk to your car in the morning and pretending that none of this ever happened. I can't imagine not sitting here with you on the couch, like we're doing now." He swallowed. "And right now, I can't imagine being in love with any other woman."

Gabby wasn't sure she'd heard him right, but when she saw the way he was staring at her, she knew he meant it. And with that, she felt the last of her defenses falling away and knew she had fallen in love with him as well.

The grandfather clock chimed in the background. Candlelight flickered on the walls, casting shadows around the room. Travis could sense the gentle rise and fall of her chest as she breathed, and they continued to stare at each other, neither one of them able to speak.

The phone rang, shattering her thoughts, and Travis turned away. Gabby leaned forward and reached for the portable phone. She answered, her voice betraying nothing.

"Oh, hey, how are you? . . . Not much . . . Uh-huh . . . I was running some errands. . . . What's been going on there?"

As she listened to Kevin's voice, a rush of guilt washed over her. Yet she found herself reaching over and placing a hand on Travis's leg. He hadn't moved or made a sound, and she could feel the muscles tense beneath his jeans as she ran her hand along his thigh.

"Oh, that's great. Congratulations. I'm glad you won . . . sounds like you had fun. . . . Oh, me? Nothing too exciting."

Hearing Kevin's voice while being so close to Travis was pulling her in two directions. She tried to concentrate and listen to Kevin, while sorting through what had just happened with Travis. The situation was too surreal to absorb.

"I'm sorry to hear that. . . . I know, I get sunburned, too. . . . Uh-huh . . . uh-huh . . . Yes, I've thought about the trip to Miami, but I don't get any vacation days until the end of the year. . . . Maybe, I don't know. . . ."

She released Travis's leg and leaned back against the couch, trying to keep her voice steady, wishing she hadn't answered, wishing he hadn't called. Knowing she was only becoming more confused. "We'll see, okay? We'll talk about it when you get back. . . . No, nothing's wrong. I'm just tired, I guess. . . . No, nothing to worry about. It's been a long weekend. . . ."

It wasn't a lie, but it wasn't the truth, either, and she knew it, which made her feel even worse. Travis was staring downward, listening but pretending not to.

"I will," she went on. "Yeah, you, too . . . Uh-huh . . . yeah, I should be around. . . . Okay . . . I do, too. And have fun tomorrow. Bye."

Hanging up the phone, she seemed preoccupied for a moment before leaning forward and putting the handset on the table. Travis knew enough not to say anything.

"That was Kevin," she finally said.

"I figured," Travis said, unable to read her expression.

"He won the best ball tournament today."

"Good for him."

Again, a silence descended between them.

"I think I need some fresh air," she finally said, rising from the couch. She made her way to the sliding glass door and stepped outside.

Travis watched her go, wondering if he should join her or

whether she needed to be alone. From his spot on the couch, her image against the railing was shadowed. He could imagine heading out to join her, only to hear her suggest that it might be best if he left, and though the thought frightened him, he needed to be with her, now more than ever.

He made his way out the door and joined her against the rail. In the moonlight, her skin was pearly, her eyes darkly luminous.

"I'm sorry," he said.

"Don't be. There's nothing for you to be sorry for." She forced a smile. "It's my fault, not yours. I knew what I was getting into."

Gabby could sense that he wanted to touch her, but she was torn about whether she wanted him to. She knew she should end this, that she shouldn't let the evening progress any further, but she couldn't break the spell that Travis's declaration had cast over her. It didn't make sense. It took time to fall in love, more time than a single weekend, yet somehow, despite her feelings for Kevin, it had happened. She sensed Travis's nervousness as he stood beside her, and she watched him fortify himself with a last sip of wine.

"Did you mean what you said earlier?" she asked. "About wanting a family?"

"Yes, I did."

"I'm glad," she said. "Because I think you'd be a great father. I didn't tell you before, but that's what I thought when I saw you with the kids yesterday. You seemed so natural with them."

"I've had a lot of experience with puppies."

Despite the tension, she laughed. She took a small step closer to him, and when he turned to face her, she slipped her arms around his neck. She could hear the little voice inside warning her to stop, telling her that it still wasn't too late to end this. But another urge had taken hold of her, and she knew it was pointless to deny it.

"Maybe so, but I thought it was sexy," she whispered.

Travis pulled her tight against him, noticing how her body seemed to fit against his. He could smell a trace of jasmine perfume on her, and as they stood holding each other, his senses seemed to come alive. He felt as if he'd reached the end of a long journey, unaware until this moment that Gabby had been his destination all along. When he whispered, "I love you, Gabby Holland," against her ear, he'd never felt more sure about anything.

Gabby sank into him.

"I love you, too, Travis Parker," she whispered, and as they stood in each other's arms, Gabby couldn't imagine wanting anything more than what was happening now, all regrets and reservations swept aside.

He kissed her, then kissed her again and again, leisurely exploring her neck and collarbone before rising to meet her lips once more. She ran her hands over his chest and shoulders, feeling the strength in the arms that held her, and when he buried his fingers in her hair, she shivered, knowing that this was what the weekend had been building toward all along.

They kissed on the deck for a long time. Finally she pulled back, and took his hand to lead him inside, past the living room and toward the bedroom. She motioned toward the bed, and as Travis lay down, she pulled a lighter from the drawer and proceeded to light the candles she'd set out earlier. Her bedroom, dark at first, gave way to a flickering glow that bathed her in liquid gold.

With shadows accentuating her every movement, Travis watched as Gabby crossed her arms, reaching for the hem of her shirt. With a single movement, she pulled the shirt over her head. Her breasts pressed against the satin outline of her bra, and her hands drifted slowly downward to the snap on her jeans. A moment later, she stepped out of the crumpled pile at her feet.

Travis was mesmerized as she moved toward the bed and playfully pushed him onto his back. She began to undo the buttons on his shirt and pulled it over his shoulders. As he wiggled his arms free, she undid the snap on his jeans, and a moment later, he felt the heat from her belly as it slid against his own.

His mouth met hers with controlled passion. Her body felt right against his, more right than anything she'd ever known, like missing pieces in a puzzle finally coming together.

Afterward, he lay beside her and said the words that had been echoing inside his head all night.

"I love you, Gabby," he whispered. "You are the best thing that's ever happened to me."

He felt her reach out for him.

"I love you, too, Travis," she whispered, and upon hearing her words, he knew that the solitary journey he'd been on for years had somehow reached its end.

With the moon still high in the sky and the silver light illuminating the bedroom, Travis rolled over, knowing instantly that Gabby was gone. It was almost four in the morning, and after noting that she wasn't in the bathroom, he got up and slipped on his jeans. He walked down the hall and peeked into the guest bedroom before poking his head into the kitchen. All the lights were off, and he hesitated for a moment before noticing that the sliding glass door was cracked open.

He stepped out onto the small deck, catching sight of a shadowed figure leaning against the deck railing off to the side of the house. He took a hesitant step toward her, unsure if she wanted to be alone.

"Hey," he heard a voice call out in the darkness. Travis saw she was wearing the bathrobe that had been hanging in the bathroom.

"Hey there," he answered quietly. "You okay?"

"I'm fine. I woke up and tossed and turned for a while, but I didn't want to wake you."

Stopping just short of her, he leaned against the rail as well, neither of them speaking. Instead, they simply watched the sky. Nothing seemed to be stirring; even the crickets and frogs were silent.

"It's so lovely out here," she finally said.

"Yes, it is," he answered.

"I love nights like this."

When she said nothing else, he moved closer and reached for her hand. "Are you upset by what happened?"

"Not at all," she said, her voice clear. "I don't regret any of it."

He smiled. "What are you thinking about?"

"I was thinking about my dad," she mused, leaning into him. "In a lot of ways, he reminds me of you. You'd like him."

"I'm sure I would," he said, uncertain where the conversation was going.

"I was thinking about the way he must have felt when he met my mom for the first time. What was going through his mind when he saw her, whether he was nervous, what he said when he approached her."

Travis stared at her. "And?"

"I have no idea."

When he laughed, she looped her arm through his. "Is the hot tub at your place still warm?" she asked.

"Should be. I haven't checked it, but I'm sure it's okay."

"Do you want to go for a dip?"

"I'd have to get my suit, but that sounds great."

She squeezed him tight against her, then leaned toward his ear. "Who said you needed a suit?"

Travis said nothing as they crossed the yard to his hot tub. As he lifted off the cover, he saw her bathrobe slip from her shoulders and glimpsed her naked body, knowing how much he loved her and that these last couple of days were somehow going to mark his life forever.

Fourteen

Though they both returned to work on Monday, over the next two days Travis and Gabby spent every free moment together. They made love on Monday morning before work, had lunch together at a small, family-owned café in Morehead City, and that evening, with Molly feeling better, they took both dogs for a walk on the beach near Fort Macon. As they walked, holding hands, Moby and Molly wandered the beach ahead like two old friends who'd grown used to their differences. When Moby chased terns and charged toward flocks of seagulls, Molly would hold her course, acting as if she wanted no part of it. After a while, Moby would realize that Molly was no longer alongside him and would bound back to her, and the two would trot happily together until Moby went nuts again and the whole thing repeated itself.

"That's kind of like the way we are, huh?" Gabby remarked as she squeezed Travis's hand. "One always chasing excitement, the other holding back?"

"Which one am I?"

She laughed and leaned into him, resting her head on his shoulder. Stopping, he took her in his arms, amazed and terrified by the strength of his feelings. But when she lifted her face to kiss him, he felt his fears begin to melt away, replaced by a growing sense of completion. He wondered whether love felt like this for everyone.

Afterward, they stopped at the grocery store. Neither of them was very hungry, so Travis picked up the makings for a chicken Caesar salad. In the kitchen, he grilled the chicken and watched Gabby rinse the lettuce leaves at the sink. Curled up on the couch after dinner, Gabby told Travis more about her family, arousing a mixture of sympathy for Gabby and anger at her mother for failing to recognize what an incredible woman Gabby had become. That night, they lay intertwined in each other's arms until long after midnight.

On Tuesday morning, Travis was at her side just as she was beginning to stir. She cracked open an eye.

"Is it time to get up?"

"I guess so," he mumbled.

They lay facing each other without moving before Travis went on. "You know what sounds good? Fresh coffee and a cinnamon roll."

"Yum," she said. "Too bad we don't have time. I've got to be at the office at eight. You shouldn't have kept me awake so long last night."

"Just close your eyes and wish real hard, and maybe your wish will come true."

Too tired to do anything else, she did what he suggested, longing for just another couple of minutes in bed.

"And there it is!" she heard him say.

"What?" she mumbled.

"Your coffee. And a cinnamon roll."

"Don't tease me. I'm starved."

"It's right there. Roll over and see for yourself."

She struggled to sit up and saw two steaming cups of coffee and a mouthwatering cinnamon roll on a plate on the nightstand.

"When did you . . . I mean, why did you . . . ?"

"A few minutes ago." He grinned. "I was awake anyway, so I raced downtown."

She reached for both the coffees and handed one to him, smiling. "I'd kiss you right now, but this smells great and I'm starved. I'll kiss you later."

"In the shower, maybe?"

"There's always a catch with you, isn't there?"

"Be nice. I just brought you breakfast in bed."

"I know," she said with a wink. She reached for her roll. "And I'm going to enjoy it."

On Tuesday evening, Travis took Gabby out on the boat, where they watched the sun go down from the waters off Beaufort. Gabby had been quiet ever since she'd returned home from work, which was why he'd suggested it; it was his way of trying to put off the conversation he knew was coming.

An hour later, seated on Travis's deck with Molly and Moby lying at their feet, Travis finally gave in to the inevitable.

"What's going to happen next?" he asked.

Gabby rotated the water glass in her hands. "I'm not sure," she said in a low voice.

"Do you want me to talk to him?"

"It's not that simple." She shook her head. "I've been trying all day to figure it out, and I'm still not sure what I'm going to do, or even what I'm going to say to him."

"You're going to tell him about us, aren't you?"

"I don't know," she said. "I really don't." She turned to Travis, her eyes filled with tears. "Don't get mad at me. Please don't. Believe me when I say that I know how this makes you feel, because it makes me feel the same way. In the last few days, you've made me feel . . . alive. You make me feel beautiful and intelligent and wanted, and no matter how hard I try, I'll never be able to tell you how much that's meant to me. But as intense as all this has been, as much as I care about you, we're not the same people, and you're not facing the same kind of decision that I am. For you, it's easy—we love each other, so we should be together. But Kevin is important to me, too."

"What about all those things you said?" Travis asked, trying not to sound as scared as he felt.

"He's not perfect, Travis. I know that. And no, things aren't great between us right now. But I can't help thinking that it's partly my fault. Can't you see that? With him, I have all these expectations, but with you . . . I don't have any. And if you reversed the equation, would any of this have even happened? What if I had expected you to marry me, but with him, I just allowed myself to enjoy being in the moment? You wouldn't have given me the time of day, and most likely I wouldn't have wanted you to."

"Don't say that."

"But it's true, isn't it?" Her smile was pained. "That's what I was thinking about today, even though it hurts me to say it. I love you, Travis, I really do. If I thought of this as a weekend fling, I'd put it behind me now and then go back to imagining a future with Kevin. But it's not going to be that easy. I have to make a choice between the two of you. With Kevin, I know what to expect. Or at least until you came along, I thought I did. But now . . ."

She paused, and Travis could see her hair moving slightly in the breeze. She hugged her arms tightly to her body.

"We've only known each other for a few days, and while we were on the boat, I found myself wondering how many other women you'd taken out like that. Not because I was jealous, but because I kept asking myself what brought those relationships to an end. And then I started wondering whether you would feel the same way about me in the future as you do right now, or whether this will just end up like all your previous relationships. As much as we think we know each other, we don't. Or at least, I don't. All I know is that I fell in love with you, and I've never been more frightened about anything in my entire life."

She stopped. Travis stayed silent, letting her words penetrate before saying anything.

"You're right," he admitted. "Your choice is different from mine. But you're wrong if you think this was just a fling for me. I might have started out thinking along those lines, but . . ." He reached for her hand. "That's not how it ended up. Spending time with you showed me what I've been missing in my life. The more time we spent together, the more I could imagine it lasting in the future. That's never happened to me before, and I'm not sure it'll ever happen again. I've never been in love with anyone before you came along—not real love, anyway. Not like this, and I'd be a fool if I let you slip away without a fight."

He ran a hand through his hair, drained.

"I don't know what else I can tell you, other than that I can imagine spending the rest of my life with you. I know that sounds crazy. I know we're just getting to know each other, and even admitting what I just did might make you think I'm nuts, but I've never been more sure about anything. And if you give me a chance—if you give *us* a chance—I'm going to live the rest of my life proving to you that you made the right decision. I love you, Gabby. And not just for the person you are, but for the way you make me think that *we* can be."

For a long moment, neither of them said anything. In the darkness, Gabby could hear the crickets calling from the foliage. Her mind was whirling—she wanted to run away, and she wanted to stay here forever, her warring instincts a reflection of the impossible bind she'd gotten herself into.

"I like you, Travis," she said earnestly. Then, realizing how it sounded, she struggled on. "And I love you, too, of course, but hopefully you already know that. I was just trying to tell you that I like the way you talk to me. I like the fact that when you say something, I know that you really mean it. I like the fact that I can tell when you're teasing or telling the truth and when you're not. It's one of your more endearing qualities." She patted his knee. "Now will you do something for me?"

"Of course," he said.

"No matter what I ask?"

He hesitated. "Yeah . . . I guess."

"Will you make love to me? And not think it might be the last time it ever happens?"

"That's two things."

She didn't dignify his answer with a response. Instead, she held out her hand to him. As they moved toward the bedroom, she broke into the tiniest of smiles, finally knowing what she had to do.

PART TWO

PART TWO

Fifteen

Travis tried to shake free of those memories from nearly eleven years ago, wondering why they'd resurfaced with such clarity. Was it because he was now old enough to realize how unusual it was to fall in love so quickly? Or simply because he missed the intimacy of those days? He didn't know.

Lately, it seemed he didn't know a lot of things. There were people who claimed to have all the answers, or at least the answers to the big questions of life, but Travis had never believed them. There was something about the assurance with which they spoke or wrote that seemed self-justifying. But if there were one person who could answer any question, Travis's question would be this: How far should a person go in the name of true love?

He could pose the question to a hundred people and get a hundred different answers. Most were obvious: A person should sacrifice, or accept, or forgive, or even fight if need be . . . the list went on and on. Still, even though he knew that all these answers were valid, none would help him now. Some things were beyond understanding. Thinking back, he recalled events he wished he could change, tears he wished had never been shed, time that could have been better spent, and frustrations he should have shrugged off. Life, it seemed, was full of regret, and he yearned to turn back the clock so he could live parts of his life over again. One thing was certain: He should have been a better husband. And as he considered the question of how far a person should go in the name of love, he knew what his answer would be. Sometimes it meant a person should lie.

And soon, he had to make his choice as to whether he would.

The fluorescent lights and white tile underscored the sterility of the hospital. Travis moved slowly down the corridor, certain that even though he'd spotted Gabby earlier, she hadn't seen him. He hesitated, steeling himself to head over and talk to her. It was the reason he'd come, after all, but the vivid parade of memories earlier had drained him. He stopped, knowing a few more minutes to collect his thoughts wouldn't make any difference.

He ducked into a small reception room and took a seat. Watching the steady, rhythmic movement in the corridor, he realized that despite the never-ending emergencies, the staff had a routine here, much as he had his own routines at home. It was inevitable for people to try to create a sense of normalcy in a place where nothing was normal. It helped one get through the day, to add predictability to a life that was inherently unpredictable. His mornings were a case in point, for every one was the same. Six-fifteen alarm; a minute to get out of bed and nine minutes in the shower, another four minutes to shave and brush his teeth, and seven minutes to get dressed. A stranger could set a watch by following his shadowed movements through his windows. After that, he'd hurry downstairs to pour cereal; he'd check backpacks for homework and make peanut-butter-and-jelly sandwiches for lunches while his sleepy daughters ate their breakfast. At exactly quarter past seven, they'd troop out the door and he'd wait with them at the end of the driveway for the school bus to arrive, driven by a man whose Scottish accent reminded him of *Shrek*. After his daughters got on and settled into their seats, he'd smile and wave, just as he was supposed to. Lisa and Christine were six and eight, a bit young for first and third grade, and as he watched them venture out to start another day, he often felt his heart clench with worry. Perhaps that was common—people always said that parenting and worrying were synonymous—but recently his worries had grown more pronounced. He dwelled on things he never had before. Little things. Ridiculous things. Was Lisa laughing at cartoons as much as she used to? Was Christine more subdued than normal? Sometimes, as the bus would pull away, he would find himself replaying the morning over and over, searching for clues to their well-being. Yesterday he had spent half the day wondering whether Lisa had been testing him by making him tie her shoes or whether she had just been feeling lazy. Even though he knew he was bordering on obsession, when he'd crept to their rooms last night to adjust their strewn-about blankets, he couldn't stop himself from wondering whether the nighttime restlessness was new or something he'd just never noticed before.

It shouldn't have been like this. Gabby should have been with him; Gabby should have been the one tying shoes and adjusting the blankets. She was good at things like that, as he'd known she would be from the very beginning. He remembered that in the days that followed their first weekend together, he would find himself studying Gabby, knowing on some deep level that even if he spent the rest of his life looking, he'd never find a better mother or more perfect complement to him. The realization often hit in the strangest of places—while pushing the cart in the fruit aisle of the grocery store or standing in line to buy movie tickets—but whenever it happened, it made something as simple as taking her hand an exquisite pleasure, something both momentous and gratifying.

Their courtship hadn't been quite as uncomplicated for her. She was the one torn between two men vying for her love. "A minor inconvenience," was the way he described it at parties, but he often wondered when exactly her feelings for him finally overwhelmed those she'd had for Kevin. Was it when they sat beside each other, gazing at the nighttime sky, and she quietly began naming the constellations she recognized? Or was it the following day, when she held him tight as they rode on the motorcycle before their picnic? Or was it later that evening, when he took her in his arms?

He wasn't sure; capturing a specific instant like that was no more possible than locating a specific drop of water in the ocean. But the fact remained that it left Gabby to explain the situation to Kevin. Travis could remember her pained expression on the morning she knew Kevin would be arriving back in town. Gone was the certainty that had guided them the previous days; in its place was the reality of what lay ahead for her. She barely touched her breakfast; when he kissed her good-bye, she responded with only the flicker of a smile. The hours had crawled by without word, and Travis busied himself at work and made calls to find homes for the puppies, knowing it was important to her. Eventually, after work, Travis went to check on Molly. As if sensing she'd be needed later, she didn't return to the garage after he let her out. Instead, she lay in the tall marsh grass that fronted Gabby's property, staring toward the street as the sun sank lower in the sky.

It was well after dark when Gabby turned in the drive. He remembered the steady way she looked at him as she stepped out of the car. Without a word, she took a seat beside him on the steps. Molly wandered up and began to nuzzle her. Gabby ran her hand rhythmically through her fur.

"Hey," he said, breaking the silence.

"Hey." Her voice sounded drained of emotion.

"I think I found homes for all of the puppies," he offered.

"Yeah?"

He nodded, and the two of them sat together without speaking, like two people who'd run out of things to talk about.

"I'm always going to love you," he said, searching and failing to find adequate words to comfort her.

"I believe you," she whispered. She looped her arm through his and leaned her head against his shoulder. "That's why I'm here."

Travis had never liked hospitals. Unlike the veterinary clinic, which closed its doors around dinnertime, Carteret General Hospital struck him as the endless turning of a Ferris wheel, with patients and employees hopping on and off every minute of every day. From where he was sitting, he could see nurses bustling in and out of rooms or clustering around the station at the end of the hall. Some were frazzled while others seemed bored; the doctors were no different. On other floors, Travis knew that mothers were giving birth and the elderly were passing away, a microcosm of the world. As oppressive as he found it, Gabby had thrived working here, energized by the steady buzz of activity.

There'd been a letter in the mailbox months earlier, something from the administrator's office announcing that the hospital planned to honor Gabby's tenth year working at the hospital. The letter didn't allude to anything specific that Gabby had accomplished; it was nothing more than a form letter, something no doubt sent out to a dozen other people who'd started working around the same time she had. A small plaque, the letter promised, would be hung in Gabby's honor in one of the corridors, along with other recipients', though as yet it hadn't happened.

He doubted that she cared. Gabby had taken the job at the hospital not because she might one day receive a plaque, but because she'd felt she hadn't much choice. Though she had alluded to some problems at the pediatrician's office during their first weekend together, she hadn't been specific. He'd let the comment pass without pressing her, but he knew even then that the problem wasn't simply going to go away.

Eventually, she told him about it. It was the end of a long day. He'd been called out the previous night to the equestrian center, where he found an Arabian sweating and pawing the ground, its stomach tender to the touch. Classic signs of equine colic, though with a bit of luck, he didn't think it would require surgery. Still, with the owners in their seventies, Travis wasn't comfortable asking them to walk the horse for fifteen minutes every hour, in case the horse became more agitated or took a turn for the worse. Instead, he decided to stay with the horse himself, and though the horse gradually improved as the day rolled on into the next evening, he was exhausted by the time he left.

He arrived home, sweaty and filthy, to find Gabby crying at her kitchen table. It took a few minutes before she was able to tell him the story—how she'd had to stay late with a patient who was waiting for an ambulance for what she was fairly certain was appendicitis; by the time she was able to leave, most of the staff had gone home. The attending physician, Adrian Melton, had not. They left together, and Gabby didn't realize that Melton was walking with her toward her car until it was too late. There, he laid a hand on her shoulder and told her that he was heading to the hospital and would update her on the patient's condition. When she forced a smile, however, he leaned in to kiss her.

It was a clumsy effort, reminiscent of high school, and she recoiled before he could finish. He stared at her, seemingly put out. "I thought this was what you wanted," he'd said.

At the table, Gabby shuddered. "He made it sound like it was my fault."

"Has it happened before?"

"No, not like this. But . . ."

When she trailed off, Travis reached over and took her hand. "Come on," he said. "It's me. Talk to me."

Her gaze remained focused on the surface of the table, but her voice was steady as she recounted the history of Melton's behavior. By the time she finished, his face was tight with barely suppressed rage.

"I'll fix this," he said without waiting for a response.

It took two phone calls to find out where Adrian Melton lived.

Within minutes, his car screeched to a stop in front of Melton's house. His insistent finger on the doorbell brought the doctor to the front door. Melton barely registered his puzzlement before Travis's fist crashed into his jaw. A woman Travis assumed was Melton's wife materialized the same instant Melton hit the floor, and her screams echoed in the hallway.

When the police arrived at the house, Travis was arrested for the first and only time in his life. He was brought to the station, where most of the officers treated him with amused respect. Every one of them had brought their pets to the clinic and were clearly skeptical of Mrs. Melton's claim that "some psycho has assaulted my husband!"

When Travis called his sister, Stephanie showed up looking less worried than amused. She found Travis sitting in a single cell, deep in discussion with the sheriff; as she approached, he realized they were talking about the sheriff's cat, who seemed to have developed a rash of some sort and couldn't stop scratching.

"Bummer," she said.

"What?"

"And here I thought I was going to find you wearing an orange jumper."

"Sorry to disappoint you."

"Maybe there's still time. What do you think, Sheriff?"

The sheriff didn't know what to think, and a moment later, he left them alone.

"Thanks for that," Travis said once the sheriff was gone. "He's probably considering your suggestion."

"Don't blame me. I'm not the one attacking doctors on doorsteps."

"He deserved it."

"I'm sure he did."

Travis smiled. "Thanks for coming."

"I wouldn't have missed it, Rocky. Or would you prefer I call you Apollo Creed?"

"How about you work on getting me out of here instead of trying to come up with nicknames?"

"Coming up with nicknames is more fun."

"Maybe I should have called Dad."

"But you didn't. You got me. And trust me, you made the right choice. Now let me go talk to the sheriff, okay?"

Later, while Stephanie was talking to the sheriff, Adrian Melton visited Travis. He'd never met the local veterinarian and demanded to know the reason for Travis's assault. Though he never told Gabby what he said, Adrian Melton promptly dropped the charges, despite protests from Mrs. Melton. Within a few days, Travis heard through the small-town grapevine that Dr. and Mrs. Melton were in counseling. Nonetheless, the workplace remained tense for Gabby, and a few weeks later, Dr. Furman called Gabby into the office and suggested that she consider trying to find another place to work.

"I know it's not fair," he said. "And if you stay, we'll somehow make it work. But I'm sixty-four, and I'm planning to retire next year. Dr. Melton has agreed to buy me out, and I doubt that he'll want to keep you on anyway, or that you'd want to work for him. I think it would be easier and better for you if you take the time to find a place where you're comfortable and simply put this awful thing behind you." He shrugged. "I'm not saying that his behavior wasn't reprehensible; it was. But even if he's a jerk, he's the best pediatrician I interviewed and the only one who was willing to practice in a small town like this. If you leave voluntarily, I'll write the finest recommendation you can imagine. You'll be able to get a job anywhere. I'll make sure of it."

She recognized the manipulation for what it was, and while her emotions cried out for retribution on her behalf and that of sexually harassed women everywhere, her pragmatic side asserted itself. In the end, she took a job in the emergency room at the hospital.

There had been only one problem: When Gabby found out what Travis had done, she'd been furious. It was the first argument they had as a couple, and Travis could still remember her outrage when she demanded to know whether he believed she was "grown-up enough to handle her own problems" and why he acted "as if she were some silly damsel in distress." Travis didn't bother trying to defend himself. In his heart, he knew he'd do the same thing again in an instant, but he wisely kept his mouth shut.

For all Gabby's outrage, Travis suspected there was part of her that had admired what he'd done. The simple logic of the act—*He bothered you? Let me at 'im*—had appealed to her, no matter how angry she'd appeared, for later that night her lovemaking had seemed particularly passionate.

Or at least, that's the way Travis remembered it. Had the evening unfolded exactly like that? He wasn't sure. These days, it seemed that the only thing he was certain about was the knowledge that he wouldn't trade his years with Gabby for anything. Without her, his life had little meaning. He was a small-town husband with a small-town occupation and his cares were no different from anyone else's. He'd been neither a leader nor a follower, nor had he been someone who would be remembered long after he passed away. He was the most ordinary of men with only one exception: He'd fallen in love with a woman named Gabby, his love deepening in the years they'd been married. But fate had conspired to ruin all that, and now he spent long portions of his days wondering whether it was humanly possible to fix things between them.

Sixteen

$\sim\!\!\sim$

Hey, Travis," said a voice from the doorway. "I thought I'd find you in here."

Dr. Stallings was in his thirties and made rounds every morning. Over the years, he and his wife had become good friends of Gabby and Travis's, and last summer the four of them had traveled to Orlando with kids in tow. "More flowers?"

Travis nodded, feeling the stiffness in his back.

Stallings hesitated on the threshold of the room. "I take it you haven't seen her yet."

"Kind of. I saw her earlier, but . . ."

When he trailed off, Stallings finished for him. "You needed some time alone?" He entered and took a seat beside Travis. "I guess that makes you normal."

"I don't feel normal. Nothing about this feels normal at all."

"No, I don't suppose it does."

Travis reached for the flowers again, trying to keep his thoughts at bay, knowing there were some things he couldn't talk about.

"I don't know what to do," he finally admitted.

Stallings put his hand on Travis's shoulder. "I wish I knew what to tell you."

Travis turned toward him. "What would you do?"

Stallings remained silent for a long moment. "If I were in your position?" He brought his lips together, considering the questions, looking older than his years. "In all honesty, I don't know."

Travis nodded. He hadn't expected Stallings to answer. "I just want to do the right thing."

Stallings brought his hands together. "Don't we all."

When Stallings left, Travis shifted in his seat, conscious of the papers in his pocket. Where once he'd kept them in his desk, he now found it impossible to go about his daily life without them nearby, even though they portended the end of everything he held dear.

The elderly attorney who drafted them seemed to find nothing unusual about their request. His small-town family law practice had been located in Morehead City, close enough to the hospital where Gabby worked to be able to see it from the windows of the paneled walls of the conference room. The meeting hadn't lasted long; the lawyer explained the relevant statutes and offered a few anecdotal experiences; later Travis could remember only the loose, almost weak way he had grasped Travis's hand on his way out the door.

It seemed strange that those papers could signal the official end of his marriage. They were codified words, nothing more, but the power afforded them now seemed almost malevolent. Where, he wondered, was the humanity in those phrases? Where was the emotion governed by these laws? Where was the acknowledgment of the life they'd led together, until everything went wrong? And why in God's name had Gabby wanted them drawn up in the first place?

It shouldn't end like this, and it was certainly not an outcome he foresaw when he'd proposed to Gabby. He remembered their autumn trip to New York; while Gabby had been at the hotel spa getting a massage and a pedicure, he'd sneaked over to West 47th Street, where he'd purchased the engagement ring. After dining at

Tavern on the Green, they'd taken a carriage ride through Central Park. And beneath a cloudy, full-moon sky, he'd asked for her hand in marriage and was overcome by the passionate way she'd wrapped her arms around him while whispering her consent over and over.

And then? Life, he supposed. In between her shifts at the hospital, she planned the wedding: Despite his friends' warnings to simply go with the flow, Travis relished being part of the process. He helped her pick out the invitations, the flowers, and the cake; he sat beside her as she flipped through albums in downtown studios, hoping to find the right photographer to memorialize the day. In the end, they invited eighty people to a small, weathered chapel on Cumberland Island in spring 1997; they honeymooned in Cancún, which ended up being an idyllic choice for both of them. Gabby wanted someplace relaxing, and they spent hours lying in the sun and eating well; he wanted a bit more adventure, so she learned to scuba dive and joined him on a day trip to see the nearby Aztec ruins.

The give-and-take of the honeymoon set the tone for the marriage. Their dream house was constructed with little stress and was completed by their first anniversary; when Gabby ran her finger over the rim of her glass of champagne and wondered aloud whether they should start a family, the idea struck him as not only reasonable, but something he desperately wanted. She was pregnant within a couple of months, her pregnancy devoid of complications or even much discomfort. After Christine was born, Gabby cut back on her hours and they worked out a schedule that ensured one of them was always home with the baby. When Lisa followed two years later, neither of them noticed much of a change, other than added joy and excitement in the house.

Christmases and birthdays came and went, the kids grew out of one outfit only to be replaced by the next. They vacationed as a family, yet Travis and Gabby also spent time alone, keeping the flame of romance alive between them. Max eventually retired, leaving Travis to take over the clinic; Gabby limited her hours even more and had enough time to volunteer at school. On their fourth anniversary, they went to Italy and Greece; for their sixth, they spent a week on safari in Africa. On their seventh, Travis built Gabby a gazebo in the backyard, where she could sit and read and watch the play of light reflecting on the water. He taught his daughters to wakeboard and ski when each was five years old; he coached their soccer teams in the fall. On the rare occasions when he stopped to reflect on his life, he wondered if anyone in the world felt as blessed as he did.

Not that things were always perfect. Years ago, he and Gabby had gone through a rough patch. The reasons were fuzzy now, lost in the recesses of time, but even then, there had never been a point when he truly believed their marriage to be in jeopardy. Nor, he suspected, had she. Marriage, each of them realized intuitively, was about compromise and forgiveness. It was about balance, where one person complemented the other. He and Gabby had that for years, and he hoped they could have it again. But right now they didn't, and the realization left him wishing there was something, anything, he could do to restore that delicate balance between them.

Travis knew he couldn't postpone seeing her any longer, and he rose from his seat. Holding the flowers, he started down the corridor, feeling almost disembodied. He saw a few nurses glance at him, and though he sometimes wondered what they thought, he never stopped to ask. Instead, he summoned his nerve. His legs were shaky, and he could feel the beginning of a headache, a dull throb at the back of his head. If he allowed himself to close his eyes, he felt sure he would sleep for hours. He was falling apart, a thought that made about as much sense as a square golf ball. He was forty-three, not seventy-two, and though he hadn't been eating much lately, he still forced himself to go to the gym. "You've got to keep exercising," his dad had urged. "If only for your own sanity." He'd lost eighteen pounds in the last twelve weeks, and in the mirror he could see that his cheeks had hollowed out. He reached the door and pushed it open, forcing himself to smile as he saw her.

"Hi, sweetheart."

He waited for her to stir, waited for any response to let him know that things were somehow returning to normal. But nothing happened, and in the long, empty silence that followed, Travis felt an ache like a physical pain in his heart. It was always like this. Stepping into the room, he continued to stare at Gabby as if trying to memorize her every feature, though he knew it was a pointless exercise. He knew her face better than his own.

At the window, he opened the blinds, allowing sunlight to spill across the floor. There wasn't much of a view; the room overlooked a small highway that bisected the town. Slow-moving cars drifted past fast-food restaurants, and he could imagine the drivers listening to music on the radio, or chatting on cell phones, or heading to work, or making deliveries, or running errands, or going to visit friends. People going about their daily lives, people lost in their own concerns, all of them oblivious to what was going on in the hospital. He had once been one of them, and he felt the loss of his previous life.

He set the flowers on the sill, wishing he had remembered to bring a vase. He had chosen a winter bouquet, and the burnt orange and violet colors seemed muted, almost mournful. The florist considered himself an artist of sorts, and in all the years Travis had used him, he'd never been disappointed. The florist was a good man, a kind man, and sometimes Travis wondered how much the florist knew about their marriage. Over the years, Travis had purchased bouquets on anniversaries and birthdays; he'd purchased them as apologies or on the spur of the moment, as a romantic surprise. And each time, he'd dictated to the florist what he wanted written on the card. Sometimes he'd recited a poem he'd either found in a book or written on his own; at other times, he'd come straight to the point and simply said what was on his mind.

Gabby had saved these cards in a tiny bundle held together by a rubber band. They were a kind of history of Travis and Gabby's life together, described in tiny snippets.

He took a seat in the chair by the bed and reached for her hand. Her skin was pale, almost waxy, her body seemed smaller, and he noted the spidery lines that had begun to form at the corners of her eyes. Still, she was as remarkable to him as she had been the first time he'd ever seen her. It amazed him that he'd known her almost eleven years. Not because the length of time was extraordinary, but because those years seemed to contain more . . . *life* than the first thirty-two years without her. It was the reason he'd come to the hospital today; it was the reason he came every day. He had no other choice. Not because it was expected—though it was—but because he couldn't imagine being anywhere else. They spent hours together, but their nights were spent apart. Ironically, there was no choice in that, either, for he couldn't leave his daughters alone. These days, fate made all his decisions for him.

Except for one.

Eighty-four days had passed since the accident, and now he had to make a choice. He still had no idea what to do. Lately he'd been searching for answers in the Bible and in the writings of Aquinas and Augustine. Occasionally he would find a striking passage, but nothing more than that; he would close the cover of the book and find himself staring out the window, his thoughts blank, as if hoping to find the solution somewhere in the sky.

He seldom drove straight home from the hospital. Instead, he would drive across the bridge and walk the sands of Atlantic Beach. He would slip off his shoes, listening as the waves crashed along the shore. He knew his daughters were as upset as he was, and after his visits to the hospital, he needed time to compose himself. It would be unfair to subject them to his angst. He needed his daughters for the escape they afforded him. When focusing on them, he didn't focus on himself, and their joy still held an unadulterated purity.

They still had the ability to lose themselves in play, and the sound of their giggling made him want to laugh and cry at the same time. Sometimes as he watched them, he was struck by how much they resembled their mother.

Always they asked about her, but usually he didn't know what to tell them. They were mature enough to understand that Mommy wasn't well and had to stay in the hospital; they understood that when they visited, it would seem as if Mommy were asleep. But he couldn't bring himself to tell them the truth about her condition. Instead, he would cuddle with them on the couch and tell them how excited Gabby had been when she'd been pregnant with each of them or remind them about the time the family played in the sprinklers for an entire afternoon. Mostly, though, they would thumb through the photo albums Gabby had assembled with care. She was old-fashioned that way, and the pictures never ceased to bring a smile to their faces. Travis would tell stories associated with each, and as he stared at Gabby's radiant face in the photos, his throat would tighten at the knowledge that he'd never seen anyone more beautiful.

To escape the sadness that overtook him in such moments, he would sometimes raise his eyes from the album and focus on the large, framed photograph they'd had taken at the beach last summer. All four of them had worn beige khakis and white button-down oxfords, and they were seated amid the dune grass. It was the kind of family portrait common in Beaufort, yet it somehow struck him as entirely unique. Not because it was his family, but because he was certain that even a stranger would find himself filled with hope and optimism at the sight, for the people in the photo looked the way a happy family should.

Later, after the girls had gone to bed, he would put away the albums. It was one thing to look at them with his daughters and tell stories in an attempt to keep their spirits up, it was another thing to gaze at them alone. He couldn't do that. Instead, he would sit alone on the couch, weighed down by the sadness he felt inside.

Sometimes Stephanie would call. Their conversations were filled with their usual banter but it was somehow stilted at the same time, for he knew she wanted him to forgive himself. Despite her sometimes flippant remarks and her occasional teasing, he knew what she was really saying: that no one blamed him, that it wasn't his fault. That she and others were worried about him. To head off her reassurances, he'd always say that he was doing fine, even when he wasn't, for the truth was something he knew she didn't want to hear: that not only did he doubt he'd ever be fine again, but he wasn't even sure he ever wanted to be.

Seventeen

W̲arm bands of sunlight continued to stretch toward them. In the silence, Travis squeezed Gabby's hand and winced at the pain in his wrist. It had been in a cast until a month ago, and the doctors had prescribed painkillers. The bones in his arms had fractured and his ligaments had torn in half, but after his first dose, he'd refused to take the painkillers, hating the woozy way they made him feel.

Her hand was as soft as always. Most days he would hold it for hours, imagining what he would do if she squeezed his in return. He sat and watched her, wondering what she was thinking or if she was thinking at all. The world inside her was a mystery.

"The girls are good," he began. "Christine finished her Lucky Charms at breakfast, and Lisa was close. I know you worry about how much they eat, since they're on the small side, but they've been pretty good about nibbling on the snacks I put out after school."

Outside the window, a pigeon landed on the sill. It walked a few steps one way, then back again, before finally settling in place as it did on most days. It seemed, somehow, to know when it was time for Travis to visit. There were times he believed it was an omen of sorts, though of what, he had no idea.

"We do homework after dinner. I know you like to do it right after school, but this seems to be working out okay. You'd be excited at how well Christine is doing in math. Remember at the beginning of the year when she didn't seem to understand it at all? She's really turned it around. We've been using those flash cards you bought pretty much every night, and she didn't miss a single question on her latest test. She's even doing her homework without me having to walk her through it. You'd be proud of her."

The sound of the cooing pigeon was barely audible through the glass.

"And Lisa's doing well. We watch either *Dora the Explorer* or *Barbie* every night. It's crazy how many times she can watch the same DVDs, but she loves them. And for her birthday, she wants a princess theme. I was thinking about getting an ice-cream cake, but she wants to have her party at the park, and I'm not sure they'd get to the cake before it melts, so I'll probably have to get something else."

He cleared his throat.

"Oh, did I tell you that Joe and Megan are thinking of having another kid? I know, I know—it's crazy considering how many problems she had with the last pregnancy and the fact that she's already in her forties, but according to Joe, she really wants to try for a little boy. Me? I think Joe's the one who wants a son and Megan's just going along with it, but with those two, you never really know, do you."

Travis forced himself to sound conversational. Since she'd been here, he'd been trying to act as naturally as he could around her. Because they talked incessantly about the kids before the accident, because they discussed what was happening in their friends' lives, he always tried to talk about them when he visited her. He had no idea whether she heard him; the medical community seemed divided on that. Some swore that coma patients could hear—and possibly remember—conversations; others said just the opposite. Travis didn't know whom to believe, but he chose to live his days on the side of the optimists.

For that same reason, after glancing at his watch, he reached for the remote. In her stolen moments when she hadn't been working, Gabby's guilty pleasure was watching *Judge Judy* on television, and Travis had always teased her about the way she took an almost perverse delight in the antics of those unfortunate enough to find themselves in Judge Judy's courtroom.

"Let me turn on the television, okay? Your show's on. I think we can catch the last couple of minutes."

A moment later, Judge Judy was speaking over both the defendant and the plaintiff, just to get them to shut up, which seemed to be the predictable, recurring theme of the show.

"She's in rare form, huh?"

When the show was over, he turned it off. He thought about moving the flowers closer, in the hope that she would smell them. He wanted to keep her senses stimulated. Yesterday, he'd spent some time brushing her hair; the day before, he'd brought in some of her perfume and added a dab to each wrist. Today, however, doing any of those things seemed to take more effort than he could summon.

"Other than that, not much new is going on," he said with a sigh. The words sounded as meaningless to him as they no doubt did to her. "My dad's still covering for me at the clinic. You'd be amazed at how well he does with the animals, considering how long ago he retired. It's like he never left. People still adore him, and I think he's happy being there. If you ask me, he never should have stopped working in the first place."

He heard a knock at the door and saw Gretchen walk in. In the past month, he'd come to depend on her. Unlike the other nurses, she maintained an undying faith that Gabby would emerge from all of this just fine and consequently treated Gabby as if she were conscious.

"Hey, Travis," she chirped. "Sorry for interrupting, but I've got to hook up a new IV."

When Travis nodded, she approached Gabby. "I'll bet you're

starving, honey," she said. "Just give me a second, okay? Then I'll give you and Travis your alone time. You know how I am about interrupting two lovebirds."

She worked quickly, removing one IV bag and replacing it with another, all the while keeping up a steady stream of conversation. "I know you're sore from your workout this morning. We really went at it, didn't we? We were like those folks you see on those infomercials. Working this, working that. I was really proud of you."

Every morning and again in the evening, one of the nurses came in to flex and stretch Gabby's limbs. Bend the knee, straighten it out; flex the foot up, then push it down. They did this for every joint and muscle in Gabby's body.

After she finished hanging the bag, Gretchen checked the flow and adjusted the sheets, then turned to Travis.

"Are you doing okay today?"

"I don't know," he said.

Gretchen seemed sorry she'd asked. "I'm glad you brought flowers," she said, nodding in the direction of the windowsill. "I'm sure Gabby appreciates it."

"I hope so."

"Are you going to bring in the girls?"

Travis swallowed through the lump in his throat. "Not today."

Gretchen pursed her lips and nodded. A moment later, she was gone.

Twelve weeks ago, Gabby was rolled into the emergency room on a gurney, unconscious and bleeding heavily from a gash on her shoulder. The physicians concentrated first on the gash because of the heavy blood loss, though in retrospect, Travis wondered whether a different approach would have changed things.

He didn't know, nor would he ever. Like Gabby, he'd been rolled into the emergency room; like Gabby, he'd spent the night unconscious. But there the similarities had ended. The following day, he woke up in pain with a mangled arm, while Gabby never woke up at all.

The doctors were kind, but they didn't try to conceal their concern. Brain injuries were always serious, they said, but they were hopeful the injury would heal and that all would be well in time.

In time.

He sometimes wondered whether doctors realized the emotional intensity of time, or what he was going through, or even that time was something finite. He doubted it. No one knew what he was going through or really understood the choice that lay before him. On the surface, it was simple. He would do exactly what Gabby wanted, exactly as she'd made him promise.

But what if . . .

And that was the thing. He had thought long and hard about the reality of the situation; he had stayed awake nights considering the question. He wondered again what love really meant. And in the darkness, he would toss and turn, wishing for someone else to make the choice for him. But he wrestled with it alone, and more often than not, he'd wake in the morning with a tear-drenched pillow in the place Gabby should have been. And the first words out of his mouth were always the same.

"I'm so sorry, sweetheart."

The choice Travis now had to make had its roots in two distinct events. The first event related to a couple named Kenneth and Eleanor Baker. The second event, the accident itself, had occurred on a rainy, windy night twelve weeks ago.

The accident was simple to explain and was similar to many accidents in that a series of isolated and seemingly inconsequential mistakes somehow came together and exploded in the most horrific of ways. In mid-November, they'd driven to the RBC Center in Raleigh to see David Copperfield perform onstage. Over the years, they'd usually seen one or two shows a year, if only to have an excuse to get away for an evening alone. Usually they had dinner beforehand, but that night they didn't. Travis was running late at the clinic, they got a late start out of Beaufort, and by the time they parked the car, the show was only minutes from beginning. In his haste, Travis forgot his umbrella, despite the ominous clouds and building wind. That was mistake number one.

They watched the show and enjoyed it, but the weather had deteriorated by the time they'd left the theater. Rain was pouring down hard, and Travis remembered standing with Gabby, wondering how best to get to their car. They happened to bump into friends who'd also seen the show, and Jeff offered to walk Travis to his car so he wouldn't get wet. But Travis didn't want him to have to go out of his way and declined Jeff's offer. Instead, he bolted into the rain, splashing through ankle-deep puddles on the way to his car. He was soaked to the bone by the time he crawled in, especially his feet. That was mistake number two.

Because it was late, and because they both had to work the following morning, Travis drove fast despite the wind and rain, trying to save a few minutes in a drive that normally took two and a half hours. Though it was difficult to see through the windshield, he drove in the passing lane, pushing past the speed limit, racing past cars with drivers who were more cautious about the dangers of the weather outside. That was mistake number three. Gabby asked him repeatedly to slow down; more than once, he did as she asked, only to speed up again as soon as he could. By the time they reached Goldsboro, still an hour and a half from home, she'd become so angry that she'd stopped speaking to him. She leaned her head back and closed her eyes, refusing to talk, frustrated at the way he was tuning her out. That was mistake number four.

The accident was next, and it could have been avoided had none of the other things happened. Had he brought his umbrella or walked with his friend, he wouldn't have run to the car in the rain. His feet might have stayed dry. Had he slowed the car, he might have been able to control it. Had he respected Gabby's wishes, they wouldn't have argued, and she would have been watching what he intended to do and stopped him before it was too late.

Near Newport, there's a wide, easy bend in the highway intersected by a stoplight. By that point in the drive—less than twenty minutes from home—the itch in his feet was driving him crazy. His shoes had laces, the knots made tighter by the moisture, and no matter how hard he tried to push them off his feet, the toe of one foot would slip from the heel of the other. He leaned forward, his eyes barely above the dash, and reached for one shoe with his hand. Glancing downward, he struggled with the knot and didn't see the light turn yellow.

The knot wouldn't come free. When it finally did, he lifted his eyes, but by then it was already too late. The light had turned red, and a silver truck was entering the intersection. Instinctively he hit the brakes, and the tail began to swerve on the rain-slicked road. Their car careened out of control. At the last instant, the wheels caught and they avoided the truck in the intersection, only to continue hurtling through the bend, off the highway, and toward the pines.

The mud was even more slippery, and there was nothing he could do. He turned the wheel and nothing happened. For an instant, the world seemed to be moving in slow motion. The last thing he remembered before he lost consciousness was the sickening sound of shattering glass and twisting metal.

Gabby didn't even have time to scream.

Travis brushed a loose strand of hair from Gabby's face and tucked it behind her ear, listening to his stomach as it gurgled. As hungry as he was, he couldn't bear the idea of eating. His stomach was perpetually knotted, and in those rare moments it wasn't, thoughts of Gabby would come rushing back to fill the void.

It was an ironic form of punishment, for during their second year of marriage, Gabby had taken it upon herself to teach Travis to eat things other than the bland food he'd long favored. He sup-

posed it had come about because she'd grown tired of his restric-
tive habits. He should have realized that changes were coming
when she started slipping in the occasional comment regarding
the tastiness of Belgian waffles on Saturday mornings or how
nothing was more satisfying on cold winter days than a plate of
homemade beef stew.

Until that point, Travis had been the chef in the family, but
little by little she began edging her way into the kitchen. She
bought two or three cookbooks, and in the evenings, Travis would
watch her as she lay on the couch, occasionally folding down the
corner of a page. Now and then, she would ask him whether something sounded particularly good. She'd read aloud the ingredients
of Cajun jambalaya or veal Marsala, and though Travis would say
they sounded terrific, the tone of his voice made it obvious that
even if she prepared these dishes, he probably wouldn't eat them.

But Gabby was nothing if not persistent, and she started making small changes anyway. She prepared butter or cream or wine
sauces and poured them over her portion of the chicken he
cooked nearly every night. Her single request was that he at least
smell it, and usually he had to admit the aroma was appetizing.
Later, she took to leaving a small amount in the serving bowl,
and after she'd poured some on her plate, she simply added some
to his whether he wanted to try it or not. And little by little, to
his own surprise, he did.

On their third anniversary, Gabby prepared a mozzarella-stuffed,
Italian-flavored meat loaf; in lieu of a gift, she asked him to eat it
with her; by their fourth anniversary, they were sometimes cooking
together. Though his breakfast and lunch were as boring as usual
and most evenings his dinners were still as bland as always, he had
to admit there was something romantic about preparing meals
together, and as the years rolled on, they started to do it at least
twice a week. Often, Gabby would have a glass of wine, and while
they cooked, the girls were required to stay in the sunroom, where
the prominent feature was a Berber carpet the color of emeralds.

They called it "green carpet time." While Gabby and Travis chopped and stirred and conversed quietly about their day, he reveled in the contentment that she had brought him.

He wondered if he'd ever get the chance to cook with her again. In the first weeks after the accident, he'd been almost frantic about making sure the evening nurse had his cell number handy. After a month, because she was breathing on her own, she was moved from the ICU to a private room, and he was certain the change would wake her. But as the days passed with no change at all, his manic energy was replaced by a quiet, gnawing dread that was even worse. Gabby had once told him that six weeks was the cutoff—that after that, the odds of waking from a coma dropped dramatically. But still he held out hope. He told himself that Gabby was a mother, Gabby was a fighter, Gabby was different from all the rest. Six weeks came and went; another two weeks followed. At three months, he knew, most patients who remained in a coma were moved to a nursing home for long-term care. That day was today, and he was supposed to let the administrator know what he wanted to do. But that wasn't the choice he was facing. His choice had to do with Kenneth and Eleanor Baker, and though he knew he couldn't blame Gabby for bringing them into their lives, he wasn't ready to think about them just yet.

Eighteen

⁓

The house they built was the kind of place in which Travis could imagine spending the rest of his life. Despite its new-ness, there was a lived-in quality from the moment they moved in. He attributed this to the fact that Gabby had worked hard to create a home that made people feel comfortable as soon as the door was opened.

She was the one who oversaw the details that had made the house come alive. While Travis conceived the structure in terms of square footage and building materials that could survive the salty, humid summers, Gabby introduced eclectic elements he'd never considered. Once, while in the process of building, they were driving past a crumbling farmhouse, long since abandoned, and Gabby insisted he pull over. By that point, he'd grown used to her occasional flights of fancy. He humored her, and soon they were walking through what was once a doorway. They stepped across floors carpeted with dirt and tried to ignore the kudzu that wove through broken walls and gaping windows. Along the far wall, however, was a fireplace, thick with grime, and Travis remembered thinking that she'd somehow known it was there. She squatted next to the fireplace, running her hand along the sides and beneath the mantel. "See this? I think it's hand-painted tile," she said. "There must be hundreds of pieces, maybe more. Can you imagine how beautiful it was when it was new?" She reached for his hand. "We should do something like this."

Little by little, the house took on accents he'd never before imagined. They didn't just copy the style of the fireplace; Gabby found the owners, knocked on their door, and convinced them to let her purchase the fireplace in its entirety for less than it cost to clean it. She wanted big oak beams and a vaulted, soft pine ceiling in the living room, which seemed to match the gabled roofline. The walls were plaster or brick or covered with colorful textures, some that resembled leather, all of them somehow resembling works of art. She spent long weekends shopping for antique furniture and knickknacks, and sometimes it seemed as if the house itself knew what she was trying to accomplish. When she found a spot in the hardwood floor that creaked, she walked back and forth, a big grin on her face, to make sure she wasn't imagining it. She loved rugs, the more colorful the pattern the better, and they were scattered throughout the house with generous abandon.

She was practical, too. The kitchen, bathrooms, and bedrooms were airy and bright and sparkly modern, with large windows framing the gorgeous views. The master bathroom had a claw-foot tub and a roomy, glass-walled shower. She wanted a big garage, with plenty of room for Travis. Guessing that they'd spend a lot of time on the wraparound porch, she insisted on a hammock and matching rockers, along with an outdoor grill and a seating area located in such a way that during storms, they could sit outside without getting wet. The overall effect was one in which a person didn't know whether he or she was more comfortable inside or out; the kind of home where someone could walk in with muddy shoes and not get in trouble. And on their first night in their new home, as they lay on the canopy bed, Gabby rolled toward Travis with an expression of pure contentment, her voice almost a purr: "This place, with you by my side, is where I'll always want to be."

* * *

The kids had been having problems, even if he didn't mention them to Gabby.

Not surprising, of course, but most of the time, Travis was at a loss as to what to do. Christine had asked him more than once whether Mommy was ever going to come home, and though Travis always assured her that she would, Christine seemed uncertain, probably because Travis wasn't sure he believed it himself. Kids were perceptive like that, and at eight years old, she'd reached an age where she knew the world wasn't as simple as she'd once imagined it to be.

She was a lovely child with bright blue eyes who liked to wear neat bows in her hair. She wanted her room to always appear just so and refused to wear clothes that didn't match. She didn't throw temper tantrums when things weren't right; instead, she was the sort of child who organized her toys or picked a new pair of shoes. But since the accident, she got frustrated easily, and temper tantrums were now the norm. His family, Stephanie included, had recommended counseling, and both Christine and Lisa went twice a week, but the temper tantrums seemed to be getting worse. And last night, when Christine went to bed, her room was a mess.

Lisa, who'd always been small for her age, had hair the same color as Gabby's and a generally sunny disposition. She had a blanket she carried with her everywhere, and she followed Christine around the house like a puppy. She put stickers on all her folders, and her work in school usually came home covered in stars. Still, for a long time she'd cry herself to sleep. From downstairs, Travis could hear her weeping on the monitor, and he'd have to pinch the bridge of his nose to keep from joining in. On those nights, he would climb the stairs to the girls' bedroom—since the accident, another change was that they wanted to sleep in the same room—and Travis would lie beside her, stroking her hair and listening as she whimpered "I miss Mommy" over and over, the saddest words Travis had ever heard. Almost too choked up to speak, he would simply say, "I know. I do, too."

He couldn't begin to take Gabby's place, and he didn't try; what that left, however, was a hole where Gabby used to be, an emptiness he didn't know how to fill. Like most parents, each of them had carved out fiefdoms of expertise when it came to child care. Gabby, he knew now, had taken a far greater share of the responsibility than he had, and he regretted it now. There were so many things he didn't know how to do, things that Gabby made seem easy. Little things. He could brush the girls' hair, but when it came to braids, he understood the concept but found them impossible to master. He didn't know what kind of yogurt Lisa referred to when she said she wanted "the one with the blue banana." When colds settled in, he stood in the aisle of the grocery store, scanning the shelves of cough syrup, wondering whether to buy grape or cherry flavoring. Christine never wore the clothes he set out. He'd had no idea that Lisa liked to wear sparkly shoes on Fridays. He realized that before the accident, he hadn't even known their teachers' names or where in the school, exactly, their classrooms were located.

Christmas had been the worst, for that had always been Gabby's favorite holiday. She loved everything about the season: trimming the tree, decorating, baking cookies, and even the shopping. It used to amaze Travis that she could retain her humor as she pushed through frenzied crowds in department stores, but at night, after the girls had gone to bed, she'd drag out the gifts with a giddy sense of glee, and together they'd wrap the items she'd purchased. Later, Travis would hide them in the attic.

There was nothing joyous about last year's holiday season. Travis did his best, forcing excitement when none was evident. He tried to do everything Gabby had done, but the effort of maintaining a happy facade was wearying, especially because neither Christine nor Lisa made things any easier. It wasn't their fault, but for the life of him, he didn't know how respond when at the top of both their holiday wish lists was the request for Mommy to get better. It wasn't like a new Leapster or a dollhouse could take her place.

In the past couple of weeks, things had improved. Kind of. Christine still threw her tantrums and Lisa still cried at night, but they'd adapted to life in the house without their mom. When they walked in the house after school, they no longer called for her out of habit; when they fell and scraped their elbows, they automatically came to him to find a Band-Aid. In a picture of the family Lisa drew at school, Travis saw only three images; he had to catch his breath before he realized there was another horizontal image in the corner, one that seemed added almost as an afterthought. They didn't ask about their mom as much as they used to, and they visited rarely. It was hard for them to go, for they didn't know what to say or even how to act. Travis understood that and tried to make it easier. "Just talk to her," he would tell them, and they would try, but their words would trail off into nothing when no response was forthcoming.

Usually, when they did visit, Travis had them bring things— pretty rocks they'd found in the garden, leaves they'd laminated, homemade cards decorated with glitter. But even gifts were fraught with uncertainty. Lisa would set her gift on Gabby's stomach and back away; a moment later, she'd move it closer to Gabby's hand. After that, she'd shift it to the end table. Christine, on the other hand, would move constantly. She'd sit on the bed and stand by the window, she'd peer closely at her mother's face, and through it all, she'd never say a single word.

"What happened at school today?" Travis had asked her the last time she'd come. "I'm sure your mom wants to hear all about it."

Instead of answering, Christine turned toward him. "Why?" she asked, her tone one of sad defiance. "You know she can't hear me."

There was a cafeteria on the ground floor of the hospital, and on most days Travis would go there, mainly to hear voices other than his own. Normally, he arrived around lunchtime, and over the past few weeks, he'd come to recognize the regulars. Most were

employees, but there was an elderly woman who seemed to be
there every time he arrived. Though he'd never spoken to her,
he'd learned from Gretchen that the woman's husband had already been in the intensive care unit when Gabby was admitted.
Something about complications from diabetes, and whenever he
saw the woman eating a bowl of soup, he thought about her husband upstairs. It was easy to imagine the worst: a patient hooked
up to a dozen machines, endless rounds of surgery, possible ampu-
tation, a man barely hanging on. It wasn't his business to ask, and
he wasn't even certain he wanted to know the truth, if only because it felt as though he couldn't summon the concern he knew
he'd need to show. His ability to empathize, it seemed to him, had
evaporated.

Still, he watched her, curious about what he could learn from her.
While the knot in his stomach never seemed to settle enough for
him to swallow more than a few bites of anything, she not only ate
her entire meal, but seemed to enjoy it. While he found it impossible to focus long enough on anything other than his own needs
and his daughters' daily existence, she read novels during lunch,
and more than once, he'd seen her laughing quietly at a passage that
had amused her. And unlike him, she still maintained an ability to
smile, one she offered willingly to those who passed her table.

Sometimes, in that smile, he thought he could see a trace of
loneliness, even as he chided himself for imagining something
that probably wasn't there. He couldn't help wondering about her
marriage. Because of her age, he assumed they'd celebrated a silver, perhaps even golden, anniversary. Most likely there were kids,
even if he'd never seen them. But other than that, he could intuit
nothing. He wondered whether they had been happy, for she
seemed to be taking her husband's illness in stride, while he
walked the corridors of the hospital feeling as if a single wrong step
would send him crumpling to the floor.

He wondered, for instance, whether her husband had ever
planted rosebushes for her, something Travis had done for Gabby

when she'd first become pregnant with Christine. Travis remembered the way she looked as she sat on the porch, one hand on her belly, and mentioned that the backyard needed flowers. Staring at her as she said it, Travis could no more have denied her request than breathed underwater, and though his hands were scraped and his fingertips bloody by the time he finished planting the bushes, roses were blooming on the day Christine had been born. He'd brought a bouquet to the hospital.

He wondered whether her husband had watched her from the corner of his eye the way Travis watched Gabby when their kids frolicked on the swings in the park. He loved the way Gabby's expression would light up with pride. Often, he'd reach for her hand and feel like holding it forever.

He wondered whether her husband had found her beautiful first thing in the morning, with her hair askew, the way Travis did when he saw Gabby. Sometimes, despite the structured chaos always associated with mornings, they would simply lie together in each other's arms for a few more minutes, as if drawing strength to face the upcoming day.

Travis didn't know whether his marriage had been especially blessed or whether all marriages were like his. All he knew was that without Gabby he was utterly lost, while others, including the woman in the cafeteria, somehow found the strength to go on. He didn't know whether he should admire the woman or feel sorry for her. He always turned away before she caught him staring. Behind him, a family wandered in, chattering excitedly and carrying balloons; at the register, he saw a young man digging through his pockets for change. Travis pushed aside his tray, feeling ill. His sandwich was only half-eaten. He debated whether to bring it with him back to the room but knew he wouldn't finish it even if he did. He turned toward the window.

The cafeteria overlooked a small green space, and he watched the changing world outside. Spring would be here soon, and he imagined that tiny buds were beginning to form on the dogwoods.

In the past three months, he'd seen every kind of weather from this very spot. He'd watched rain and sun and seen winds in excess of fifty miles an hour bend the pine trees in the distance almost to the point of snapping. Three weeks ago, he'd seen hail fall from the sky, only to be followed minutes later by a spectacular rainbow that seemed to frame the azalea bushes. The colors, so vivid they seemed almost alive, made him think that nature sometimes sends us signs, that it's important to remember that joy can always follow despair. But a moment later, the rainbow had vanished and the hail returned, and he realized that joy was sometimes only an illusion.

Nineteen

By midafternoon, the sky was turning cloudy, and it was time for Gabby's afternoon routine. Though she'd completed the exercises from the morning, and a nurse would come by later in the evening to do another workout, he'd asked Gretchen if it would be okay if he did the same thing in the afternoon as well.

"I think she'd like that," Gretchen had said.

She walked him through the process, making sure he understood that every muscle and every joint needed attention. While Gretchen and the other nurses always started with Gabby's fingers, Travis started with her toes. He lowered the sheet and reached for her foot, flexing her pinkie toe up and down, then again, before moving to the toe beside it.

Travis had come to love doing this for her. The feel of her skin against his own was enough to rekindle a dozen memories: the way he'd rubbed her feet while she'd been pregnant, the slow and intoxicating back rubs by candlelight during which she'd seemed to purr, massages on her arm after she'd strained it lifting a bag of dog food one-handed. As much as he missed talking to Gabby, sometimes he believed that the simple act of touch was what he missed

most of all. It had taken him over a month before he'd asked
Gretchen's permission to help with the exercises, and during that
time, whenever he'd stroked Gabby's leg, he'd felt somehow as if
he were taking advantage of her. It didn't matter that they were
married; what mattered was that it was a one-sided act on his part,
somehow disrespectful to the woman he adored.

But this . . .

She needed this. She *required* this. Without it, her muscles
would atrophy, and even if she woke—when she woke, he quickly
corrected himself—she would find herself permanently bedrid-
den. At least, that's what he told himself. Deep down, he knew
he needed it as well, if only to feel the heat from her skin or the
gentle pulse of blood in her wrist. It was at such times he felt
most certain that she would recover; that her body was simply
repairing itself.

He finished with her toes and moved to her ankles; when that
was done, he flexed her knees, bending them both to her chest and
then straightening them. Sometimes, while lying on the couch and
glancing through magazines, Gabby would absently stretch her leg
in exactly the same way. It was something a dancer would do, and
she made it look just as graceful.

"Does that feel good, sweetheart?"

That feels wonderful. Thanks. I was feeling a little stiff.

He knew he'd imagined her answer, that Gabby hadn't stirred.
But her voice seemed to arise from nowhere whenever he worked
with her like this. Sometimes he wondered whether he was going
crazy. "How are you doing?"

*Bored out of my head, if you want to know the truth. Thanks for the
flowers, by the way. They're lovely. Did you get them from Frick's?*

"Where else?"

How are the girls? Tell me the truth this time.

Travis moved to the other knee. "They're okay. They miss
you, though, and it's hard on them. Sometimes I don't know
what to do."

You're doing the best you can, right? Isn't that what we always tell each other?

"You're right."

Then that's all I expect. And they'll be okay. They're tougher than they look.

"I know. They take after you."

Travis imagined her looking him over, her expression wary.

You look skinny. Too skinny.

"I haven't been eating much."

I'm worried about you. You've got to take care of yourself. For the girls. For me.

"I'll always be here for you."

I know. I'm afraid of that, too. Do you remember Kenneth and Eleanor Baker?

Travis stopped flexing. "Yes."

Then you know what I'm talking about.

He sighed and started again. "Yes."

In his mind, her tone softened. *Do you remember when you made us all go camping in the mountains last year? How you promised that the girls and I would love it?*

He began working on her fingers and arms. "What brought that up?"

I think about a lot of things here. What else can I do? Anyway, do you remember that when we first got there, we didn't even bother to set up camp—just kind of unloaded the truck—even though we heard thunder in the distance, because you wanted to show us the lake? And how we had to walk half a mile to get there, and right when we reached the shore, the sky opened up and it just . . . poured? Water gushing out of the sky like we were standing under a hose. And by the time we got back to camp, everything was soaked through. I was pretty mad at you and made you take us all to a hotel instead.

"I remember."

I'm sorry about that. I shouldn't have gotten so mad. Even though it was your fault.

"Why is it always my fault?"

He imagined her winking at him as he gently rolled her neck from side to side.

Because you're such a good sport when I say it.

He bent over and kissed her on the forehead.

"I miss you so much."

I miss you, too.

His throat clenched a little as he finished the exercise routine, knowing Gabby's voice would begin to fade away again. He moved his face closer to hers. "You know you've got to wake up, right? The girls need you. I need you."

I know. I'm trying.

"You've got to hurry."

She said nothing, and Travis knew he'd pressed too hard.

"I love you, Gabby."

I love you, too.

"Can I do anything? Close the blinds? Bring you something from home?"

Will you sit with me a while longer? I'm very tired.

"Of course."

And hold my hand?

He nodded, covering her body with the sheet once more. He sat in the chair by the bed and took her hand, his thumb tracing it slightly. Outside, the pigeon had come back, and beyond it, heavy clouds shifted in the sky, transforming into images from other worlds. He loved his wife but hated what life with her had become, cursing himself for even thinking this way. He kissed her fingertips one by one and brought her hand to his cheek. He held it against him, feeling her warmth and wishing for even the tiniest of movements, but when nothing happened, he moved it away and didn't even realize that the pigeon seemed to be staring at him.

Eleanor Baker was a thirty-eight-year-old housewife with two boys she adored. Eight years ago, she'd come into the emergency room vomiting and complaining about a blinding pain in the back of her head. Gabby, who was covering a friend's shift, happened to be working that day, though she didn't treat Eleanor. Eleanor was admitted to the hospital, and Gabby knew nothing about her until the following Monday, when she realized that Eleanor had been placed in the intensive care unit when she didn't wake up on Sunday morning. "Essentially," one of the nurses said, "she went to sleep and didn't wake up."

Her coma was caused by a severe case of viral meningitis.

Her husband, Kenneth, a history teacher at East Carteret High School who by all accounts was a gregarious, friendly guy, spent his days at the hospital. Over time, Gabby got to know him; at first it was only a few niceties here and there, but as time wore on, their conversations grew longer. He adored his wife and children, and always wore a neat sweater and pressed Dockers when he visited the hospital, and he drank Mountain Dew by the liter. He was a devout Catholic, and Gabby often found him praying the rosary by his wife's bedside. Their kids were named Matthew and Mark.

Travis knew all this because Gabby spoke about him after work. Not in the beginning, but later, after they'd become something like friends. Their conversations were always the same in that Gabby wondered how he could continue to come in each and every day, what he might be thinking as he sat in silence beside his wife.

"He seems so sad all the time," Gabby said.

"That's because he is sad. His wife is in a coma."

"But he's there all the time. What about his kids?"

Weeks turned into months, and Eleanor Baker was eventually moved to a nursing home. Months eventually passed into a year, then another. Thoughts of Eleanor Baker may have eventually slipped away, if not for the fact that Kenneth Baker shopped at the same grocery store as Gabby. They would occasionally bump into each other, and always the conversation would turn to how Eleanor was doing. There was never any change.

But over the years, as they continued to run into each other, Gabby noticed that Kenneth had changed. "She's still going," was the way he began to casually describe her condition. Where there had once been a light in his eyes when he spoke about Eleanor, there was now only blankness; where once there was love, now there seemed to be only apathy. His black hair had turned gray within a couple of years, and he'd become so thin that his clothes hung off him.

In the cereal aisle or frozen food section, Gabby couldn't seem to avoid him, and he became something of a confidant. He seemed to need her, to tell her what was happening, and in those moments they met, Kenneth mentioned one horrible event after another: that he'd lost his job, lost his house, that he couldn't wait to get all the kids out of the house, that the older one had dropped out of high school and the younger one had been arrested again for dealing drugs. *Again*. That was the word Gabby emphasized when she told Travis about it later. She also said she was pretty sure he'd been drunk when she'd run into him.

"I just feel so bad for him," Gabby said.

"I know you do," Travis said.

She grew quiet then. "Sometimes I think it might have been easier if his wife had died instead."

Staring out the window, Travis thought about Kenneth and Eleanor Baker. He had no idea whether Eleanor was still in the nursing home or whether she was still alive. Since the accident, he'd replayed those conversations in his head nearly every day, remembering the things Gabby had told him. He wondered whether somehow Eleanor and Kenneth Baker had been brought into their lives for a reason. How many people, after all, knew anyone who'd been in a coma? It seemed so . . . *fantastic*, no more likely than visiting an island filled with dinosaurs or watching an alien spaceship blowing up the Empire State Building.

But Gabby worked in a hospital, and if there was some sort of reason for the Bakers to have come into their lives, what was it? To warn him that he was doomed? That his daughters would lose their way? Those thoughts terrified him, and it was the reason he made sure he was waiting when his daughters came home from school. It was the reason he would be taking them to Busch Gardens as soon as school let out, and it was the reason he let Christine spend the night at her friend's house. He woke every morning with the thought that even if they were struggling, which was normal, he still insisted they behave at home and in school, and it was the reason that when they misbehaved, both of them were sent to their rooms for the night as punishment. Because those were the things Gabby would have done.

His in-laws sometimes thought he was being too hard on the girls. That wasn't surprising. His mother-in-law, in particular, had always been judgmental. While Gabby and her dad could chat on the phone for an hour, conversations with her mother were always clipped. In the beginning, Travis and Gabby spent the mandatory holidays in Savannah and Gabby always came home stressed; once their daughters were born, Gabby finally told her parents she wanted to start her own holiday traditions and that while she would love to see them, her parents would have to come to Beaufort. They never did.

After the accident, however, her parents checked into a hotel in Morehead City to be close to their daughter, and for the first month, the three of them were often in Gabby's room together. While they never said they blamed him for the accident, Travis could feel it in the way they seemed to keep their distance. When they spent time with Christine and Lisa, it was always away from the house—outings for ice cream or pizza—and they seldom spent more than a couple of minutes inside.

In time, they had to go back, and now they sometimes came up on weekends. When they did, Travis tried to stay away from the hospital. He told himself that it was because they needed time alone with their daughter, and that was partly true. What he didn't like to admit was that he also stayed away because they continually, if unintentionally, reminded him that he was responsible for Gabby being in the hospital in the first place.

His friends had reacted as he'd expected. Allison, Megan, and Liz prepared dinners in shifts for the first six weeks. Over the years, they'd grown close to Gabby, and sometimes it seemed as if Travis had to support them. They would show up with red eyes and forced smiles, holding Tupperware containers filled to the brim with lasagna or casseroles, side dishes, and desserts of every kind. They always made a special point to mention that chicken was always used in place of red meat, to ensure that Travis would eat it.

They were particularly good with the girls. In the beginning, they often held the girls as they cried, and Christine grew especially fond of Liz. Liz braided her hair, helped her make beaded bracelets, and usually spent at least half an hour with Christine, kicking the soccer ball back and forth. Once inside, they would begin to whisper as soon as Travis left the room. He wondered what they said to each other. Knowing Liz, he was certain that if she felt it was something important, she'd tell him, but usually she'd simply say that Christine wanted to talk. Over time, he found himself simultaneously thankful for her presence and envious of her relationship with Christine.

Lisa, on the other hand, was closer to Megan. They would color at the kitchen table or sit beside each other watching television; sometimes Travis would watch Lisa curl her body against Megan's in the same way she did with Gabby. In moments like those, they almost looked like mother and daughter, and for the briefest of moments, Travis would feel as if the family were reunited again.

Allison, on the other hand, was the one who made sure the girls understood that even if they were sad and upset, they still had responsibilities. She reminded them to pick up their rooms, helped them with their homework, and always prompted them to bring their dishes to the sink. She was gentle about it, but firm as well, and while his daughters sometimes avoided their chores on the nights Allison didn't come, it happened less frequently than Travis would have guessed. On a subconscious level, they seemed to realize they craved structure in their lives, and Allison was exactly what they'd needed.

Between them and his mother—who was there every afternoon and most weekends—Travis was seldom alone with his daughters in the aftermath of the accident, and they were able to function as parents in a way that he simply couldn't. He'd needed them to do that for him. It was all he could do to get out of bed in the morning, and most of the time, he felt on the verge of crying. His guilt hung heavy, and not simply because of the accident. He didn't know what to do or where he was supposed to be. When he was at the hospital, he wished he were at home with his daughters; when he was at home with his daughters, he wished he were visiting Gabby. Nothing was ever right.

But after six weeks of dumping excess food in the garbage cans, Travis finally told his friends that while they were welcome to continue visiting, he no longer needed his dinners prepared. Nor did he want them coming by every day. By that point, with visions of Kenneth Baker playing in his mind, he knew that he had to take control over what was left of his life. He had to become the father he once had been, the father Gabby wanted him to be, and little by little, he did. It wasn't easy, and while there were still times when Christine and Lisa seemed to miss the attention from the others, it was more than offset by the attention Travis began to show again. It wasn't as if everything had reverted to normal, but now, at the three-month mark, their lives were as normal as could be expected. In taking responsibility for the care of his daughters, Travis sometimes thought he'd saved himself.

On the downside, since the accident, he'd left little time for Joe, Matt, and Laird. While they still dropped by occasionally for a beer after the girls had gone to bed, their conversations were stilted. Half the time, everything they said seemed to be . . . *wrong*, somehow. When they asked about Gabby, he wasn't in the mood to talk about her. When they tried to talk about something else, Travis wondered why they seemed to be avoiding talking about Gabby. He knew he wasn't being fair, but while spending time with them, he was always struck by the differences between their lives and his. Despite their kindness and patience, despite their sympathy, he would find himself thinking that in a little while, Joe would head home to Megan and they'd talk quietly while curled up in bed; when Matt put his hand on his shoulder, he would wonder whether Liz was glad that Matt had gone over or whether she'd needed him to do something at home. His relationship with Laird was exactly the same, and despite himself, he was often unaccountably angry in their presence. While he was forced to live constantly with the unthinkable, their concern could be switched on and off, and for the life of him, he couldn't escape his rage at the unfairness of it all. He wanted what they had and knew they would never understand his loss, no matter how hard they tried. He hated himself for thinking these things and tried to hide his fury, but he got the sense that his friends realized that things had changed, even if they were uncertain what was really going on. Gradually, their visits became shorter and more infrequent. He hated himself for that, too, for the wedge he was creating between them, but he didn't know how to repair it.

In quiet moments, he wondered about his anger toward his friends, while he felt only gratitude toward their wives. He would sit on the deck pondering it all, and last week he'd found himself gazing at the crescent moon, finally accepting what he'd known all along. The difference, he knew, had to do with the fact that Megan, Allison, and Liz focused their support on his daughters, while Joe, Matt, and Laird focused their support on him. His daughters deserved that.

He, however, deserved to be punished.

Twenty

$\sim$

Sitting with Gabby, Travis glanced at his watch. It was coming up on half-past two, and normally he would be getting ready to say good-bye to Gabby so he could be home when the girls came back from school. Today, however, Christine was visiting a friend's house, and Lisa was going to a birthday party at the aquarium in Pine Knoll Shores, so neither would be home until just before dinner. The fact that his daughters had plans for today was fortunate, since he needed to stay longer anyway. Later, he had to meet with the neurologist and the hospital administrator.

He knew what the meeting was about, and he had no doubt they'd be in full-sympathy mode, complete with moderate, reassuring tones. The neurologist would tell him that because there was nothing more the hospital could do for Gabby, she would have to be transferred to a nursing home. He would be assured that since her condition was stable, the risk would be minimal and that a physician would check in on her weekly. Additionally, he would probably be told that the staff who worked in nursing homes were fully capable of providing the care she would need daily. If Travis protested, the administrator would probably step in and note that unless Gabby was in the intensive care unit, their insurance covered only a three-month stay in the hospital. He might also shrug and mention that since the hospital was meant to serve the local community, there wasn't room to keep her long-term, even if she had once been an employee. There was really nothing else he could do. Essentially, by teaming up, they wanted to make sure they got their way.

What neither of them realized was that the decision wasn't quite that simple. Beneath the surface lurked the reality that while Gabby was in the hospital, it was assumed that she would wake up soon, for this was where temporary coma patients always stayed. Patients in temporary comas needed physicians and nurses nearby to quickly monitor changes that would signify the improvement they'd known was coming all along. In a nursing home, it would be assumed that Gabby would never wake up. Travis wasn't ready to accept that, but it seemed as if he weren't going to be given a choice.

But Gabby had a choice, and in the end, his decision wasn't going to be based on what either the neurologist or the administrator said to him. He would base his decision on what he thought Gabby would want.

Outside the window, the pigeon was gone, and he wondered whether it went off to visit other patients, like a doctor making his rounds, and if it did, whether the other patients noticed the pigeon the way he did.

"Sorry about crying earlier," Travis whispered. As he stared at Gabby, he watched her chest rising and falling with every breath. "I couldn't help it."

He was under no illusions he would hear her voice this time. It happened only once a day.

"Do you know what I like about you?" he asked. "Aside from pretty much everything?" He forced a smile. "I like the way you are with Molly. She's all right, by the way. Her hips haven't given out, and she still likes to lie in the tall grass whenever she can. Whenever I see her doing that, I think about those first few years we were together. Remember when we used to take the dogs on walks down the beach? When we'd go out early so we could let them off the leash and they could run around? Those were always such . . . restful mornings, and I used to love watching you laugh as you chased Molly in circles, trying to tap her butt. She used to go crazy when you did that, and she'd get this gleam in her eye with her tongue hanging out, waiting for you to make your move."

He paused, noting with surprise that the pigeon had returned. It must like listening to him talk, he decided.

"That's how I knew you'd be great with kids, by the way. Because of how you were with Molly. Even that first time we met . . ." He shook his head, his mind flashing back. "Believe it or not, I've always liked the fact that you stormed over to my place that night, and not just because we ended up getting married. You were like a mama bear protecting her cub. It's impossible to get that angry unless you're capable of loving deeply, and after watching how you were with Molly—lots of love and attention, lots of worry, and nobody on earth better mess with her—I knew you'd be exactly the same way with kids."

He traced his finger along her arm. "Do you know how much that's meant to me? Knowing how much you love our daughters? You have no idea how much comfort that gave me over the years."

He leaned his face close to her ear. "I love you, Gabby, more than you'll ever know. You're everything I've ever wanted in a wife. You're every hope and every dream I've ever had, and you've made me happier than any man could possibly be. I don't ever want to give that up. I can't. Can you understand that?"

He waited for a response, but there was nothing. There was always nothing, as if God were telling him that his love was somehow not enough. Staring at Gabby, he suddenly felt very old and very tired. He adjusted the sheet, feeling alone and apart from his wife, knowing he was a husband whose love had somehow failed her.

"Please," he whispered. "You've got to wake up, sweetheart. Please? We're running out of time."

"Hey," Stephanie said. Dressed in jeans and a T-shirt, she looked nothing like the successful professional she'd become. Living in Chapel Hill, she was the senior project manager at a rapidly growing biotechnology firm, but in the last three months, she'd spent three or four days a week in Beaufort. Since the accident, she'd been the only one Travis could really talk to. She alone knew all his secrets.

"Hey," Travis said.

She crossed the room and leaned over the side of the bed. "Hey, Gabby," she said, kissing her on the cheek. "You doing okay?"

Travis loved the way his sister treated Gabby. Except for Travis, she was the only one who'd always seemed comfortable in Gabby's presence.

Stephanie pulled up another chair and slid it closer to Travis. "And how are you doing, big brother?"

"Okay," he said.

Stephanie gave him the once-over. "You look like hell."

"Thanks."

"You're not eating enough." She reached in her handbag and pulled out a bag of peanuts. "Eat these."

"I'm not hungry. I just had lunch."

"How much?"

"Enough."

"Humor me, okay?" She used her teeth to tear open the bag. "Just eat these and I promise I'll shut up and won't bother you again."

"You say that every time you're here."

"That's because you keep looking like hell." She tilted her head toward Gabby. "I'll bet she said the same thing, too, right?" She'd never questioned Travis's claims about hearing Gabby's voice, or if she did, her tone reflected no concerns about it.

"Yeah, she did."

She forced the bag toward him. "Then take the peanuts."

Travis took the bag, lowering it to his lap.

"Now put some in your mouth, then chew and swallow."

She sounded like their mother. "Did anyone ever tell you that you can be a little bit too pushy at times?"

"Every day. And believe me, you need someone to be pushy with you. You're just lucky you have me in your life. I'm quite the blessing for you."

For the first time all day, he gave a genuine laugh. "That's one word for it." He poured out a small handful of nuts and began to chew. "How are things with you and Brett?"

Stephanie had been dating Brett Whitney for the past two years. One of the most successful hedge fund managers in the country, he was wildly wealthy, handsome, and considered by many to be the most eligible bachelor south of the Mason-Dixon Line.

"We're still going."

"Trouble in paradise?"

Stephanie shrugged. "He asked me to marry him again."

"And you said?"

"The same thing I said before."

"How did he take it?"

"Fine. Oh, he did his 'I'm hurt and angry' thing again, but he was back to normal in a couple of days. We spent last weekend in New York."

"Why don't you just marry him?"

She shrugged. "I probably will."

"Here's a hint, then. You might want to say yes when he asks."

"Why? He'll ask again."

"You sound so certain when you say that."

"I am. And I'll say yes when I'm positive he wants to marry me."

"He's asked you three times. How much more positive can you get?"

"He just thinks he wants to marry me. Brett is the kind of guy who likes challenges, and right now, I'm a challenge. As long as I stay a challenge, he'll keep asking. And when I know he's really ready, that's when I'll say yes."

"I don't know . . ."

"Trust me," she said. "I know men, and I have my charms." Her eyes glittered with mischief. "He knows that I don't need him, and it practically kills him."

"No," he said. "You definitely don't need him."

"So, changing the subject, when are you going back to work?"

"Soon," he mumbled.

She reached into his bag of peanuts and popped a couple in her mouth. "You are aware that Dad's not exactly a spring chicken anymore."

"I know."

"So . . . next week?"

When Travis didn't respond, Stephanie folded her hands in front of her. "Okay, here's what's going to happen, since you obviously haven't made up your mind. You're going to start showing up at the clinic, and at the very least, you're going to stay every day until at least one o'clock. That's your new schedule. Oh, and you can close the office on Friday at noon. That way, Dad's only there for four afternoons."

He squinted at her. "I can see you've been giving this a lot of thought."

"Someone has to. And just so you know, this isn't just for Dad. You need to go back to work."

"What if I don't think I'm ready?"

"Too bad. Do it anyway. If not for you, do it for Christine and Lisa."

"What are you talking about?"

"Your daughters. Remember them?"

"I know who they are. . . ."

"And you love them, right?"

"What kind of a question is that?"

"Then if you love them," she said, ignoring his question, "you've got to start acting like a parent again. And that means you have to go back to work."

"Why?"

"Because," she said, "you have to show them that no matter what horrible things happen in life, you still have to go on. That's your responsibility. Who else is going to teach them that?"

"Steph . . ."

"I'm not saying it's going to be easy, but I am saying you don't have a choice. After all, you haven't let them quit, have you? They're still in school, right? You're still making them do homework, right?"

Travis said nothing.

"So, if you expect them to handle their responsibilities—and they're only six and eight—then you've got to handle yours. They need to see you getting back to normal, and work is part of that. Sorry. That's life."

Travis shook his head, feeling his anger rise. "You don't understand."

"I understand completely."

He brought his fingers to the bridge of his nose and squeezed. "Gabby is . . ."

When he didn't continue, Stephanie put her hand on his knee. "Passionate? Intelligent? Kind? Moral? Funny? Forgiving? Patient? Everything you ever imagined in a wife and mother? In other words, pretty much perfect?"

He looked up in surprise.

"I know," she said quietly. "I love her, too. I've always loved her. She's not only been the sister I never had, but my best friend, too. Sometimes she felt like my only real friend. And you're right—she's been wonderful for you and the kids. You couldn't have done any better. Why do you think I keep coming down here? It's not just for her, or for you. It's for me. I miss her, too."

Unsure how to respond, he said nothing. In the silence, Stephanie sighed.

"Have you decided what you're going to do?"

Travis swallowed. "No," he admitted. "Not yet."

"It's been three months."

"I know," he said.

"When's the meeting?"

"I'm supposed to meet with them in half an hour."

Watching her brother, she accepted that. "Okay. I'll tell you what. I'll let you think about it some more. I'll just head over to your place and see the girls."

"They're not there, but they should be back later."

"You mind if I wait around?"

"Go ahead. There's a key—"

She didn't let him finish. "Beneath the plaster frog on the porch? Yeah, I know. And if you're curious, I'm pretty sure most burglars could figure that out, too."

He smiled. "I love you, Steph."

"I love you, too, Travis. And you know I'm here for you, right?"

"I know."

"Always. Anytime."

"I know."

Staring at him, she finally nodded. "I'll just wait for you, okay? I want to know what happens."

"Okay."

Standing, she reached for her purse and flung it over her shoulder. She kissed her brother on the top of his head.

"We'll see you later, okay, Gabby?" she said, not expecting an answer. She was halfway out of the room when she heard Travis's voice again.

"How far should you go in the name of love?"

Stephanie half turned. "You've asked me that question before."

"I know." Travis hesitated. "But I'm asking what you think I should do."

"Then I'll tell you what I always do. That it's your choice how you handle this."

"What does that mean for me?"

Her expression seemed almost helpless. "I don't know, Trav. What do you think it means?"

Twenty-one

It was a little more than two years ago when Gabby bumped into Kenneth Baker on one of those summer evenings for which Beaufort was famous. With live music playing and dozens of boats tied up at the docks on a summer night, it had seemed like the perfect night to bring Gabby and the kids downtown for ice cream. While they stood in line with the kids, Gabby casually mentioned that she'd seen a beautiful print in one of the stores they'd passed. Travis smiled. By then, he'd grown used to her hints.

"Why don't you check it out," he'd said. "I've got the girls. Go ahead."

She was gone longer than he'd expected, and when she returned, her expression was troubled. Later, after they'd gone home and put the girls to bed, Gabby sat on the couch, clearly preoccupied.

"Are you okay?" he asked.

Gabby shifted on the couch. "I ran into Kenneth Baker earlier today," she admitted. "When you were getting ice cream."

"Oh yeah? How's he doing?"

She sighed. "Do you realize that his wife's been in a coma for six years now? Six *years*. Can you imagine what that must be like for him?"

"No," Travis said. "I can't."

"He looks like an old man."

"I'm sure I'd age, too. He's going through something terrible."

She nodded, her expression still troubled. "He's angry, too. It's like he resents her. He said he only visits her now and then. And his kids . . ." Lost in thought, she seemed to lose track of her sentence.

Travis stared at Gabby. "What's this about?"

"Would you visit me? If something like that happened to me?"

For the first time, he felt a pang of fear, even though he wasn't quite sure why. "Of course I would."

Her expression was almost sad. "But after a while, you'd visit less."

"I'd visit you all the time."

"And in time, you'd resent me."

"I'd never resent you."

"Kenneth resents Eleanor."

"I'm not Kenneth." He shook his head. "Why are we even talking about this?"

"Because I love you."

He opened his mouth to respond, but she raised her hand. "Let me finish, okay?" She paused, collecting her thoughts. "When Eleanor first went into the hospital, it was obvious how much Kenneth loved her. That's what I noticed whenever we spoke, and over time, I think he told me their entire story—how they'd met at the beach the summer after graduation; that when he first asked her out, she'd said no, but he somehow finagled her number anyway; that he first told her he loved her on her parents' thirtieth anniversary. But he didn't just tell the stories—it was like he was reliving them over and over. In a way, he reminded me of you."

Gabby reached for his hand. "You do the same thing, you know. Do you know how many times I've heard you tell someone about the first time we met? Don't get me wrong—I love that about you. I love the fact that you keep those memories alive in your heart and that they mean as much to you as they do to me. And the thing is . . . when you do, I can feel you fall in love with me again. In some ways, it's the most touching thing you do for me." She paused. "Well, that and cleaning the kitchen when I'm too tired to do it."

Despite himself, he laughed. Gabby didn't seem to notice.

"Today, though, Kenneth was just so . . . bitter, and when I asked about Eleanor, I got the sense that he wished she were dead. And when I compare that to the way he used to feel about his wife, and what's happened to his kids . . . it's terrible."

When her voice died away, Travis squeezed her hand. "That's not going to happen to us. . . ."

"That's not the point. The point is, I can't live knowing that I didn't do what I should have done."

"What are you talking about?"

She ran her thumb over his hand. "I love you so much, Travis. You're the best husband, the best person, that I've ever known. And I want you to make me a promise."

"Anything," he said.

She looked directly at him. "I want you to promise that if anything ever does happen to me, you'll let me die."

"We already have living wills," he countered. "We did those when we did our regular wills and power of attorney."

"I know," she said. "But our lawyer retired to Florida, and as far as I know, no one but the three of us knows that I don't want my life prolonged in the event I can't make my own decisions. It wouldn't be fair to you or the kids to put your lives on hold, because in time, resentment would be inevitable. You would suffer and the kids would suffer. Seeing Kenneth today convinced me of that, but I don't want you to ever be bitter about anything we shared. I love all of you too much for that. Death is always sad, but it's also inevitable, and that's why I signed the living will in the first place. Because I love all of you so much." Her tone became softer and yet more determined. "And the thing is . . . I don't want to feel like I have to tell my parents or my sisters about the decision I made. The decision we made. I don't want to have to find another attorney and redraft the documents. I want to be able to trust that you'll do what I want. And that's why I want you to promise me that you'll honor my wishes."

The conversation struck him as surreal. "Yeah . . . sure," he said.

"No, not like that. I want you to promise me. I want you to make a vow."

Travis swallowed. "I promise to do exactly what you want. I swear it."

"No matter how hard it is?"

"No matter how hard."

"Because you love me."

"Because I love you."

"Yes," she said. "And because I love you, too."

The living will Gabby had signed in the attorney's office was the document Travis had brought with him to the hospital. Among other things, it specified that her feeding tubes were to be removed after twelve weeks. Today was the day he had to make his choice.

Sitting beside Gabby in the hospital, Travis recalled the conversation he'd had with Gabby that night; he remembered the vow he'd made to her. He'd replayed those words a hundred times over the last few weeks, and as the three-month mark approached, he'd found himself growing ever more desperate for Gabby to wake. As had Stephanie, which was why she was waiting for him at home. Six weeks ago, he'd told her about the promise he'd made to Gabby; the need to share it had become unbearable.

The next six weeks passed without relief. Not only didn't Gabby stir, but she'd shown no improvement in any of her brain functions. Though he tried to ignore the obvious, the clock had moved forward, and it was now the hour of his decision.

Sometimes, during his imaginary conversations with her, he'd tried to get her to change her mind. He'd argue that the promise hadn't been a fair one; that the only reason he'd said yes was that the prospect seemed so unlikely, he'd never believed it would come up. He confessed that had he been able to predict the future, he would have torn up the documents she'd signed in the attorney's office, for even if she couldn't respond, he still couldn't imagine a life without her.

He would never be like Kenneth Baker. He felt no bitterness toward Gabby, nor would he ever. He needed her, he needed the hope he felt whenever they were together. He drew strength from visiting her. Earlier today, he'd been exhausted and lethargic; as the day wore on, his sense of commitment had only grown stronger, leaving him certain that he would have the ability to laugh with his daughters, to be the father Gabby wanted him to be. It had worked for three months, and he knew he could do it forever. What he didn't know was how on earth he could go on knowing that Gabby was gone. As strange as it seemed, there was a comforting predictability to the new routine of his life.

Outside the window, the pigeon paced back and forth, making him think it was pondering the decision with him. There were times when he felt a strange kinship with the bird, as if it were trying to teach him something, though what, he had no idea. Once, he had brought some bread with him, but he hadn't realized the screen would prevent him from tossing it onto the ledge. Standing before the glass, the pigeon had eyed the bread in his hand, cooing slightly. It flew away a moment later, only to return and stay the rest of the afternoon. After that, it showed no fear of him. Travis could tap the glass and the pigeon would stand in place. It was a curious situation that gave him something else to think about when sitting in the quiet room. What he wanted to ask the pigeon was this: Am I to become a killer?

This was where his thoughts inevitably led, and it was what differentiated him from others who were expected to carry out the desires outlined in living wills. They were doing the right thing; their choice was rooted in compassion. For him, however, the choice was different, if only for logical reasons. If A and B, then C. But for his commission of one mistake after the next, there would have been no car accident; had there been no accident, there would have been no coma. He was the proximate cause of her injury, but she hadn't died. And now, with the flourish of some legal documents from his pocket, he could finish the job. He could be responsible for her death once and for all. The difference turned his stomach inside out; with every passing day, as the decision approached, he ate less and less. Sometimes it seemed not only that God wanted Gabby to die, but that He wanted Travis to know that it had been entirely his fault.

Gabby, he was certain, would deny it. The accident was just that—an accident. And she, not he, had made the decision as to how long she wanted a feeding tube. Yet he couldn't shed the crushing weight of his responsibility, for the simple reason that no one, aside from Stephanie, knew what Gabby wanted. In the end, he alone would make the choice.

The grayish afternoon light gave the walls a melancholy cast. He still felt paralyzed. Buying time, he removed the flowers from the windowsill and brought them to the bed. As he laid them across Gabby's chest and took his seat, Gretchen appeared in the doorway. She moved into the room slowly; as she checked Gabby's vitals, she didn't say a word. She jotted something in the chart and smiled briefly. A month ago, when he was doing Gabby's exercises, Gabby had mentioned that she was pretty sure Gretchen had a crush on him.

"Is she going to be leaving us?" he heard Gretchen ask.

Travis knew she was referring to a transfer to a nursing home; in the halls, Travis had heard whispers that it would be coming soon. But there was more to her question than Gretchen could possibly understand, and he couldn't summon the will to answer.

"I'm going to miss her," she said. "And I'm going to miss you, too."

Her expression was brimming with compassion.

"I mean it. I've worked here longer than Gabby, and you should have heard the way she used to talk about you. And the kids, too, of course. You could tell that even though she loved her job, she was always happiest when it was time to go home at the end of the day. She wasn't like the rest of us, who were excited to be done for the day. She was excited to go home, to be reunited with her family. I really admired that about her, that she had a life like that."

Travis didn't know what to say.

She sighed, and Travis thought he saw the glisten of tears. "It breaks my heart to see her like this. And you, too. Do you know that every nurse in the hospital knows you sent your wife roses every anniversary? Pretty much every woman here wished that her husband or boyfriend would do things like that. And then, after the accident, the way you are with her . . . I know you're sad and angry, but I've seen you do the exercises with her. I've heard what you say, and . . . it's like you and she have this connection that can't be broken. It's heartbreaking and yet beautiful. And I feel so horrible for what you're both going through. I've been praying for you both every night."

Travis felt his throat close.

"I guess what I'm trying to say is that you two make me believe that true love really exists. And that even the darkest hours can't take that away." She stopped, her expression revealing that she felt she'd said too much, and she turned away. A moment later, as she was about to leave the room, he felt her place a hand on his shoulder. It was warm and light and lingered for just an instant, and then it was gone, and Travis was alone with his choice once more.

It was time. Looking at the clock, he knew he couldn't wait any longer. The others were waiting for him. He crossed the room to shut the blinds. Habit led him to turn on the television. Though he knew the nurses would turn it off later, he didn't want Gabby to lie alone in a room more silent than a tomb.

He'd often imagined himself trying to explain how it happened. He could see himself shaking his head in disbelief while sitting at the kitchen table with his parents. "I don't know why she woke up," he heard himself saying. "As far as I can tell, there is no magical answer. It was just like every other time I visited . . . except that she opened her eyes." He could imagine his mother crying tears of joy, he could picture himself making the call to Gabby's parents. Sometimes it was as clear to him as if it had actually happened, and he would hold his breath, living and experiencing the feeling of wonder.

But now he doubted that it would ever be possible, and from across the room, he stared at her. Who were they, Gabby and he? Why had it all turned out this way? There had been a time when he would have had reasonable answers to those questions, but that time was long past. These days, he understood nothing. Above her, the fluorescent light hummed, and he wondered what he was going to do. He still didn't know. What he knew was this: She was still alive, and where there was life, there was always hope. He focused on her, wondering how someone so close and so present could remain so remote.

Today, he had to make his choice. To tell the truth meant Gabby would die; to tell a lie meant that Gabby's wish would be denied. He wanted her to tell him what to do, and from somewhere far away, he could imagine her answer.

I already have, sweetheart. You know what you have to do.

But the choice, he wanted to plead, had been based on faulty assumptions. If he could go back in time, he would never have made that promise, and he wondered whether she would have even asked him to. Would she have made the same decision if she'd known that he would cause her coma in the first place? Or if she'd known that pulling the feeding tube and watching her slowly starve to death would certainly kill a part of him? Or if he told her that he believed he could be a better father if she remained alive, even if she never recovered at all?

It was more than he could bear, and he felt his mind begin to scream: *Please wake up!* The echo seemed to shake the very atoms of his being. *Please, sweetheart. Do it for me. For our daughters. They need you. I need you. Open your eyes before I go, while there's still time. . . .*

And for a moment, he thought he saw a twitch, he would swear he saw her stir. He was too choked up to speak, but as always, reality reasserted itself, and he knew it had been an illusion. In the bed, she hadn't moved at all, and watching her through his tears, he felt his soul begin to die.

He had to go, but there was one more thing he had to do. Like everyone, he knew the story of Snow White, of the kiss from the Prince that broke the evil spell. That's what he thought of every time he left Gabby for the day, but now the notion struck him as imperative. This was it, his very last chance. Despite himself, he felt a tiny swell of hope at the thought that somehow, this time would be different. While his love for her had always been there, the finality had not, and maybe the combination constituted the magical formula that he'd been missing. He steadied himself and moved toward the bed, trying to convince himself that this time it would work. This kiss, unlike all the others, would fill her lungs with life. She would moan in momentary confusion, but then she would realize what he was doing. She would feel his life pouring into hers. She would sense the fullness of his love for her, and with a passion that surprised him, she would begin to kiss him in return.

He leaned closer, their faces drawing near, and he could feel the heat of her breath mingling with his. He closed his eyes against the memory of a thousand other kisses and touched his lips to hers. He felt a kind of spark, and all at once he felt her slowly coming back to him. She was the arm that held him close in times of trouble, she was the whisper on the pillow beside him at night. It was working, he thought, it was really working . . . and as his heart began to race in his chest, it finally dawned on him that nothing had changed at all.

Pulling back, all he could do was lightly trace her cheek with his finger. His voice was hoarse, barely above a whisper.

"Good-bye, sweetheart."

Twenty-two

How far should a person go in the name of love?

Travis was still turning this question over in his mind when he pulled into the drive, even though he'd already made his decision. Stephanie's car was parked out front, but except for the living room, the rest of the house was dark. An empty house would have been too much to bear.

The chill was biting as he stepped out of his car, and he pulled his jacket tighter. The moon had yet to rise, and the stars glittered overhead; if he concentrated, he knew he could still remember the names of the constellations that Gabby had once traced for him. He smiled briefly, thinking back on that evening. The memory was as clear as the sky above, but he forced it away, knowing he didn't have the strength to let it linger. Not tonight.

The lawn was shiny with moisture, promising a heavy frost overnight. He reminded himself to put out the girls' mittens and scarves so he wouldn't have to rush around in the morning. They would be home soon, and despite his fatigue, he missed them. Tucking his hands in his pockets, he made his way up the front steps.

Stephanie turned when she heard him enter. He could feel her trying to read his expression. She started toward him.

"Travis," she said.

"Hey, Steph." He removed his jacket, realizing he couldn't remember the drive back home.

"Are you okay?"

It took him a moment to respond. "I don't know."

She put her hand on his arm. Her voice was gentle. "Can I get you something to drink?"

"A glass of water would be great."

She seemed relieved to be able to do something. "Be back in a jiffy."

He sat on the couch and leaned his head back, feeling as drained as if he'd spent the day in the ocean, fighting waves. Stephanie returned and handed him the glass.

"Christine called. She's running a little late. Lisa's on her way."

"Okay," he said. He nodded before focusing on the family portrait.

"Do you want to talk about it?"

He took a drink of water, realizing how parched his throat had become. "Did you think about the question I asked you earlier? About how far someone should go in the name of love?"

She considered the question for a moment. "I think I answered that."

"You did. Sort of."

"What? You're telling me it wasn't a good enough answer?"

He smiled, thankful that Stephanie was still able to talk to him as she always had. "What I really wanted to know is what you would have done if you were in my position."

"I knew what you wanted," she said hesitantly, "but . . . I don't know, Trav. I really don't. I can't imagine having to make that kind of decision, and to be honest, I don't think anyone can." She exhaled. "Sometimes I wish you'd never told me."

"I probably shouldn't have. I had no right to burden you with that."

She shook her head. "I didn't mean it like that. I know you had to talk to someone about it, and I'm glad you trusted me. It's just that it made me feel terrible for what you've been going through. The accident, your own injuries, worries about the kids, your wife in a coma . . . and then to have to make a choice whether or not to honor Gabby's wishes? It's too much for anyone to handle."

Travis said nothing.

"I've been worried about you," she added. "I've barely slept since you told me."

"I'm sorry."

"Don't apologize. I should be the one apologizing to you. I should have moved back here as soon as it happened. I should have visited Gabby more often. I should have been around every time you needed to talk to someone."

"It's all right. I'm glad you didn't walk away from your job. You worked hard to get there, and Gabby knew that, too. Besides, you were here a lot more than I thought you would be."

"I just feel so sorry for what you've been going through."

He slipped his arm around her. "I know," he said.

Together, they sat in silence. In the background, Travis heard the heater click on as Stephanie sighed. "I want you to know that no matter what you decided, I'm with you, okay? I know, more than almost anyone, how much you love Gabby."

Travis turned toward the window. Through the glass, he could see the lights from his neighbors' houses gleaming in the darkness. "I couldn't do it," he finally said.

He tried to collect his thoughts. "I thought I could, and I even rehearsed the words I would say when telling the doctors to remove her feeding tube. I know that's what Gabby wanted, but . . . in the end I just couldn't do it. Even if I spend the rest of my life visiting her in the nursing home, it's still a better life than one I could spend with anyone else. I love her too much to let her go."

Stephanie gave him a wan smile. "I know," she said. "I could see it on your face when you walked in the door."

"Do you think I did the right thing?"

"Yes," she answered without hesitation.

"For me, or for Gabby?"

"Both."

He swallowed. "Do you think she'll wake up?"

Stephanie met his eyes. "Yes, I do. I've always believed that. The two of you . . . there's something uncanny about the way you are with each other. I mean everything—the way you look at each other, the way she relaxes when you put your hand on her back, the way you both seem to know what the other is always thinking . . . it's always struck me as extraordinary. That's another reason I keep putting marriage off. I know I want something like what you two share, and I'm not sure I've found it yet. I'm not sure I ever will. And with love like that . . . they say anything's possible, right? You love Gabby and Gabby loves you, and I just can't imagine a world where you're not together. Together the way you're meant to be."

Travis let her words sink in.

"So what's next?" she asked. "You need help burning the living will?"

Despite the tension, he laughed. "Maybe later."

"And the lawyer? He won't come back to haunt you, right?"

"I haven't heard from him in years."

"See, that's another sign you did the right thing."

"I guess."

"What about nursing homes?"

"She'll be transferred next week. I just have to make the arrangements."

"Need help?"

He massaged his temples, feeling unbearably tired. "Yeah," he said. "I'd like that."

"Hey—" She gave him a little shake. "You made the right decision. Don't feel guilty about a single thing. You did the only thing you could do. She wants to live. She wants the chance to get back to you and the girls."

"I know. But . . ."

He couldn't finish his sentence. The past was gone and the

future had yet to unfold, and he knew he should focus his life on the present . . . yet his day-to-day existence suddenly struck him as endless and unbearable.

"I'm scared," he finally admitted.

"I know," she said, pulling him close. "I'm scared, too."

Epilogue

The muted landscape of winter had given way to the lush colors of late spring, and as Travis sat on the back porch, he could hear birds. Dozens, maybe hundreds, were calling and chirping, and every so often a flock of starlings would break from the trees, flying in formations that nearly seemed choreographed.

It was a Saturday afternoon, and Christine and Lisa were still playing on the tire swing that Travis had hung the week before. Because he wanted a long, slow arc for the girls—something different from the regular swing set—he'd cut a few of the low branches before securing the rope as high in the tree as possible. He'd spent an hour that morning pushing the swing and listening to his daughters squeal in delight; by the time he'd finished, the back of his shirt was slick with perspiration. And still the girls wanted more.

"Let Daddy rest for a few minutes," he'd wheezed. "Daddy's tired. Why don't you push each other for a while."

Their disappointment, etched so clearly on their faces and in the droop of their shoulders, lasted only moments. Soon they were squealing again. Travis watched them swing, his mouth curling into a slight smile. He loved the musical sound of their laughter, and it warmed his heart to see them playing so well together. He hoped they would always remain as close as they were now. He liked to believe that if he and Stephanie were any indication, they would grow even closer in later years. At least that was the hope. Hope, he'd learned, was sometimes all a person had, and in the past four months, he'd learned to embrace it.

Since he'd made his choice, his life had gradually returned to a kind of normalcy. Or at least a semblance thereof. Along with Stephanie, he'd toured half a dozen nursing homes. Prior to those visits, his preconceptions of nursing homes were that they were all dimly lit, filthy places where confused, moaning patients wandered the halls in the middle of the night and were watched over by orderlies who bordered on the psychotic. None of which turned out to be true. At least, not in the places he and Stephanie visited.

Instead, most were bright and airy, run by thoughtful, reflective middle-aged men or women in suits who went to great pains to prove their facilities were more hygienic than most homes and that the staff was courteous, caring, and professional. While Travis spent the tours wondering whether Gabby would be happy in a place like this or whether she'd be the youngest patient in the nursing home, Stephanie asked the hard questions. She asked about background checks for the staff and emergency procedures, she wondered aloud how quickly complaints were resolved, and as she strolled the halls, she made it obvious that she was well aware of every code and regulation that had been mandated by law. She offered hypothetical situations that might come to pass and asked how they'd be handled by the staff and director; she asked how many times Gabby would be turned in the course of a day, so as to prevent bedsores. At times, she struck Travis as being like a prosecutor trying to convict someone of a crime, and though she ruffled the feathers of a few directors, Travis was grateful for her vigilance. In his state of mind, he was barely able to function, but he was dimly aware that she was asking all the right questions.

In the end, Gabby was transferred by ambulance to a nursing

home run by a man named Elliot Harris, only a couple of blocks from the hospital. Harris had impressed not only Travis, but Stephanie as well, and Stephanie had filled out most of the paperwork in his office. She'd insinuated—true or not—that she knew people in the state legislature and ensured that Gabby was given a gracious private room that overlooked a courtyard. When Travis visited her, he rolled the bed toward the window and puffed up her pillows. He imagined that she enjoyed the sounds from the courtyard, where friends and families met, along with the sunlight. She'd said that to him once when he'd been flexing her legs. She'd also said that she understood his choice and that she was glad he'd made it. Or, more accurately, he'd imagined that she had.

After placing her in the home and spending most of another week with her while they both got acclimated to her new environment, he'd gone back to work. He took Stephanie's suggestion and began working until early afternoon four days a week; his father filled in after that. He hadn't realized how much he'd missed interaction with other people, and when he had lunch with his father, he found he was able to finish nearly all of his meal. Of course, working regularly meant he had to juggle his schedule with Gabby. After seeing the girls off to school, he went to the nursing home and spent an hour there; after work, he spent another hour with Gabby before the girls got home. On Fridays, he was there most of the day, and on weekends, he usually made it in for a few hours. That depended on the girls' schedules, which was something Gabby would have insisted on. Sometimes on the weekends they wanted to join him, but most times they didn't want to or didn't have the time because of soccer games or parties or roller-skating. Somehow, without the choice of whether Gabby would live or die hovering over him, their growing distance didn't bother Travis as much as it once had. His daughters were doing what they needed to do to heal and move on, just as he was. He'd lived long enough to know that everyone handled grief in different ways, and little by little, they all seemed to accept their new lives. And then, one afternoon nine weeks after she'd been admitted to the nursing home, the pigeon appeared at Gabby's window.

At first, Travis didn't believe it. Truth be told, he wasn't even positive it was the same bird. Who could tell? Gray and white and black with dark, beady eyes—and, okay, most of the time a pest— they all looked pretty much alike. And yet, staring at it . . . he *knew* it was the same bird. It *had* to be. It paced back and forth, showing no fear of Travis when he approached the glass, and it had a coo that sounded . . . *familiar* somehow. A million people could tell him he was crazy, and part of him would know they were right, but still . . .

It was the same pigeon, no matter how crazy it sounded.

He watched it in wonder, amazed, and the following day, he brought some Wonder Bread and scattered a few pieces on the sill. After that, he glanced at the window regularly, waiting for the pigeon to reappear, but it never did. In the days following its visit, he found himself depressed by its absence. Sometimes, in fanciful moments, he liked to think that it had simply come to check on them, to make sure Travis was still watching over Gabby. Either that, he told himself, or it came to tell him not to give up hope; that in the end, his choice had been correct.

On the back porch, remembering that moment, he marveled that he could stare out at his happy daughters and experience so much of their joy himself. He barely recognized this sense of well-being, the feeling that all was right in the world. Had the appearance of the pigeon heralded the changes that took hold of their lives? He supposed it was only human to wonder about such things, and Travis figured that he'd be telling the rest of the story as long as he lived.

What happened was this: It was midmorning, six days after the pigeon had reappeared, and Travis was working at the clinic. In one room was a sick cat; in another, a Doberman puppy needing shots. In the third room, Travis was suturing a mutt—half Labrador, half golden retriever—that had received a gash while crawling through barbed wire. He finished the final stitch, tied off the knot, and was about to tell the owner how to keep the gash from getting infected when an assistant entered the room without knocking. Travis turned in surprise at the interruption.

"It's Elliot Harris," she said. "He needs to talk to you."

"Can you take a message?" Travis asked, glancing at the dog and its owner.

"He said it can't wait. It's urgent."

Travis apologized to the client and told the assistant to finish up. He walked to his office and closed the door. On the phone was a flashing light signaling Harris on hold.

Thinking back, he wasn't sure what he'd expected to hear. He did feel, however, something ominous as he raised the receiver to his ear. It was the first—and the only—time Elliot Harris had ever called him at the office. He steadied himself, then pressed the button.

"Travis Parker speaking," he said into the phone.

"Dr. Parker, it's Elliot Harris," the director said. His voice was calm and unreadable. "I think you should come down to the nursing home as quickly as you can."

In the short silence that followed, a million thoughts raced through Travis's mind: that Gabby had stopped breathing, that she'd taken a turn for the worse, that somehow all hope had been lost. In that instant, Travis gripped the phone as if trying to ward off whatever might come next.

"Is Gabby okay?" he finally asked, the words sounding choked.

There was another pause, probably only a second or two. A blink of an eye that was years in the making, is the way he described it now, but the two words that followed made him drop the phone.

He was eerily calm as he left his office. At least, that's what his assistants would tell him later: that in looking at him, he gave no clues as to what had happened. They said that they'd watched as he drifted past the front desk, oblivious to those who were watching him. Everyone, from the staff to the owners who'd brought their animals to the clinic, knew that Travis's wife was in the nursing home. Madeline, who was eighteen and worked at the front desk, stared at him with wide eyes as he approached her. By that point, nearly everyone in the office knew that the nursing home had called. In small towns, news is nearly instantaneous.

"Would you call my dad and tell him to come in?" Travis asked. "I have to go to the nursing home."

"Yes, of course," Madeline answered. She hesitated. "Are you all right?"

"Do you think you could drive me? I don't think I should be behind the wheel right now."

"Sure," she said, looking frightened. "Just let me make the call first, okay?"

As she punched the number, Travis stood as if paralyzed. The waiting room was silent; even the animals, it seemed, knew something had happened. He heard Madeline speaking to his dad as if from a great distance; in fact, he was only dimly aware of where he was. It was only when Madeline hung up the phone and told him that his father would be right in that Travis seemed to recognize his surroundings. He saw the fear on Madeline's face. Maybe because she was young and didn't know better, she asked the question that everyone seemed to be thinking.

"What happened?"

Travis saw empathy and concern etched on their faces. Most of them had known him for years; some had known him since he was a child. A few, mostly the staff, knew Gabby well and, after the accident, they had gone through a period that almost resembled mourning. It wasn't anyone's business and yet it was, because his roots were here. Beaufort was their home, and looking around, he recognized everyone's curiosity as something akin to familial love. Yet he didn't know what to say to them. He'd pictured this day a thousand times, but now, however, everything was blank. He could hear himself breathing. If he concentrated hard enough, he believed that he would even be able to feel his heart beating in his chest; but his thoughts seemed too far away to grasp, let alone put into words. He wasn't sure what to think. He wondered if he'd heard Harris correctly or if it had all been a dream; he wondered if he'd somehow misunderstood. In his mind, he replayed the conversation, hunting for hidden meanings, trying to grasp the reality behind the words, but try as he might, he couldn't seem to focus long enough to even feel the emotion he was supposed to. Terror kept him from feeling anything at all. Later, he would describe the way he was feeling then as like being on a teeter-totter, with ultimate happiness on one end and ultimate loss on the other, while he was stuck in the middle, his legs on both sides, thinking that a single wrong move in either direction would send him tumbling off.

In the clinic, he put his hand on the counter to steady himself. Madeline rounded the counter with her keys dangling. Travis looked around the waiting room, then at Madeline, then at the floor. When he raised his eyes, all he could do was mimic exactly what he'd heard on the phone only moments before.

"She's awake," he finally said.

Twelve minutes later, after thirty lane changes and three traffic lights that were definitely yellow and perhaps even red, Madeline brought Travis to a halt at the entrance to the nursing home. He hadn't said a word since he'd been in the car, but he smiled his thanks as he pushed open the car door.

The drive had done nothing to clear his mind. He hoped beyond hope and was excited beyond all measure; at the same time, he couldn't shake the thought that somehow he'd misunderstood. Maybe she woke for an instant and was in a coma again; maybe someone had gotten the information wrong in the first place. Maybe Harris had been referring to some obscure medical condition that improved brain function, rather than the obvious. His head spun with alternating scenarios of hope and despair as he made his way toward the entrance.

Elliot Harris was waiting for him and seemed far more in control than Travis imagined himself ever being again.

"I've already called the physician and the neurologist, and they're going to be here in a few minutes," he said. "Why don't you go up to her room?"

"She's okay, right?"

Harris, a man Travis barely knew, put a hand on his shoulder, ushering him forward. "Go see her," he said. "She's been asking for you."

Someone held the door open for him—no matter how hard he tried, he couldn't even remember whether it had been a male or a female—and Travis entered the facility. A quick right led him to the stairs, and he bounded up them, becoming more wobbly the higher he got. On the second floor, he pulled open the door and saw both a nurse and an orderly waiting, as if expecting him. By their excited expressions, he assumed they must have seen him come in and wanted to tell him what was happening, but he didn't stop, and they let him pass. As he took the next step, he felt as if his legs were about to give way. He leaned against the wall to steady himself for a moment, then took another step toward Gabby's room.

It was the second room on the left, and her door stood open. As he got closer, he heard the murmur of people talking. At the door, he hesitated, wishing he'd at least brushed his hair but knowing it didn't matter. He stepped inside, and Gretchen's face lit up.

"I was at the hospital next to the doctor when he got the page, and I just had to come see. . . ."

Travis barely heard her. Instead, all he could register was the sight of Gabby, his wife, propped up weakly on her hospital bed. She seemed disoriented, but her smile when she saw him told him everything he needed to know.

"I know you two have a lot of catching up to do . . . ," Gretchen went on in the background.

"Gabby?" Travis finally whispered.

"Travis," she croaked. Her voice sounded different, scratchy and hoarse from disuse, but somehow, it was Gabby's voice just the same. Travis moved slowly toward the bed, his eyes never leaving hers, unaware that Gretchen was already backing out, shutting the door behind her.

"Gabby?" he repeated in near disbelief. In his dream, or what he thought was a dream, he watched as she moved her hand from the bed to her stomach, as if that took all the strength she had.

He sat on the bed beside her.

"Where were you?" she asked, the words slurry but nonetheless full of love, unmistakably full of life. Awake. "I didn't know where you were."

"I'm here now," Travis said, and at that he broke down, his sobs coming out in heaving bursts. He leaned toward Gabby, aching for her to hold him, and when he felt her hand on his back, he began to cry even harder. He wasn't dreaming. Gabby was holding him; she knew who he was and how much she meant to him. It's real, was all he could think, this time, it's real. . . .

With Travis unwilling to leave Gabby's side, his dad covered for him at the clinic for the next few days. Only recently had he returned to something resembling a full-time schedule, and on weekends like this, with his daughters running and laughing in the yard and Gabby in the kitchen, he sometimes caught himself grasping for details of the past year. His memories of the days he spent in the hospital had a blurry, hazy quality to them, as if he'd been only slightly more conscious than Gabby.

Gabby hadn't emerged from her coma unscathed, of course. She had lost a great deal of weight, her muscles had atrophied, and a numbness persisted on most of her left side. It took days before she could stand upright without support. The therapy was maddeningly slow; even now, she spent a couple of hours daily with the physical therapist, and in the beginning, she often grew frustrated that she could no longer do simple things she'd once taken for granted. She hated her gaunt appearance in the mirror and commented more than once that she looked as if she had aged fifteen years. In moments like those, Travis always told her she was beautiful, and he'd never been more sure of anything.

Christine and Lisa took a bit of time to adjust. On the afternoon that Gabby woke up, Travis asked Elliot Harris to call his mother so she could pick up the girls from school. The family was reunited an hour later, but when they stepped into the room, neither Christine nor Lisa seemed to want to get close to their mother. Instead, they clung to Travis and offered monosyllabic answers to whatever Gabby asked. It took half an hour before Lisa finally crawled onto the bed alongside her mother. Christine didn't open up until the following day, and even then she kept her feelings at bay, as if she were meeting Gabby for the first time. That night, after Gabby had been transferred back to the hospital and Travis brought the girls home, Christine asked whether "Mommy was really back, or if she'd go back to sleep again." Though the physicians made it clear they were fairly certain she wouldn't, they hadn't ruled it out completely, at least for the time being. Christine's fears reflected his own, and whenever he found Gabby sleeping or simply resting after a grueling round of therapy, Travis's stomach would clench. His breathing would get shallow, and he'd nudge her gently, growing increasingly panicked that she wouldn't open her eyes. And when she finally stirred, he couldn't mask his relief and gratitude. While Gabby accepted his anxieties in the beginning—she admitted the thought scared her as well—it had begun to drive her crazy. Last week, with the moon high in the sky and crickets chirping, Travis began to stroke her arm as she lay beside him. Her eyes opened and she focused on the clock, noting it was a little after three in the morning. A moment later, she sat up in bed and glared at him.

"You've got to stop doing this! I need my sleep. Unbroken, regular sleep, like everyone else in the world! I'm exhausted, can't you understand that? I refuse to live the rest of my life knowing that you're going to nudge me awake every hour!"

That had been the extent of her comments; it couldn't even be classified as an argument, since he didn't have time to respond before she'd rolled over with her back to him, muttering to herself—but it struck Travis as so . . . *Gabby-like* that he breathed a sigh of relief. If she no longer worried about slipping into a coma again—and she swore she didn't—then he knew he shouldn't, either. Or, at the very least, he could let her sleep. If he was honest with himself, he wondered whether the fear would ever disappear completely. Now, in the middle of the night, he simply listened to the way she breathed, and when he noticed differences in the pattern, differences that hadn't occurred when she'd been in a coma, he was finally able to roll over and go back to sleep.

They were all adjusting, and he knew that would take time. Lots of it. They had yet to talk about the fact that he'd disregarded the living will, and he wondered whether they ever would. He had yet to tell Gabby the extent of the imaginary conversations she'd had with him while she was in the hospital, and she had little to say about the coma itself. She didn't remember anything: no aromas, no sounds from the television, nothing about his touch. "It's like time just . . . *vanished.*"

But that was fine. It was all as it should be. Behind him, he heard the screen door creak open and he turned. In the distance, he could see Molly lying in the tall grass off to the side of the house; Moby, old guy that he was, was sleeping in the corner. Travis smiled as Gabby spied her daughters, noting her content expression. As Christine pushed Lisa on the tire swing, both of them giggling madly, Gabby took a seat in the rocker beside Travis.

"Lunch is ready," she said. "But I think I'll let them play for a few more minutes. They're having such a good time."

"They are. They wore me out earlier."

"Do you think that maybe later, when Stephanie gets here, we can all head over to the aquarium? And maybe have some pizza afterward? I've been dying for pizza."

He smiled, thinking he could stay in this moment forever. "That sounds good. Oh yeah, that reminds me. I forgot to tell you that your mom called when you were in the shower."

"I'll call her back in a little while. And I've got to call about the heat pump, too. The girls' room just wouldn't cool off last night."

"I can probably fix it."

"I don't think so. The last time you tried to fix it, we had to buy a whole new unit. Remember?"

"I remember you didn't give me enough time."

"Yeah, yeah," she teased. She winked at him. "Do you want to eat out here or inside?"

He pretended to debate the question, knowing it wasn't really important. Here or there, they would all be together. He was with the woman and daughters he loved, and who could ever need or want anything more than that? The sun shone bright, flowers were blooming, and the day would pass with a careless ease that had been impossible to imagine the winter before. It was just a normal day, a day like any other. But most of all, it was a day in which everything was exactly the way it should be.

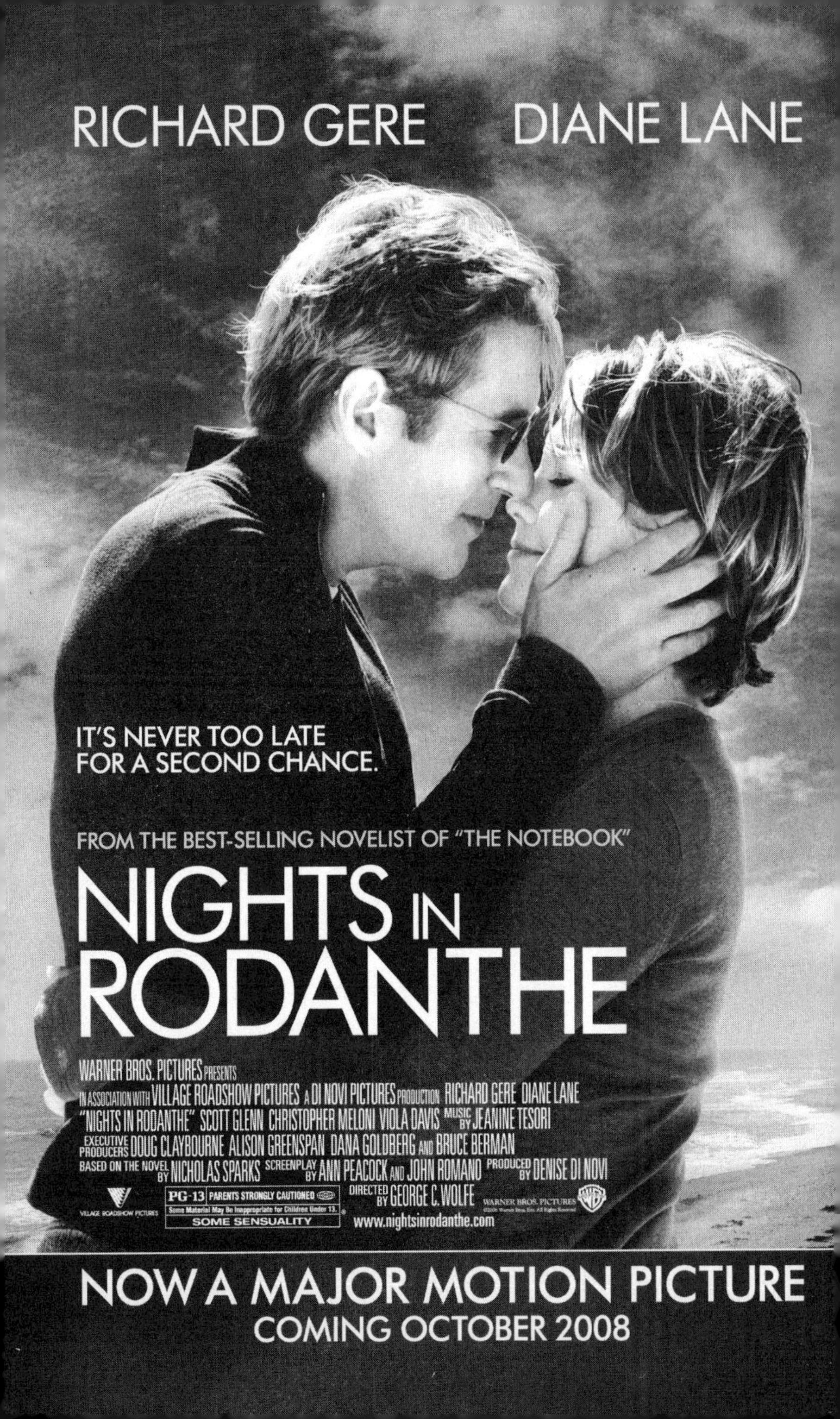
RICHARD GERE
DIANE LANE
IT'S NEVER TOO LATE
FOR A SECOND CHANCE.
FROM THE BEST-SELLING NOVELIST OF "THE NOTEBOOK"
NIGHTS IN
RODANTHE
WARNER BROS. PICTURES PRESENTS
IN ASSOCIATION WITH VILLAGE ROADSHOW PICTURES A DI NOVI PICTURES PRODUCTION RICHARD GERE DIANE LANE
"NIGHTS IN RODANTHE" SCOTT GLENN CHRISTOPHER MELONI VIOLA DAVIS MUSIC BY JEANINE TESORI
EXECUTIVE PRODUCERS DOUG CLAYBOURNE ALISON GREENSPAN DANA GOLDBERG AND BRUCE BERMAN
BASED ON THE NOVEL BY NICHOLAS SPARKS SCREENPLAY BY ANN PEACOCK AND JOHN ROMANO PRODUCED BY DENISE DI NOVI
VILLAGE ROADSHOW PICTURES
PG-13 PARENTS STRONGLY CAUTIONED
Some Material May Be Inappropriate for Children Under 13.
SOME SENSUALITY
DIRECTED BY GEORGE C. WOLFE
WARNER BROS. PICTURES
www.nightsinrodanthe.com
NOW A MAJOR MOTION PICTURE
COMING OCTOBER 2008